RESIST

USA TODAY BESTSELLING AUTHOR

K.A KNIGHT

Resist

Copyright © 2025 by K.A. Knight

All rights reserved.

No part of this book may be reproduced in any form or by any electronic or mechanical means, including information storage and retrieval systems, without written permission from the author, except for the use of brief quotations in a book review.

Written by K.A. Knight.

Edited By Jess from Elemental Editing and Proofreading.

Proofreading by Norma's Nook.

Internal Formatting by The Nutty Formatter.

Art by Dily Iola Designs

Cover by Moonstruck Cover Design & Photography

READER CONSIDERATIONS

This is a very dark book not meant for anybody under the ages of 18.

Content includes: explicit sex, explicit violence, stalking, sexual assault, dubious consent, depression, drug missue, alcohol misuse, blackmail, revenge porn and much more.

PROLOGUE

I turn the TV off and let the hotel room lapse into silence, the darkness surrounding me only interrupted by my bandmate's snores. The rhythmic sound is as familiar as my own breathing, but it's not enough to relax my troubled soul for me to sleep tonight.

My eyes land on the bed I should be sleeping in, one side of the covers pulled back, the other wrapped tightly around him.

He's the reason I can't sleep.

I stare at his unmoving form, wishing he were as troubled as I am and understood why everything is changing yet staying the same all at once.

We are on our way to the top and finally getting our big break with this tour. The world knows our names, and all the tiny shows and empty seats are finally worth it, but I can't help missing the simplicity of our lives then.

The contract we signed today burns a hole in my bag, the words echoing in my head and heart, reminding me why I'm so restless.

I can't have him.

It wasn't blatantly stated in so many words, but it might as well have been.

Can I stop these urges and feelings?

I have to if we want to make it to the top. This is our time, and I won't ruin that for us all because of this forbidden love inside me.

He isn't mine, and he can't be, so why do I wish he were?

Why do I wish he loved me like I love him?

No, I must resist.

I have to.

SANCTUARY

ONE

RYKER

A year ago . . .

My voice fills the club, along with the pounding drums and shredding guitars as we perform. I slide my hand down my torso, my oversized black shirt coming loose, exposing my muscles underneath. My leather pants are so tight, they leave nothing to the imagination as I thrust and dance.

I feel Fox before the crowd cheers.

He presses against my back, but I continue to sing, trying not to mess up the lyrics as his hand slides around me, taking over from where I was, and I shudder under his caress. The crowd gasps as he rips open the rest of my shirt, exposing my slick chest and abs. I lean back into him, seeking his warmth and strength.

It doesn't help that his hand keeps sliding down, and anticipation fills me along with desire. It's wrong to get hard on stage, and it's wrong how much I love the show he puts on for the fans, especially since it isn't real. We only do this on stage, but it feels real, leaving me flustered and panting as I sing. His long, talented fingers that spend hours plucking strings stroke my skin lower and lower for the crowd as our lead guitarist flirts with their favorite lead singer.

I don't know when we became like this. It just happened, our flirting getting worse, and the crowd, no matter the size, eats it up every time, but Fox has started to push how far he takes it. My eyes widen as he slides his hand lower and grabs my dick through my jeans.

I jerk, but he keeps me in place, holding my cock as he grinds with me to the music as the crowd claps and sings along. Die-hard fans know the lyrics, while others just dance. His mouth brushes my ear, making me shiver as I drop the mic for the drum solo.

I should pull away, but I don't. Instead, I lean into his touch, and his lips tilt in a smile. His words are just for me, nobody else.

"You feel good, dirty boy." He places a teasing kiss against my pulse and releases me, moving past me as he grabs his guitar. Swinging it around, he appears totally unaffected while I pant and gawk at him.

Before Fox, I was always the ever cool, unaffected Ryker, the bad boy of Sanctuary, but something about him puts me on edge, and I'm unable to fake it with him.

Fox, on the other hand, smirks at the crowd and drops to his knees as he leans back, shredding his solo, his built chest glistening with sweat and ink under the lights. His hair is a deep, midnight blue at the moment, and it's slicked back with sweat and gel. His eyes are outlined and darkened with liner, and his lips are bright red with two spikes in his bottom lip.

More piercings line his ears on both sides, and he has one in his nose and one in his eyebrow. He looks like every rock star should, with a perfect fucking face that drives everyone wild and bulging muscles in his arms as he works the guitar.

There is nothing sexier than the way Fox plays, and he knows it.

He eats it up, working the crowd like he works me.

Dash comes over and leans into me. "You good?"

I startle from my musings and grin at our bassist. "Always, brother." I smirk as I swing the mic up as he strums the bass. I glance at Strike to see him hitting the drums so hard, he'll be bleeding later.

We always give it our all, acting like every performance is our last, because it could be.

When Fox starts to reach the end of his part, I step behind him, determined to return the favor. Gripping his hair in one hand, I tip his head back as I begin to sing the last chorus, but my eyes are on him as he smirks up at me.

It's a filthy fucking smirk that makes me think thoughts I should not be thinking about my bandmate.

When the last note of the song dies out, Fox pushes to his feet, winking at me as he returns to his stand and takes a drink. I search for mine, but it's gone, and when I go to grab another, Fox is there, his guitar over his shoulder. He pinches my chin and tilts my head back since he's taller than me, and as the audience watches, he moves closer, almost pressing our lips together, and lets the water dribble from his mouth to mine.

Some drips over my lips and down my chin, and as I swallow, he leans down and licks it away before stepping back and swinging his guitar around for the final song. I recover as quickly as I can, grinning at the crowd as the next song on our set kicks in.

This one is fast, and I hop around the stage, shouting into the mic, the beat coursing through my veins until I become the music.

I am the music. Everything else is gone.

Fox rolls his hips into his guitar as I lean into him, our eyes meeting as something passes between us—something we never talk about. My lips press to the mic as my gaze drops to *his* lips as he mouths the lyrics. His sweaty skin slides over mine as we dance to the beat of the rock song.

His arm slips around my waist from behind as I lean back, hitting the last note. I lean farther into him, allowing myself that moment of weakness before the spotlight fades and the last note dies.

I pull away, knowing the unwritten rules for both of us—this ends when we leave the stage—and peer at the crowd once more.

"Thank you for coming and goodnight! We are Sanctuary!" I yell into the mic, dismayed by the dismal clapping and cheers from the small crowd. The venue is a dive bar, but it's dead even though it's a Saturday night. It's just another set in a long line of empty shows and hopeless performances, but we bound off stage with smiles since we got to perform. All of us pretend we aren't rapidly losing hope that we will ever be successful.

The high of performing quickly wears off when the bar hands us a measly hundred bucks. We smile and pack our shit into our van, which also doubles as our bedroom while we tour from city to city, trying to catch our big break. It's a tight fit, and when we give up trying to find somewhere to park for the night and just pull over on the side of the road farther out of the city, Strike and Dash collapse in the back, asleep in seconds. Snores fill the van as Fox heads outside. I watch him go. It's the only time I allow myself to look at him like this.

He's quiet and withdrawn tonight, which isn't like him. Checking the van and pulling on the privacy curtains, I hesitate before I climb onto the shared mattress in the back, and instead, I leave Strike and Dash so I can check on Fox.

Strike's and Dash's snores reach us as I wander over to Fox and sit carefully on the rail next to him. He holds a beer in one of his hands as he looks over the city and its dazzling lights.

"Another quiet night," he murmurs. "Just the few die-hard fans that follow us from place to place. Hell, they probably sleep better than we do." He glances back at the van with a small smile, the sight making me gulp. This close, I can see the freckle right below his left eye, the one that drives me insane. Something about it only makes him that much more beautiful.

It isn't something I ever thought I would call a man, but he really is beautiful, even away from the lights and makeup.

"True." I force the word out and look back at the city so he doesn't catch me staring.

Bandmates. Friends.

I remind myself that we are nothing more. I've never felt this way about another guy before. When he took the lead guitarist spot after our last one quit, I knew he was trouble. I just had no idea how much. Before he arrived, I could flirt with my band, dance, and sing to get attention, but with him it's different—it means something, at least for me.

I might want Fox in a way I've never wanted another, but I know our deal, so I won't act on it. We are bandmates, and nothing comes before that, not even my own desire. Instead, I fulfill that urge everywhere else, trying to forget the way he touches me and stop myself from imagining the way he would taste.

As always, though, it's his eyes I see when I fuck strangers.

"Hmm, the smallest we've seen," I say, feeling the dejection as well. We've been performing together for years. Fox only joined us in the last six months, but Sanctuary was around for long before that. We have a small devoted fan base, but it isn't enough. I'm starting to think that we'll never make it.

Just because we have talent as a band doesn't mean we'll get fame and fortune, and I'd be lying if I said that wasn't why I do it. Yes, music is my soul, and I can't do anything but sing, but it would sure as fuck be nice if we could earn a living from it.

Fox's eyes swing to me for a moment as he hands me a beer. "Despite it all, I kind of love it. I wouldn't give it up for anything, even if only one person came to see us . . . I got to play and sing with all of you. I got to make music and do what I love. I just wish we could do better—not for me, but for you and the guys who gave up everything to chase this dream."

"So did you," I remind him, nudging his shoulder as I play with my beer. "Yeah, you joined us later, but you're still one of us, chasing the dream. You left your home and a stable future just like we did to be here."

He nods, looking back at the city. "I guess every band has to do this, right? Work their asses off just to get noticed. It's normal, but it's starting to feel a little hopeless."

I frown at his remark. If there is one thing Fox is, it's endlessly hopeful. He's always smiling and making everyone else laugh. Honestly, it used to drive me insane, but now I hate the frown on his lips.

His beautiful face wasn't made to cry, and I'd do anything to see his bright smile.

"We'll make it. I promise." I drape my arm over his shoulders, wanting him closer, though I never look too closely at why, and keep my eyes on the city. "We have the talent, and one day, we'll be out there with our name in lights and thousands of people screaming it. Until then, we have each other, cold beers, and music." I tap my bottle to his.

"And each other," he adds, leaning into me. "You're right. The music is all that matters. I have to trust in that . . . in us." His eyes meet mine for a moment, and I swallow words I can never say.

The night closes in around us as we stare into each other's eyes, lost in one another.

SANCTUARY

TWO

FOX

I struggle to sleep, staring up at the ceiling of the overly warm van. Ry stayed up with me as long as he could before dragging me to bed since we need to spend tomorrow working on the next bar. As usual, the covers were kicked off us since we are all practically shoved together, stripped down to our jeans and boxers just in case the police come to move us. Dash and Strike snore to my right, pressed together since there's no room. Ryker shifts to my left, sighing in his sleep and rolling over, lying across my chest.

I try to ignore the way my body reacts.

It's normal. We are in a tiny space where we need to squeeze together, and besides, we are friends. This is totally normal.

Why does it feel anything but?

He slides up my body, resting his head on my shoulder, his warm breath blowing across me. When I turn my head to look at him, our lips almost meet.

He looks so much younger, more innocent, as he sleeps than when he's gyrating on stage, spitting filthy lyrics. It's a side of him many don't get to see, but it's one of my favorites. I love the dirty, slutty singer, but this is all for me, a part of him I claim from others that even he doesn't know about.

His shoulder-length, black hair curls from the humidity. The deep midnight color is almost purple. His thick brows furrow in his sleep, pulled down over deep brown eyes the color of earth. His pale skin is unmarred, and his high cheekbones and thick jaw are clean-shaven. His plush, plump lips are still stained from the blush we use and slightly parted.

He's pretty, and he knows it.

He's skinnier than I am and slightly shorter, but not by much, with sleeker muscles compared to mine. The sight of his bare chest has me swallowing hard, trying to push back my desire, so I bring my eyes back to his face, allowing myself to stare when I normally wouldn't.

I am obsessed with him. I know it's useless, but it doesn't stop me craving him. Ryker is a goddamn work of art, and he knows it. He uses his looks like a fucking weapon against everyone—he just doesn't know how damn well it works on me too. As his friend, it shouldn't, but I never wanted to be just friends.

My eyes widen as he moves closer, closing the small distance until his lips innocently press to mine. I freeze and stare at him until reality sets in.

I scoot away as much as I can. I want to kiss him, but not like this, not while he's asleep.

Besides, Ry will never be mine. We flirt and act, but everyone knows he's straight, including me, with how he fucks his way through every city. No, it's just a one-sided obsession that I can't seem to get over, and I get my own back the only way I can—on stage, showing him what I can never say.

He thinks it's just an act, but for me, it isn't.

Forcing my eyes shut, I try to sleep, but despite my exhaustion, my mind whirs, fear mingling with my insecurities. When I finally do drift off, the sun is almost up and Ryker is still pressed to my side like a safety blanket.

"Guys, wake the fuck up!"

I jerk upright, hitting my head with a groan. I frown at Strike and Dash, who sit on the bumper, their toothbrushes forgotten. Ryker groans next to me, curling into my side.

"Ry." I shake him. "What is it? Cops?"

"No, look at this." Dash holds out his phone. Rubbing my eyes, I pull from Ry's grip and crouch in the back of the open van, early morning sunlight streaming in. "Our set last night is going viral—I mean fucking viral. Our songs have already been played everywhere, and my phone is blowing up. We went from five thousand followers to close to a million overnight."

"Fuck, what?" I rub my head. "Why? We didn't do anything different. Was there a scout there?"

Dash and Strike share a grin and look behind me to a still sleeping Ryker. "Uh-uh, no. Look." He scrolls back to the top, and I sit down on the end of the mattress, blinking at the videos.

They are of Ryker and me.

Our music was edited to them, and my eyes widen. Hundreds of videos from different angles and different parts of the set show us flirting and playing together.

"Looks like the internet is shipping you and going crazy."

I take the phone, continuing to look through it as Dash kicks Ryker, who groans, sitting up and looking far too cute and grumpy. I force my eyes away from him, and he shuffles my way as Dash explains.

He looks over my shoulder, and I'm acutely aware of the warmth of his body pressing against my back. I lift my knees to hide my reaction to him, though no one seems to notice. Everyone else's eyes are locked on the phone.

"We look good together," Ryker teases, leaning his head on my shoulder as he watches the videos I scroll through. We know the power of social media and have been trying to use it for years, but we never hit anything like this.

I nod mutely, unsure what to say. Seeing us like that . . . Yeah, it's hot as fuck, but it also makes me a little sad. It's just an act, but this is good. It could be the chance we need. Obviously, they think the same

"This could be our big break!" Dash exclaims.

I swallow hard, gripping the phone, and meet Ry's eyes over my shoulder as he glances from them to me. Something passes between us, making my heart race.

It isn't excitement for what this means, but something more.

Something darker.

Hunger.

SANCTUARY

THREE

RYKER

A month later...

The power of the internet and how fast everything moved after we blew up overnight was insane. We had labels and interviewers calling us continually, and we were gobsmacked. We knew we needed to seize the moment and rise to the top, but none of us expected this.

We were signed to a label and thrust into the limelight as swiftly as possible.

We've done more interviews than I can count and filmed more social media content than I even knew was possible. Our songs have been reworked, and we've had vocal and movement coaches.

I glance from my reflection in the mirror to the dressing room to look at Fox. His hair is a little different now but no less beautiful. It's messy and longer, falling into his face and eyes, giving him a bad boy look that drives everyone crazy. The roots are a blackish gray, then the color fades to a deep midnight blue at the ends. His lips tilt in a friendly smile as he nods at the makeup artist touching up his lips. When she lowers to her feet after standing on her tiptoes to reach him, she stumbles, and he automatically catches her, checking to make sure she's okay. I can't help but smile. He looks like a complete asshole, but Fox is all sweetness.

As if he feels my gaze, he raises his eyes to mine in the mirror, those dark orbs speaking words neither of us dare to utter.

The white crop top he wears rises as he moves, flashing his abs and tan chest, our logo proudly sprayed across the front. His leather pants match mine and dip low, exposing so much skin it's hard to breathe. All of his fingers are covered in rings, and chains drape across his ears. Every part of him is refined, and part of me misses the grungy before Fox, but I know that's mean. I'm not the same either.

I pull my eyes from his and glance down at the loose vest, which shows my arms and sides, and despite its ripped appearance, I know it's designer, as are my boots and jewelry. I don't feel like myself, and my insecurities raise their heads for a moment. As if he feels them, a warm hand lands on my shoulder. I look up, my gaze once more clashing with Fox's as he rests his chin on my shoulder, his cheek almost touching mine.

"You're going to be amazing, Ry," he promises.

"You think?" I ask nervously.

"I know it, and I'll be right there with you." He turns his face, his warm, soft lips pressing to my cheek in a comforting kiss. He lingers, and suddenly there's a flash. We jolt apart and turn in confusion to find a grinning Mabel, our new temporary manager.

"Perfect. I'll post this now. The fans will love it!" She smiles, and I swallow hard, hating that they will see this. It wasn't for them or even for the music. It was for us, and as Fox steps away, closing down, I can tell he feels the same. Our stolen moment was taken from us and changed to something to sell our image. I know it's part of the job, but as Fox walks over to Dash and Strike, I find myself watching him forlornly.

I wish no one else had seen that and it was just for us.

"Here." I glance over at Fox as he hands me the open bottle of water, the cap in his hand. Smiling, I take a big sip and pass it back, watching as he drains it halfway, his Adam's apple bobbing with the movement before he tightens the cap and leans back into the couch next to me.

Our thighs touch, and for a moment, I stare at them before I bring my head up, blushing as I realize all the cameras are trained on us.

"Sorry, what was the question?" I ask.

Embarrassment takes over even as they laugh, but luckily Fox saves me. "I think Ry is a little in shock from all the love here tonight. Let's show him how excited you are." The crowd goes wild, and he winks at me to let me know he has my back. I smile in gratitude and focus on the interview. The questions are easy, and I relax the more we talk, sharing stories of our shows before this and what it's like trying to get into the industry now.

"And there he was, butt naked. The police were staring, and all he could do was grab a pineapple to cover himself." I chuckle at the memory. It was a good night, and Fox is right. That pineapple didn't cover much, not that the police cared.

I smack Fox's thigh automatically, and we lean together, grinning widely before it fades. We continue to stare at each other before I clear my throat and smile at the others as they continue talking, telling the story for us.

"Okay, okay, we have to talk about the elephant in the room." I smile tightly as the interviewer, Sarah, winks at the crowd. "I think we have all seen that viral clip of you two on stage, right?"

The crowd shouts, and I grin at them, blowing kisses and eating it up. Inside, though, something in me tightens. Every time it's mentioned, I feel excited since it got us here, but I also feel a little . . . sad that something natural between us has been taken and sold. That's the business though, right? Not even our bodies are our own. It's the price we pay to make music, one we all agreed to, even Fox. I still glance at him in worry.

The interview today is important. It's the biggest one we have ever had. They have guests on here people usually see on red carpets. We can't mess this up. It's a hard launch for our band to get our name out there, and we'll either sink or swim.

I want to fucking swim.

My eyes land on Fox before I smile at Sarah. "Which clip is that?" I tease.

"Oh, come on now." She laughs. "I think we can all admit we've watched it more than once, right?" The crowd agrees, and I smirk as I lean back into Fox. They aren't the only ones. I won't admit it, but I might have the edits saved on my phone. "We have to know, and it's the question everyone has been asking.... Are you guys an item?"

She stares at us, and everyone goes quiet, but I let them wait it out. PR from the label said they want us to play this up, but we can't answer confirm or deny since that will make people mad. They want to ship us, but they also want to make sure we are available and give them the illusion that we can be theirs, all the while still being loyal to each other. It's tricky, and I'll probably slip up, so I go with my instinct.

"Now, that would be telling, wouldn't it?" I rest my hand on Fox's thigh, and the crowd screams. My eyebrows rise at the reaction, and Fox spares me a tight look before grinning at the crowd. His hand covers mine, playing into it, and I turn my hand over, interlacing our fingers before sliding them between our thighs on the sofa. He tries to tug his away, but I keep hold out of sight of the cameras while I wink at the crowd.

"Fox, marry me!" someone yells.

Our heads jerk around as everyone laughs. Fox smiles and blows a kiss. I pretend to catch it as I wag my finger at the crowd. "You can't have him. He's mine."

It's a joke, or it's supposed to be, but when he glances at me, I realize I meant it.

No one can have him but me.

"So what's next for Sanctuary?" Sarah asks when the audience dies down.

"World domination," Dash says, making us all laugh.

"We want to continue to make music, and we've been very lucky that Pulse Entertainment sees that and has given us the chance," Fox replies diplomatically, smiling with happiness. "We are just going with the flow at the moment. I think we are all still shocked by how fast everything has happened, and we know we wouldn't be here without our fans and supporters, both new and old. We'll honor and thank them the best way we can—with our music."

"Fox is right." I smile at him. That's one thing we always agree on—our love for music. "Music is what brought us all together and always will. It's our passion, our reason for never giving up, and that's what we will continue to do—make music and steal hearts."

"Well, I think we can all agree that's exactly what we want!" Sarah exclaims.

The interview wraps up quickly after that. We play some games, take some pictures, and then thank the crowd, all while I hold Fox's hand, refusing to let go despite him trying to pull away.

"Thank you!" I call once more, waving emphatically at the crowd. It might not be the image they want from us, but I don't care. All these people came out to see and support us, and I'll never forget that or the way I want to cry when I realize we are finally making our dream a reality.

I continue to hold Fox's hand as we walk off stage, waving and eating up the attention, but as soon as we are out of the spotlight, he tugs his hand away, shooting me an annoyed look before he storms past Mabel and toward the dressing room. I watch him go, my chest hurting even though I smile and nod at Mabel's praises, my eyes on his retreating form.

Yes, everything has changed since that night, and I'm not sure it's for the better.

I finally feel like we are reaching our dreams, but I also feel like I'm losing him in the process.

FOUR

FOX

It shouldn't surprise me that we are now being invited to parties we only saw online previously, but it does, especially when we pull up at a mansion overflowing with rock and roll legends, models, actors, and basically every "it" celebrity at the moment. We leave our run-down tour van as far away as we can and, still wearing the clothes from our interview, head toward the open doors, feeling very out of place—or at least I do. The others act like this is a normal thing for them, especially Ryker. When we step inside, Dash and Strike gape, almost giddy as they hurry away to talk to everyone and get drunk, leaving me alone with Ryker, which is somewhere I don't want to be for once.

I'm not mad at him. I'm just unsure how to act. It was never a problem before, and if he flirted like that with me outside of the interview, I wouldn't have cared, but something about it being for the cameras and the fans felt . . . wrong, like he was taking something special and monetizing it, and I don't know if I liked it.

I liked the way it felt when he held my hand and the way he looked at me. I liked it too much, in fact, and maybe that's why I'm on edge. For him, it was a PR move, but for me, it was real.

"What should we do first?" Ry asks, rubbing his hands together with an evil villain laugh, and despite my reservations, I can't stay mad at him. It isn't fair to take my emotions out on him, and it also isn't his fault that I like him. He's just doing what we all agreed on, which is helping make our dreams come true.

"How about a drink?" I suggest, slinging my arm around his shoulders to show we're okay. The bright smile he aims my way as he leans into me makes me realize I worried my best friend, and that's not okay. "Then we can make some rounds, shake some hands, all that shit."

"Sounds good to me."

"Oh my gosh! You're Sanctuary, right? Ryker and . . ." We both turn our heads up as a leggy blonde stops before us, teetering on her heels while clutching a glass of Champagne that is definitely not her first. She's drop-dead gorgeous and knows it. I'm guessing she's a model or an actress.

"Fox," I say with a smile.

She grins widely at me before her gaze lands back on Ry like he's her target, and I see a glint in her eye that tells me he is exactly that. "I've seen you guys everywhere online, but you are much better looking in person."

"So are you. I've seen your work before, and you are even more beautiful in person," Ryker flirts, offering her his usual charming grin —one he's never aimed at me.

"You're so sweet." She steps forward and stumbles on her high heels.

"Whoa, I've got you." Ryker catches her as she trips, her hand landing on his chest, and she giggles as she strokes it.

"Wow, your muscles . . ."

He grins down at her. "How about we find somewhere for you to sit, and I can get a drink as well?"

"I know a place," she gushes, taking his hand and suddenly able to walk now. She winks back at me as she leads Ryker away, and he doesn't even spare me a look.

I stare after him, and I realize very rapidly that this is what our life will be like—me staring after him, wishing I were on his arm while he fucks his way through Hollywood.

My heart clenches so hard I struggle to breathe, hoping he'll turn back and prove me wrong. I just want things to be the way they were, but I'm starting to think they never will be.

"I need a fucking drink," I mutter.

I make my way through the party. Barely anyone pays me any mind, since I'm a nobody to them. We might be making waves, but these people are the gods above us. I grab a bottle of Jack and wander the ground floor, finding Dash and Strike playing games with other people at a poker table. I watch for a little bit before wandering around, looking for him.

Where could he be?

I tell myself it's just to make sure he's okay, but when I finally find him, my heart sinks and I wish I had never looked. He's surrounded by women on a sofa deep in the house, his head thrown back as he laughs. Their hands slide over his body possessively, their nails scraping his arms and chest.

Taking a massive drink, I swish it in my mouth as bitterness fills me, then I turn away before I do something stupid. I head through some closed sliding doors, leaning against the railing on a balcony overlooking a huge backyard.

I sip the bottle as I let the fresh air try to wash away the sick feeling inside me. I knew this would happen. I mean, it's no secret Ryker likes sex and blondes are his favorite. It's one of the reasons I dyed my hair from my natural blond after a while. I didn't want to be another conquest to him.

I'm good enough to play with, but when the lights are down, he's gone. He'll never be mine, and I need to accept that, but my head is a fucking mess, and this new act we have to put on doesn't help.

Something draws my gaze back inside, and whatever was left of my heart cracks inside my chest as I watch Ry head upstairs, guided by that same leggy blonde. It doesn't take a genius to guess what they are doing, and as I turn forward, I down half the bottle and hope it numbs this pain.

It doesn't work, though, and I want to fuck up this pretty house just to feel something, but I don't. I stand on the balcony as silent as a statue while the man I love goes upstairs with someone else, wishing it were me the entire time.

Still, I wouldn't change this pain for anything, because it would mean he isn't in my life, but I don't know how long I can go on like this.

I realize I can't be his friend, not when I'm in love with him.

I'll have to be, though, even if it breaks my heart.

Staring at the sky, I force myself not to go after him. Ryker is meant to shine in the spotlight. I need to remember that, even when it's hard.

"Shit, you stole my hiding spot." I whirl at the feminine voice and watch a grinning Reign Harrow step outside. She shuts the door and mutes the frivolity and music inside. "Mind if I hide here with you?"

I blink in shock. Reign Harrow is a fucking rock legend. If I were straight, I'd be all over her in an instant. She's hot as hell but also engaged. Nodding silently, I watch her walk over and lean against the railing like I am. She gazes at the sky, holding a full, untouched glass in her hand. As I stare at her profile in shock, I notice she looks sad and tired.

Does anyone else see that? When she glances at me, I realize they probably don't. She doesn't let them, but I'm a nobody, so she doesn't bother hiding it. "Crazy, right? The party."

"Oh, uh, yeah." I nod, glancing back at the sky so she doesn't think I'm a creeper.

"I would say you get used to it but . . ." She laughs humorlessly. "I suppose you do in a way. I don't know which is worse, that this becomes normal or the fakeness of it all."

I nod again, unsure what to say. A nobody like me doesn't speak to Reign Harrow.

"Sorry, ignore my rant. Anyway, what are you hiding from?" My eyes swing to hers, and she grins. "You don't come out here unless you're hiding."

"What are you hiding from?" I ask.

The sad smile she gives me makes me blink. "You know, you're the first person to ever ask me that." She turns back to the sky, and I think she won't answer, that I've overstepped, and I curse myself silently.

"My fiancé," she admits, "and the adoring crowd and cameras that follow us around all the time. I just needed peace, you know?" She glances at me. "You get tired of it all after a while, no matter how much you wanted it."

"I can see that," I murmur. "I won't talk. You can hide here with me."

She smiles brightly, and even I can admit how fucking beautiful she is. "What about you?" she asks. "Distract me from my own life. What are you hiding from?"

I debate what to say, but then I think, *Fuck it*. It's obvious she wants her privacy too, and I don't see her spilling my secrets. Besides, I'm betting she doesn't even know who I am. Taking a drink, I glance at the stairs once more. "From the truth. Tonight, I realized that the person I love will never love me back or be mine, and I'll have to watch from the sidelines for the rest of our lives as he loves everyone else but me."

She's quiet, and when I glance at her, Reign's eyes are locked on me. "Are you sure? Did you ask him?"

"I don't need to." I offer her the bottle, and she takes a sip. "I was just being delusional. It hurts, so I'm hiding. I'm not good company tonight. Tomorrow, I'll have to go back to being what they want, but tonight . . ."

"Tonight you want to be you." She nods. "I get that." She nudges my arm. "Wearing a mask all the time can be exhausting—trust me on that—and lonely too. Find someone to have in your corner."

"Do you have someone?" I ask.

"I think so." She glances at the ring on her finger with a contemplative look in her eyes. "Although sometimes it doesn't feel like it. Sometimes I wish I'd never found fame . . . Maybe I'd be happier."

"A-fucking-men." I toast her, and we both drink in silence for a while.

"If he doesn't love you, then find someone who does. You deserve to be happy. Live your life your way, not for him, and if he really doesn't feel the same, then he should let you know. He shouldn't play with your feelings no matter what. That's just a dick move."

I nod but find myself defending him. "He's actually nice, and he cares about everything. He's always looking after me, but everything is changing, and I'm scared," I tell her. "Scared it will change him, change us . . . change me."

"Change is inevitable," she replies. "Everyone changes—sometimes for the better, sometimes not. It's the only constant we can actually rely on, and change can be terrifying, but sometimes it's good too. Sometimes life gives you exactly what you need, even if you don't know it." She leans next to me, her arm touching mine. There is nothing sexual about it, just offering comfort. "Either way, I hope you find your happiness."

"I hope you do too," I say. "You don't seem very happy, and like you said, everyone should be happy."

She blinks at me. "I don't seem happy?"

"Not at all," I admit slyly. "Are you?"

She swallows hard, searching my eyes. "I don't know." Her voice is small, scared.

"Find out," I tell her, "before it's too late." My eyes go back to the stairs inside before I turn away. "Don't break your own heart. It fucking sucks."

We're quiet for a bit, both lost in our own thoughts, before she grins at me. "Want to know everyone's dirty, funny, messy secrets? It can be intimidating coming into this world, but once you know them, it makes them so much more human, and you'll never be scared of them. I mean, how can you be scared of Yulen Miller when you know he collects unicorns and plays with them?"

I burst into laughter, and she joins in. "What else?" I ask greedily, happy for the distraction.

"Okay, so there's Griselda, the actress, right . . ."

FIVE

RYKER

Drying my hands on my pants, I hurry down the steps before she can get her claws into me again. She dragged me upstairs, saying she needed my help going to the bathroom, and I couldn't say no, not with all the eyes on me. I need to be the best I can manage for Fox and the others so we can make as many connections as we can, but as soon as we got upstairs, she pushed me onto one of the beds. She didn't want me, she wanted what I stood for, and it made me feel sick. I managed to get out from under her and make an escape. I need to find Fox. I'll stay at his side, and we can speak to some of the idols about maybe working with them.

I freeze on the bottom step, my gaze locked on the glass doors. Fox is on the balcony, laughing, and my lips want to tilt into a smile at the sight, but it's the person he's laughing with that bothers me.

Reign Harrow holds onto his arm, talking away, her eyes glittering as she stares up at him. I can feel the connection between them from here, and when I see her slap his side, I swallow the bile in my throat. I hurried down here, not wanting to leave him alone, and there he is, completely fine, flirting away. Did he even care when I was pulled away? Did he even look for me?

He acts like he cares and looks at me like I'm the only person in his universe, but then he does shit like this. He didn't even stop me from being taken upstairs.

"Hey, there you are, man," Dash calls, slapping my arm to draw my attention to him. "Have you seen Fox?" He follows my gaze and whistles. "Goddamn, did Fox pull Reign fucking Harrow? Bastard, I knew he was too much of a pretty boy. They all want him. You should see the way everyone has been asking about him."

Stuffing down the jealousy I feel, I glance at him. "What do you mean?"

Dash clears his throat, pitching his voice high. "Oh my god, where is Fox? Is Fox with you? He's here, right? He's so hot. I'm obsessed." He rolls his eyes then coughs. "That's all I keep getting asked. It seems Fox is their superstar. I guess we all thought it was you, huh?"

"Right." My eyes go back to Fox as he throws his head back and laughs hard at something she said. His dimples appear, something I've only ever seen with me.

Clearing my throat, I force a smile. "Let's get drunk and enjoy the party."

"Smartest thing you've said ever." Dash drapes his arm around me, and we follow Strike through the crowd. I force a smile, accepting drinks and being dragged into conversations, but I continue to glance outside, wondering if he will take her or if he's just playing along for the cameras.

Is anything we share real, or is it just an act?

The blonde, Sash, leans closer to me, her eyes dilated with either drugs or alcohol. She's an actress starring in some hit book remake, and it's obvious she loves being the center of attention. She homed in on us when we found ourselves sitting on the couch, surrounded by people vying for our attention. It almost feels like blades are aimed at us, carving us into little bite-sized pieces for their own enjoyment.

"So you and Fox . . . are you a thing?" she asks with a secretive giggle. "It's cool if you are. Hell, I'd even let you share me."

The idea of us sharing her makes me sick. It would mean ruining something so real and perfect.

"We are . . . friends," I answer lamely, the word sounding pathetic even to me.

Have Fox and I ever been just friends?

I thought there was something between us, but maybe I was wrong.

"Oh." She giggles again, leaning into me. "It's totally okay. We've all experimented," she whispers. "Anything goes in Hollywood. Besides, the course I went to for sensitivity told me it's all the rage these days to be open and experimenting." She nods. "It would be a shame, though. You are both so hot."

I need another fucking drink.

I nod tightly and go to stand when Fox appears, happy and relaxed. "Hey, there you guys are." He offers us all beers, and I accept one, holding the bottle tightly. My knuckles turn white from the force as I eye him. Reign Harrow isn't with him, but he's been gone awhile.

Did they hook up? She's engaged, but it doesn't seem to stop people in this crowd. Things like commitment and boundries mean nothing to them, and everything is a game, even people's feelings.

I try to bite my tongue, but it spills out like word vomit.

I need to know.

"Where have you been?" I ask, my voice accusatory, and the looks I get make me plaster on a smile. "You are missing all the fun!" I tack on, sounding overly joyful.

Fox's eyebrow arches, and he eyes me curiously. "Just getting some fresh air."

I want to snap, *Liar!*

He sits on the other side of the blonde, the only free seat, and I force myself to smile at the conversation. I make myself laugh and act happy to give them what they want and so I'm not labeled as moody or problematic. These people can make or break a career, and yeah, it's a party, but it's also a chance for us to network and find our place. I can't spend it being bitter and jealous.

I glance at Fox to see Sash's attention is now on him, her hand stroking his chest. He doesn't seem to mind as he smiles at her as they talk.

"Ryker?" someone prompts, and it's clear it's not the first time they have called my name.

"Sorry, what?" I grin, turning back.

"Are you guys playing any gigs soon?" the person asks.

"Oh, I'm not sure. We haven't received our schedule yet."

"Oh." They share a look. "Have fun with that." They laugh. "You'll miss the time when you were nobodies. Trust me, the schedules are killer."

"Right." I smile tightly.

I won't regret it. This is everything we wanted—fame, recognition, and the chance to play our music for thousands . . . .

I suddenly feel hollow at the thought.

"Can I take a drink?" Sash's syrupy sweet voice draws my attention, and I see her reaching for Fox's beer.

He offers her the bottle with an arched brow, but before she can take it, I snatch it and wrap my lips around the rim where his just were. I down it before wiping my mouth. "Sorry, I don't like to share." I wink at her as she blinks, looking between us before forcing a tight smile onto her face.

Fox eyes me, frowning, then glances at her. "Want me to get you a drink?"

"Oh my gosh, that is so sweet! Yes." He stands, and she hops up. "I'll help you."

I watch them wander off together, anger filling me before I drag my gaze away.

I don't care.

I don't.

Fox can fuck whomever he wants. It has nothing to do with me. Everything we do is for the act—nothing more, nothing less. He can have all the fun he wants now that we are climbing to the top.

I know I'm not making a good impression, but I can't seem to wear that fake persona even though I know I should, and it makes me even more annoyed and miserable. Before I know it, I'm standing.

"I think we are heading back, guys." There's a chorus of boos and people demanding we stay. "We have to be up for a meeting with our label." I force a smile. "You know how it is. We can't get into trouble on the first day." I wink. "But I can't wait to stay next time and play."

Dash and Strike extract themselves with frowns. "Aww, we can stay for a little bit longer," Dash says.

"Stay?" Fox appears at my side, eyeing me, but I can't bring myself to meet his gaze, afraid of what he might see. "Are we leaving?"

"Yeah, we have to be up early," I remind them.

"Since when did you become the responsible one?" he scoffs, nudging me.

Since you decided to stop caring about me, I think.

"True, stay!" someone yells.

"At least give us something before you go," another adds.

"I know! They should kiss! Kiss! Kiss! Kiss!" The chant starts, and I share a wide-eyed look with Fox.

I glance at his lips as I move closer. "They won't stop until we do." It's an excuse. I want to taste the beer on his lips, and I want them all to know he's mine.

His eyebrows draw together as he looks at the chanting crowd and then me as I move closer. My eyes are on his lips, but he steps back, and I freeze. He turns away from me, smiling tightly at the crowd. "Ah, you want me to kiss you?" He heads their way jokingly as they laugh. "Maybe next time." He winks as he waves. "Thanks for having us. It's been a blast. I'm sure I'll see you fuckers around." He turns and forces his way through the crowd.

I watch him go before waving and following after him, my heart pounding for some unknown reason.

"Fox!" I grab his arm. "What's the problem? It's just a game."

He jerks from my grip, frowning at me. "I shouldn't have to play games just to get them to like me. They don't matter that much to me. I don't care what they think or want."

"But we act like that together," I start, feeling frustrated.

"Out of choice, not because someone is forcing us to. It makes me feel sick to even think about it," he snaps.

His words feel like a bucket of cold water was dumped over me as I stare into his eyes, which are hard and distant.

"It made you sick to think about kissing me?" I know my voice is sharp, but something inside me cracks.

"Under these circumstances? Yes," he retorts, eyeing me. "You would have done whatever they wanted and played along."

"We need them to like us. We got this far, and we can't fail now. I'll do whatever it takes to get us to the top," I admit. I would do anything to give him his dream and get us there together.

He looks me over like he's seeing me for the first time, and I don't like what I see in his gaze.

"Good to know," he finally says, withdrawing as he steps away from me. "I know where we stand now."

"Come on, guys, enough. Let's go." Strike grabs us, wrapping his arms around our necks. "Just another night in Hollywood," he teases, but it falls flat. It's then I realize how many eyes are on us, and I let him lead us away.

I wonder what Fox meant and why I'm consumed by fear.

SANCTUARY

SIX

FOX

The house we are renting is massive. We each have our own room, and there's even a backyard and a garage. I know it isn't like some of the mansions the other bands have, but it still blows me away. We are used to sharing beds or sleeping in a van together, so the space feels like a mansion.

I'm not used to the quiet of my dark room or sleeping alone. The sheets are pushed down to my waist, my arms crossed under my head as I stare at the white ceiling. I need some noise.

I know it's an excuse.

Instead, I'm replaying everything that happened tonight.

It didn't surprise me to find Ryk surrounded by people when I went inside, all hanging on his every word. He's effortless with people, laughing, joking, and stealing hearts. I have no doubt he had fun upstairs, so when the little blonde at his side turned her attention to me, I let her.

I flirted with her to make him jealous. I wanted to see his reaction, wanted him to know he isn't the only one people find desirable.

It backfired, though, and when he almost kissed me just for their fun, it made me feel sick. I want to kiss Ryker more than I want to breathe, but the idea of doing it like that made me feel dirty, used, and downright angry. We didn't even speak when we got back despite him trying. I just couldn't look at him.

Is that really who Ryker is?

I know it's an act between us, but it always felt natural. We did it for fun because we liked it, but doing it on command for strangers?

No.

Groaning, I cover my eyes with my arm, trying to work through my muddled thoughts, when a creak reaches me. I drop my arm and look at my door, which is partially ajar. Ryker hesitates on the threshold, wearing one of our oversized tanks and boxers, holding a pillow under one arm.

"Are you asleep?" he whispers.

I look him over. "No," I reply. Something about the darkness, the silence, and the privacy steals my anger and my stupid jumbled feelings. One look at his worried face and big round eyes and I want to reach for him.

I want to protect him and love him, but I hesitate. Everything is changing so fast between us, I don't even know if I could or should do that, but he shuffles into my room, shutting the door and hesitating once more.

"Can I stay here with you? It's weird without you next to me. I'm still not used to it." The fact that he will get used to sleeping without me one day makes my stomach roll. I shouldn't cross this line again. It will only confuse both of us, but I've always been unable to resist Ryker.

I lift the covers without a word. Ryker rushes over, relief in his eyes, and climbs into my bed, placing his pillow next to mine and scooting closer. I drop the covers, tuck them around him, and go back to staring at the ceiling.

I can feel him watching me, and I hear the bedding rustling as he moves closer. He rests his head on my pillow, his warm breath wafting over my cheek. "Are you mad at me?" he asks, sounding vulnerable.

Everyone else sees the big, bad, sexy rock star, dancing and singing on stage. They don't see this side of him, and maybe it's greedy, but I love how he lets himself be open with me, trusting me to keep it between us.

"No, I'm just tired," I admit, and I am, but I don't tell him it's of this game between us, wondering if he wants me the way I want him.

He moves again, and I stiffen as he notches his head just under my chin so effortlessly, his leg thrown over mine. It's such a familiar pose that's natural for us, but does he know it drives me crazy?

I drop my arm and wrap it around his back, holding him against me, and he sighs, snuggling closer. Can he feel my desire? If he does, he doesn't comment on it. It's an unspoken rule—do not give voice to the feelings between us.

Closing my eyes, I force myself to relax.

One day he'll stop doing this and I'll lose him, so until then, I'll hold on as tightly as I can.

When I wake to sunlight streaming through the curtainless window, he is gone. My bed is empty, and his pillow is gone along with him.

Isn't that how it goes for us?

We are together in the dark, but when the light arrives, we are through.

It's a dark secret.

SEVEN

RYKER

I now understand the jokes and looks we got last night when we mentioned not having our schedule yet. Our label demanded an early morning meeting, and we are all nursing coffee and Red Bull while sitting around the glass table in our management's skyscraper, facing off with two women and a man—Mrs. Noel, Miss Wilson, and Po Freen, our new manager. We have only been here an hour, and my head is already pounding from an information overload.

We are used to doing our own thing and being in charge of ourselves. I knew it would be an adjustment, but I never realized how much. What we wear and eat will be decided by them, not to mention what we perform and when. We have lost a lot of artistic control, but the trade-off is their expertise, money, and help, so I swallow my protests and smile. There are a lot of bands out there that would kill for this shot, so we have to grab it with both hands.

We need to sign our updated contract, and until then, we need to behave. Everything else was such a rush that this is one of the first official meetings we are having. Fox sits to my left, Dash is to my right, and Strike is next to him. The people across from us are wearing suits and dresses, while we are in band shirts, jeans, and shoes. We probably look how they imagined we would, and the same could be said for them.

They have been nothing but welcoming though.

"Do you need a break or another drink before we carry on?" Po asks before sharing a look with the two women at his side, who are going to help him manage our band. Apparently, he will be with us from now on. If we need anything, we go to him.

He's a few years older than us, with glowing dark skin, a buzzed head, an 80s tash that he somehow makes work, and a power suit. I don't know how he'll fit with us, but he seems to have adapted already. It's clear he's good, which is what we need. We need someone willing to do what it takes to get us to higher levels and who has the connections and understanding that we lack.

"I'm good. Do you guys want anything?" I glance at the others as they shake their heads. Dash's eyes are wide, staring around at all the awards, Strike is fighting sleep, and Fox is taking notes.

"Good, okay. So you have the house now, but if you need anything added or changed, just ask me. You have your new phones, and we have taken over your socials. Just run everything past me, remember?" I nod, and he smiles. "Good, so let's move onto your upcoming schedule. We have taken the liberty of planning this year so far. We can adapt when needed, but we would like to keep as many of the events as possible. Right now, you're trending, and we need to keep that hype up. That means shoving you into the public eye at every chance and giving them what they want." He clicks a button on his laptop, and the screen loads with a timeline that makes my eyes widen. "I know it looks terrifying, but I swear it's manageable. It's actually calmer than some wanted it to be, but I want to make sure you enjoy your music. However, it's about finding a balance between work and events and keeping you relevant. It won't be easy, but I know you guys understand hard work or you wouldn't be here."

My eyes stay wide as he runs through dates and events for the entire year, down to when we can have days off or time away, which is very rare. He goes over a social media marketing strategy next and then looks at us.

"As for music, when can we expect a new album?"

"Uh . . ." I blink, feeling Dash and Strike looking at me, but I'm still stuck on the schedule and trying to remember what they want from us.

"We would need time to work on it. As the schedule now stands, there isn't much. Could we review it and put a plan in place for this and then answer?" Fox takes over, and I give him a grateful look. He winks at me as Po grins.

"Absolutely. Great answer. If you promised me something immediately, I would be worried," he admits. "Okay, so the heavy stuff is out of the way. I know it's a lot, but I'll be on the other end of the phone for any questions. We know this is all new to you, and there will be a transition period, but we are here to help you. Now, we've done this a little backwards, since we moved so fast, but here are your updated contracts. The ones you signed before were just to get you in the label, but this is the finalized one. Please review them and sign, and we'll get going." He slides one across to each of us.

"Going where?" Dash asks.

"A photoshoot," Po responds with a smile. "For PR and promotion. It's just a general one. Don't worry, it will be fun. I'd also like to film some TikTok videos and reels before you go so I can schedule them for the next two weeks. Of course, as discussed, feel free to film anything that comes up and then send them to me so I can edit and approve before we post. I already have some ideas for you, Fox and Ryker."

"I bet," Strike scoffs. "Oh, can we do a dancing one? I always see them on my page, and they look like fun."

"You can't dance for shit." Dash grins, nudging him as I turn the first page of the contract, half listening as I scan the legal shit, although I don't understand most of it.

If I thought the schedule was insane, it has nothing on our new contract.

"Do you understand any of this?" Strike whispers to Dash.

"Nah, just sign it," he replies as they scribble their names.

After reaching the last page, I lift my pen to sign when one of the final clauses catches my eye, and I drag them up, meeting Po's.

"Yes, Ryker, you have a question?"

"This last clause . . ." I point at it, unable to look at Fox or the others, even as I feel them staring at me. "I don't understand," I finish, unable to say it out loud.

"Oh." Po opens his copy, scanning it for what I'm referring to. "Ah, that. It's a typical clause we have. We know it probably isn't needed, but it's better to be safe than sorry. Basically, there is no dating within the band. It just prevents excess drama or breaking up if something goes wrong."

"We are prohibited from dating?" Fox frowns.

"Just each other. Anyone else is fine, though we do ask you not to promote your relationships for a while, since your selling point right now is your sex appeal and availability." Po winces.

"Damn, our love is out," Dash teases Strike.

I nod, glancing back at it then Fox. He meets my gaze, his eyes holding a million questions I can't answer. He waits for me to make up my mind. Turning away, I sign my name before I chicken out or second-guess myself.

We aren't dating anyway.

It's just an act.

When he signs, though, it hurts.

Forcing a tight smile, I shut my contract and slide it back. "So what now?" I ask, unable to look at Fox.

Whatever we had was extinguished with that signature.

We can be nothing more than bandmates now.

Po wasn't joking. Dash and Strike filmed four videos while we were looking over the proposals, actual proposals, for ours.

"Are you okay with that?" Po asks for the tenth time after we review the next one. "With pretending to kiss?"

"It isn't anything we haven't done before," Fox scoffs, but he's been quiet, shaking his head every now and again. I guess he feels weird seeing how we need to act written out. Usually, we do what we feel, but now we are doing what they are telling us to so fans can ship us and create rumors.

"Okay, then let's film the first one."

Nodding, I head over to a white booth, followed by Fox. We have been to hair and makeup and even wardrobe, which took hours. Fox's eyes are darkened so much, his bright orbs pop, his blue hair is perfectly messy, and his lips are painted deep red. He has on a choker and so many rings, they clink as he moves his fingers.

He wears leather pants with white writing and drawings all over them, and they are tucked into metal boots. His shirt is black, the sleeves are rolled back, and only one button is fastened so most of his chest is exposed. It's a good look, but I want to reach out and smear Fox's makeup to make him look like my Fox, not this perfected version of him.

I wear matching pants with a thick belt and chains. My shirt is mesh, with safety pins down each side and the front, and it shows more skin than fabric. My eyes are lined, my lips are pink, and my hair is swept back.

"Okay, are you guys ready?" Po calls as they turn on the lights. It's blinding, and I glance around nervously before meeting Fox's eyes. He smiles reassuringly, and I take a deep breath, nodding to him and Po.

"Okay, three, two, one . . ." He goes quiet, and I dramatically turn away from Fox.

His hand grips my chin, and he drags me back to face him as I breathe heavily. For a moment, I stare into his eyes and beg him to kiss me. His head tilts as if he actually will before he looks at the camera and grins, covering the lens with his hand and pushing it away. I turn my head so he doesn't see the disappointment in my gaze.

"Amazing! One more take," Po tells us. "That was so good, guys. Ryker, this time, keep your eyes on Fox. Don't look away. He's your entire focus."

Licking my lips, I nod then glance at Fox. He rolls his eyes but moves back to the starting spot, and we run it again.

"Amazing! You guys are so hot! Next!"

The next video is supposed to look like it was captured naturally, so Fox stands by the snack table, browsing it as I hold the phone and film myself walking over. I lift my fingers to my lips to shush the audience as I sneak up on him and kiss his cheek. He turns, looking from me to the camera, feigning shock and shaking his head as I go to kiss his cheek again, only for him to turn, then I catch his lips before running off while he shouts my name.

We shoot three more videos before Dash and Strike join us, and then we film some quick band reels.

"Okay, awesome, onto the photoshoot! The photographers will be here in a moment," Po calls. "Just act naturally. You all have amazing charisma, so I told them to capture you however you guys want. Just be yourselves—flirt, laugh, or joke. Let's get some incredible shots!"

We get a ten-minute break, where I shovel down some food before we are told they are ready. I glance at the others who look just as nervous as I am, so I straighten my shoulders.

"Do those little cameras scare you?" I tease them as I grab Dash in a headlock. He struggles and laughs, and I hear the cameras snap as Strike leaps onto my back to try to save Dash, while Fox watches us before wading in. He plucks Strike off me and drags me away from Dash. My back hits his chest and my head tips backwards, an involuntary response, before my eyes meet his as his arm bands across my chest. I search his face, everything else fading away as he looks down at me. The flash of a camera brings me back to the present, and he starts to pull away, but I want this.

If this is the only way I can have him, then I will take it.

He might think it's for the cameras, but I don't care. Turning in his arms, I cup his jaw and press my forehead to his. "I like the outfit," I murmur. "It makes it easy to do this." My hand slides down his throat and into his shirt. He shudders against me, his eyes widening at how brazen I am, but it's almost as if he forgets the cameras, his own hand sliding down my spine before gripping my ass and tugging me closer. I shiver, and goosebumps erupt on my skin. My gaze drops to his lips as a strong urge to taste him courses through me. He tilts his head, ready to kiss me.

"Amazing, the chemistry is so incredible!" someone remarks, and we break apart, both of us suddenly remembering where we are.

Fox moves back to Dash and Strike as the camera continues to snap. I watch him the entire time, wondering if he would have done it if they hadn't called out.

I flirt with Fox, giving him lingering touches and looks that I hope he knows are real. I wish I could tell him, wish I could be like this, but now our contract prohibits it.

This is the only way I can have him.

It will have to be enough.

EIGHT

FOX

As soon as the cameras stop flashing, Ryker steps away from me, turning to talk to the photographer and Po. I remain where I am, staring at him as everyone else returns to their lives, while I'm stuck here.

It was all for the cameras.

He was doing it all for them, and now that it's over, he's back to acting like nothing happened and it meant nothing to him.

It meant everything to me. Looking into his eyes like that wasn't an act for me. It was the truth. The way I touch him, orbit around him, isn't a performance to me. It's the truth hidden behind actions. How can he touch me like that and feel nothing?

I turn and stalk away, needing some quiet time to myself. I make my way to a glass-covered walkway that connects to the next building. Leaning against the railing, I stare out at the city as the sun shines on it. I think I liked things better before.

Yeah, we were flirting and acting, but it was for us and no one else. It didn't feel so wrong, like my feelings were being exploited, used, and sold, packaged for the masses.

Shit, I shouldn't complain. This is everything we want, but it hurts so much.

"Hey, brother, are you okay?" I glance to my left as Strike leans into my side, handing over a water bottle. I accept it with a grateful nod, sipping it as I stare out at the city.

"I'm okay," I answer. "It's just—"

"A lot?" He laughs, and we share a smile. "I guess we dreamed about it so much that it's almost surreal. I thought it would be more . . . rock and roll, you know? But we should give it a chance. We get to make the music we want, so that's something." He nudges my arm as I smile.

He's right. Strike has this innocent happiness about him that's infectious. "True." I turn to look at him. "Are you okay with it all?"

"With being adored and waited on? It's so hard," he jokes, making me chuckle as I look at the city once more. "Did you ever think we would be here?" he murmurs after a moment.

"I hoped so, but it doesn't feel real yet," I reply. "I guess we should get used to it."

"*Can* you get used to it?" I glance at him to see he's serious for once. "I mean, this, how we are now, how you and Ry are now . . . can you adapt to it? Because if these new rules risk breaking up and losing our band, then I don't want them, fame or not. All I want is for us to be happy and together as a family, making music. Whether that's in empty clubs or sold-out stadiums, I don't care. I just want us to be together."

"I know you do." I know Strike well enough to understand that all he wants is a family. He's an orphan who grew up in the system, and he turned to music to find a way to forget, but he discovered that being in a band makes him happy. He's told me many times how thankful he is for us. He's our glue, always mediating our fights and keeping us together in a humble manner, so if I ask him to, he would give it all up as long as he gets to keep us.

It's one of the many reasons I love this man like a brother.

Tugging him close, I give him a hug. "I'm not going anywhere, and neither is Ry. We are all in this together, so we'll figure it out."

"But I don't want you to hurt," he murmurs innocently, fear in his eyes. "I know how you feel about Ry." He peers up at me as I swallow. "I'm not blind, Fox. We all know. We don't say shit because it isn't our business, but I don't want my brother hurting, not for any reason, so I'm not asking if you can handle this. I'm just asking if you are okay."

"I'll be fine," I promise. "These feelings will go away. I don't plan to act on them. I wouldn't hurt us for my own selfish reasons."

"And what about hurting yourself?" he questions. "You are willing to do that to keep us together?"

"I have been since I joined," I respond truthfully. "Since I fell in love with that clueless idiot. Don't worry, nothing will change. It's us, remember?"

"Against the world." He nods, and we both look out over the city, but his words roll through my head.

They all know . . .

Does he?

Does he pretend not to, or is he truly clueless? I don't know which is worse.

"Are you guys ready? Apparently, we have to catch a plane." We both turn, and I meet Ryker's questioning gaze before I smile at Dash and Po at his side.

"Sure, let's go." I keep my arm around Strike, sensing his anxiety and wanting to ease it.

I'll ignore this. I'll keep us together. I won't hurt them like that.

We are all damaged toys, and like our name, this is our sanctuary, but as I glance over at my bandmates, I wonder how this will change us.

What will we become now?

I send up a prayer that no matter what storm comes our way, we will weather it together because without each other, our dream means nothing.

I switch off the TV, letting the hotel room lapse into silence. The darkness surrounding me is only interrupted by my bandmates' snores. Atlas Records, our label, put us up in a shared room after an interview in another city, and everyone else crashed once we reached it. It was crazy from the moment we signed our contract, and it was almost three in the morning before our heads hit the pillows—everyone but me. The rhythmic sound is as familiar as my own breathing, but it's not enough to relax my troubled soul enough for me to sleep tonight.

My eyes land on the bed I should be sleeping in, one side of the covers pushed back and empty, the other wrapped tightly around him.

He's the reason I can't sleep.

I stare at his unmoving form, wishing he were as troubled as I am and understood why everything is changing yet staying the same all at once.

We are on our way to the top and finally getting our big break with this tour. The world knows our names, and all the tiny shows and empty seats are finally worth it, but I can't help missing the simplicity of our lives then.

The contract we signed today burns a hole in my bag, the words echoing in my head and heart, reminding me why I'm so restless.

I can't have him.

It wasn't blatantly stated in so many words, but it might as well have been.

Can I stop these urges and feelings?

I have to if we want to make it to the top. This is our time, and I won't ruin that for us all because of this forbidden love inside me.

He isn't mine, and he can't be, so why do I wish he were?

Why do I wish he loved me like I love him?

No, I must resist.

I have to.

RESIST

Six months later

Everything has changed.

In just six months, our band and image have grown. Our label is pushing us hard, and it's been a blur of back-to-back events, recording, and rehearsing. We barely have time for anything else, but Ryker finds his own ways to party and fuck his way through Hollywood—discreetly of course. We can't have the illusion of him and me ruined.

Our actual bond . . . yeah, that's long since ruined, or tainted at the very least.

He doesn't crawl into bed with me anymore. Hell, he isn't usually home, too busy fucking his way through the masses. He's become the sex symbol of rock, and I've lost him and whatever we had. He let the fame go to his head.

We still play for the cameras and shows, and every now and again, there are stolen touches and longing looks that remind me of what we had before, but it all seems so far away now. We are more like bandmates than anything else, and it hurts to see the man I love pulling away, falling in love with other people, and enjoying his life while I'm haunted by what could have been.

Instead, I focus on my music, writing us new songs and pushing myself harder for our future, and I work on keeping our band together when we feel like we are drifting apart. We spend less and less time together, and I hate it. I know Strike does as well, but we don't know how to fix it. There isn't one thing forcing a wedge between us. It's just time and fame, something we can't battle.

When the call comes, I'm almost relieved about what it means for us.

It's another chance to get close again and spend time together.

It's an opportunity to find our passion, love, family, and the reason we started.

NINE

RYKER

I hurry into the meeting room to find the others already there. Brushing my hair back, I sit heavily in the empty chair on the end, the farthest from Fox. He does that now, sits farther away from me. I hate it. It's the only time I can be close to him without raising suspicion.

"What's up, boss?" I call to Po, who grins at us.

"I have amazing news—incredible, actually. All your hard work has paid off." We wait with bated breath, and he grins. "You are going on tour as backup for Dead Ringers! It's sold-out, set to be the biggest of the year."

Strike and Dash whoop, hugging each other, but my eyes are on Fox as he drums his fingers on the table. "They are going ahead with the tour? I heard there were issues."

Does he know I watch him all the time? Things are different between us now, but it's for the best. Flirting was fun, but it wasn't worth risking our futures over. The label was serious. I saw firsthand what happens if you break their rules, so I refused to. Instead, I pulled away from Fox. I play the part they want, but I forced myself to stop reaching for him. It wasn't easy, and I've found myself in many other beds, trying to forget him. I know I hurt him and our band, which I hate, but this is the only way I can keep us moving to the top, our future within grabbing distance. I will not be the reason our band fails.

Not when I don't know if what we had was real or not.

We can be friends and bandmates; that isn't a problem. I never crossed the line with him—hell, I don't even know if I wanted to or just enjoyed the chase—so I stay away, but as he speaks, my eyes drift to his lips.

The actress's bed I just left feels far away, all that momentary pleasure fading as I look at him. It messes me up inside. I don't like guys, but I like him. I want him but I don't.

"The Dead Ringers have a . . . problematic past, but they are a huge name in the industry, and this tour is all anyone can talk about. It's a big deal and our chance to push you into many rock lovers' hearts. They are the perfect fit, and it's a great way to welcome you into touring life. You will have a bus and travel with them. Some nights you will stay in hotels, and others you'll be on the bus. It will be long and hard, but it will be worth it. I promise. We need to prepare some new songs to be ready by then, and we will rehearse twenty-four seven. Understood?" Po explains.

For a moment, Fox's eyes drift to me. "We can do that, can't we?"

Dash and Strike nod, but I know he's speaking to me. I don't spend time with them if I can help it. It's just too hard. I know they wonder why, Strike even cried one night when he was drunk and begged me to tell him what they did wrong so they could fix it. I never wanted to hurt them.

I just wanted to protect them.

Po is right. This is good news. It will give me a chance to fix everything between us and drive us to the top, where we belong. I don't understand my feelings for Fox, but I can have this with them . . . with him.

"Of course we can. We're Sanctuary." I smirk. "Let's do it, boss man."

"Then let's do it. You have today to celebrate. I'll pick you up bright and early tomorrow for an interview to announce your tour." Po stands. "Good job, guys. You're killing it. Remember the rules. No arrests or headlines tonight. Behave as much as you can." He eyes me, and I smile.

When he leaves, Dash and Strike hurry out. Fox stands and heads my way, his eyes locked on me. I can't breathe or move as he advances on me.

Being the center of Fox's attention is all-consuming. He's just that strong. "You better be there in the morning. This is important."

"I will," I murmur, my voice hoarse.

His hand drifts out, and I swear my heart skips a beat. I lean in, hoping he's going to touch me like the old days, but his skin doesn't even touch mine as he grabs my designer shirt.

He lifts it, righting it for me. "The scratch marks were showing," he says, his voice cold and distant. I glance down and see he's right. She must have done a number on my back as well as my front, and for some reason, I want to apologize, but he's already gone.

I feel like I've betrayed him somehow.

They say actions speak louder than words—so what are his actions saying, and why does it make my heart clench so painfully that I struggle to breathe?

Have I finally lost Fox?

TEN

FOX

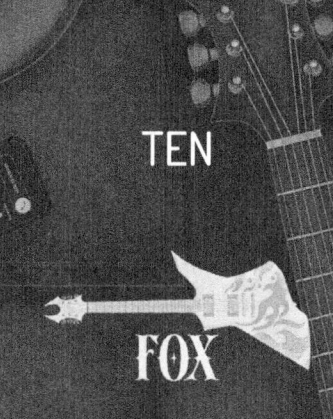

"Oh, come on, please, Fox," Strike whines, placing his hands together in a prayer as he pouts at me. "One night to celebrate. Your lyrics and scribbles will still be here when you get back. You don't even have to drink."

"We have to be up early for the interview. You guys can go if you want to," I mutter, focusing on my notepad. Don't they understand I need to work? I have to write songs so we can keep growing.

"Fox," Ry snaps as he turns from the mirror where he was fussing with his hair. I don't know why. It always looks perfect. Heading my way, he places his ring-covered hands on my arms. "This is great news. We should celebrate like we used to—together as a band. Po is right. This is important. It's our chance. Don't you want to celebrate with us? We worked so hard for this. Come on, it will be like old times."

My heart skips a beat then slams in my chest as I stare into his eyes. It's the closest we've been without a camera on us in ages. I can smell his whiskey scent and feel his warmth. My eyes sweep over his stunning face, desire pooling low in my belly as I remember the way it felt pressed against my chest as he slept. His smile drops, and he glances at my lips as if remembering as well, and my gaze moves lower, watching his Adam's apple bob.

My eyes drop to his partially opened shirt, and I see the scratch marks there, making my heart go cold. The desire and want I felt disappear, so I steel myself and glare at him.

"What's wrong?" he asks quietly, no doubt sensing the change in me.

At this point, I'd rather die than admit that I'm in love with him.

I eye his hands on my arms, and he leans back, removing them. "Please?" he cajoles. "Just a few drinks, some music, and then we'll come back. No getting drunk or misbehaving."

I scoff, not believing him. He doesn't know how to control himself anymore. He can't lie to me.

"I promise," he begs, standing next to Strike and copying his pose. Dash quickly joins in on his other side. "Just us tonight to celebrate how far we've come. Don't make us go without you. We're a family."

I want to ask when we became a family again, but the hope in their eyes is my undoing. I don't want to make them sad or disappoint them. This is big news, and they are right. We should celebrate. It's not their fault I have feelings for that idiot.

"Fine, give me five," I mutter as I stand.

I head upstairs to my room, ignoring their cheers. I'm back down in under four minutes, my hair loose and wavy. The blue was only refreshed this morning for the interview, so it looks good. I have my rings, earrings, and necklaces in place and wear leather pants with a big belt, a sheer shirt, and my usual leather jacket. I ignore the eyes on me, refusing to look as I pull my boots on and head out the door.

"Are you coming?" I call.

"It's party time!" I hear Dash yell, and I can't help but smile.

Ryker picked the place, since he knows all the clubs and hangout spots. He spends all his nights in them so he should. There's a line when we get out of the car, and it stretches all the way down the block. I hesitate when I see how busy the converted church is, but Ryker ignores the line and heads right to the door. Sighing, I follow him. I hear whispers, and I even see some people snapping pictures. "Are we okay here?" I ask him.

He turns his head, and I have to jerk back to prevent his lips from crashing into mine. His eyes widen, and he doesn't speak for a minute. "Ry?"

"Oh, um . . ." He blinks and laughs. "Yeah, only celebrities are allowed, and no photos, so we are fine." Turning back to the bouncer, he flashes his smile, and the door is opened despite the extensive line.

"How often do you come here for them to know you on sight?" Dash chuckles, slinging an arm around Ry as he heads through the ancient-looking church door.

Strike loops his arm with mine and grins at me. "Come on. Forget everything else, let's have a good night."

"Sure," I mutter, trying to force myself to cheer up since he's so excited, but he frowns, obviously sensing my mood. I lean closer and murmur, "I promise I'm fine. Let's have a good night."

That perks him up, and when I glance back, Dash and Ry are waiting for us. Dash is smiling, but Ry's eyes are hard as he glances between Strike and me. My frown deepens, but he turns away and heads through another set of chapel doors, and we have no choice except to follow.

Once through the next set, the beat flows through me. There is a famous punk song playing, and that makes my eyebrows rise. I don't know what I expected, but it isn't the Gothic, satanic church vibe they have going, with a huge demon at the back wrapped around a cross, blowing fire. The red lights only add to the atmosphere. The bar is painted black, and there are cages hanging from the ceiling with dancers inside.

The stained-glass windows are a mocking reminder as celebrities dance or sprawl across casual sofas and even some pews.

I can't help but stare. It's fucking amazing.

"I thought you might like this place," Ry yells into my ear, leaning up to be heard. "I've wanted to bring you here for a while."

He kept asking, and I kept saying no.

His hand slides down my arm, and his fingers twine with mine as he tugs me along. "Come on, let's grab a table." I stare at our joined hands, and he tugs me, so I let him pull me after him. The warmth of his palm against mine causes desire and joy to course through me, right up until a beautiful woman steps into our path. Her eyes are sparkling and familiar as she looks at Ryker.

"Hi, Ryker. I'm Chelsea. Remember me?" She smiles seductively, caressing her hand along his forearm. He doesn't push her away, but he grips my hand tighter.

"Uh, yeah, sure," he replies, sounding uncertain before he turns the charm on. "You look beautiful tonight."

She giggles and clutches his arm, refusing to let go, and she's basically dragged between us.

We both know who will win, so I bow out.

Pulling my hand free, I smile at them. "I'm going to grab a drink."

"Fox, wait—" I ignore his voice and head over to the bar with Strike and Dash.

They pull me between them. "What are you drinking?" Dash asks.

"Just a beer, thanks," I call over the music as a man in a waistcoat and not much else comes over and leans into Dash to take his order. I glance behind us, unable to help myself. Despite his words, Ry doesn't seem too bothered about me leaving. Chelsea is plastered against him, stroking his chest as she grins up at him while he smiles down at her. Looks like he's found his latest in a long line.

Turning away in annoyance, I nod my thanks to the bartender and drain some of my beer. "Want to grab a table?" Dash asks, oblivious to my inner turmoil.

I shouldn't have come. I knew what I would see, which is exactly why I don't go out with him or them. I'm trying to move on from my feelings for Ry, but I'm not strong enough to watch him fuck around right in front of me. Knowing it and seeing it are two very different things.

"Don't let him ruin your night," Strike murmurs to me, smiling sadly.

I nod and force another smile, not wanting to ruin Strike's. Draping my arms around him and Dash, I turn back to the club. "Let's do this. Where do you want to sit?"

"Oh, over there." Dash points at a square selection of sofas, and I let him lead us across the dance floor. As soon as we sit, people flock to us. It's something I'm still not used to, but even amongst celebrities, we seem to be popular. I don't know if it's because we are new or if they genuinely like us, but it's hard to tell, and none of it ever appears genuine or real.

Just like my and Ry's relationship, it's all for show.

I smile and talk with them, never going too deep. I joke and laugh, letting Strike and Dash lead the conversation until Dash leans forward. "Sorry, lovers, we are out celebrating tonight. It's a band night, you understand?"

They wander away and leave us in peace, and I sip my beer as I tap my foot to the music until Ryker suddenly appears.

"Sorry about that." He offers us a grin and slides onto the couch next to me, sitting so close our thighs touch despite there being room on the other side.

"Managed to escape the one-night stand?" Dash jokes.

I feel Strike's eyes on me, but I ignore him as I sip my beer. It doesn't hurt me anymore. At least, that's what I tell myself.

"Something like that," Ryker mutters, and then he leans into me. "Did you get me a drink?"

"Bar's there, get your own," I grumble, and then I lean into Strike. "Did you see that Olly is over there, from Scar Head?"

"I did. Is it weird if we fanboy and go over?" Strike laughs, leaning into me and giving me the out I need from Ry. I feel his eyes on me, but I ignore him. I'm not his slave, nor his boy. I'm his bandmate, and at this point, I'm barely that. He made it this way, so he has to live with it.

"Oh, I met him the other night. Want me to introduce you?" Ryker offers hopefully, butting in. Strike and I share a look, and I sit back and nurse my beer. Ry seems to slump. "I can. He's really nice."

"It's okay," Strike replies. "I'm sure we'll meet him later."

"Okay." Ry slumps further, looking at us before perking up. "You guys want another drink?"

"Sure," Dash answers, and Ry hops up, grinning at us. "Strike? Fox?"

"I'm good," I murmur, scanning the crowd.

"I'm okay, thanks," Strike tells him.

I feel Ry staring, but then he's gone, and I take another sip of my beer. He returns quickly and sits right next to me again, sipping some fruity cocktail. "Good club, right?" He's trying too hard, and I respect that. We've all been distant recently, so I relax a little and try to be his friend.

As the night goes on, though, he gets bolder. He leans into me, touches me, and teases me. It could be friendly banter, but when you're in love with someone, it's hard not to take things like that to heart.

Does he even realize how much it hurts every time he turns that wide grin on me and touches my arm?

"Dance with me?" he pleads abruptly. It's something we did all the time before.

"No, I'm okay," I reply and see the shock in his eyes as the rejection sets in. I don't want to hurt him, but I can't dance with his hands all over me and mine all over him like nothing is different between us. It would be crossing the line he drew, and I won't do that again.

I've been burnt enough.

"Please, Foxy?" he implores. "We can burn it up like old times—"

"I'm good," I interrupt. I don't need a trip down memory lane, especially not tonight when I'm already on edge. If I danced with him, I'd end up taking it too far.

He looks so crestfallen, I have to avert my eyes, and Dash laughs awkwardly. "How about I dance with you?"

"Sure," Ry agrees, but he looks back at me as they walk to the dance floor.

"You did the right thing," Strike murmurs.

"I know." I down my drink. "I'm going to get another." I leave Strike there, but by the time I'm halfway to the bar, he's surrounded by others again. My eyes find Dash and Ry as they dance and laugh on the floor before I focus on the bar and lean against the sticky top.

Someone moves to my right, waiting to order as well. I place mine and wait. When my beer appears, I grab it just as someone backs into me on my left. My beer tips, falling all over the person on my right.

"Shit, sorry." I grab some napkins and wipe the man's arm. He chuckles, the warm sound making my head jerk up and my eyes widen.

Shit. He's fucking pretty.

"Thank you."

I blink. He has bright green eyes, wavy, shoulder-length blond hair, and a muscular build with a killer smile. He's not my usual type, but damn he's hot.

"Fuck, I said that out loud, didn't I?" I mutter.

"You did, but I liked it. Don't worry." He gives me a crooked grin. "I'm Team."

"Team?" I echo.

He laughs. "I know. My parents were hippies and thought it was funny. What's your name?"

I blink in surprise. "You don't recognize me?" I'm not arrogant. It's just a fact that we tend to get recognized a lot, and it's tiring.

How do you know if someone is getting close for real or as an act?

"Sorry, I'm kind of a hermit, so I don't recognize you," he replies, and fuck if that isn't attractive. This isn't someone trying to align themselves with me. It's a genuine interaction, and maybe that's why I relax.

"Fox, my name's Fox," I tell him with a grin.

"Well, Fox, let me replace that beer." Before I can speak, he holds his hand up and orders for me.

"You didn't have to," I say.

"It was totally my fault." He winks. "Besides, I want to buy you a drink. Are you here alone?"

"Oh, smooth. Trying to find out if I'm single?" I chuckle, leaning into the bar.

"Maybe. Is it working?" He leans closer as the music thumps.

"I'm here with my band. You?"

"Oh, now the tables are turning." He takes a drink from a wine glass as he runs his eyes down my body before meeting mine again. "I'm single, no bodies—figuratively or literally—in my past, not closeted, and definitely your type."

"Cocky. I didn't ask for all that." I smirk as I take a sip of my beer.

"Just getting it out there in case you were interested." He leans closer, opening his mouth, when someone suddenly appears between us, shoving us apart.

"I'm thirsty." Ry presses between us, his back to Team, and drains my beer before wiping his mouth. "Come dance."

"I'm good here. You go on," I say, frowning at my bottle and then him.

"I'm thirsty too." Dash grins from his side and downs Team's drink before dragging Ry back to the dance floor, but his eyes are on me the entire time. I watch them go before turning to Team, surprised he didn't run away.

"Sorry about them," I mutter. "Let me get you another."

"It's okay. They seem fun," he remarks, "and I'm not easily scared off."

"You sure there aren't any bodies in your past? You aren't a serial killer, are you?" I tease.

"No, but I might eat you alive if you ask nicely," he flirts.

Fuck.

I almost choke on air, so I turn away to hide my surprised blush, and when I turn back, he's grinning. "So, Fox, are we going to stand at the bar all night, or can I make you sit with me?"

"Ask nicely," I retort as I hand him his drink. I realize I'm flirting, and it feels . . . good. He isn't doing it for an act. He looks fucking interested.

He might just be the distraction I need. Besides, Ry is definitely taking someone home tonight, so maybe it's time I do as well. I don't usually do one-night stands, but it can't be hard, right? If he's able to fuck like nothing is wrong, then so can I.

Team's mouth brushes my ear, making me shiver. "Please come sit with me, Fox." He drags out my name, and when he leans back, his eyebrow arches.

Gripping my beer, I turn and begin to walk away from the bar, but then I glance back. "Are you coming?"

He follows me with a laugh, slipping his hand around my waist as I head to a booth next to ours since not many others are free.

After sliding in, I expect him to sit on the opposite side, but he scoots in right next to me and turns to face me, his arm draped along the back. He's good, I'll give him that. He knows exactly how to make someone look at him.

"Model, right?" I guess.

"How did you know?" he responds, his eyes widening in surprise.

"You know how to pose." I gesture down at him, and he blushes.

"Habit." He sounds embarrassed. "But it also means I look good without clothes on."

I can't help but laugh. "You're really forward."

"What's the point in holding back? I know exactly what I want, and I always get it. Besides, being shy never got me anywhere."

"And what do you want?" I ask.

"Isn't that obvious?" he murmurs, placing his hand on my thigh and squeezing. "For you to take me home tonight."

Rolling my lips in, I eye him. Can I do it? Can I take him home?

Can I be the sort of person who takes something and leaves? It wouldn't have expectations, just pleasure and fun, but under it all . . . would I be imagining it's *him*?

Am I trying to fill the hole Ryker left with others? I probably won't even remember Team's face or name, but I'd remember the way it felt to fuck someone, wishing it were my bandmate.

Fuck, I'm so messed up inside.

I don't know what Team sees on my face, but he leans in. "How about we talk a bit more first? There's no need to rush this. I have all night, so let's have some fun."

"I can do that," I reply.

Sitting next to Team, I cross my legs and lean back. His arm on the back of the sofa touches my shoulder, and I don't move away. He leans in to be heard over the music, and his eyes seem to darken. "I have to admit something."

"Oh?" I lift my beer as I wait.

"I knew who you were at the bar." I blink, and he grins. "I didn't think you'd talk to me if I admitted that . . . and I wanted to talk to you—badly."

I groan. "You aren't an obsessed fan, are you?" We get some of them, especially for Ry and me. Some even attacked Ry after they saw him walking with one of our friends in public, joking around. They are very protective over our "ship."

"No, but I might just become one." He winks.

"No, I want another! I can decide how much I fucking drink," Ry yells behind me. I glance back and see Strike and Dash sharing a worried look as Ry downs two drinks and then heads to the bar.

"Everything okay?" Team asks, drawing my gaze back to him. "Do you need to deal with that?"

"No, not at all," I murmur as I smile at him. "He's an adult, and he can look after himself."

"Then where were we . . . ? Ah, so being a rock god, what's it like?"

I burst into laughter.

For the next hour, we talk about everything and anything, just flirty, fun conversation, and it's nice. He looks at me, smiles, and touches me. He's very obvious about what he wants, and it's nice to have someone who wants me like that.

It makes me feel good and desired, not tossed aside and discarded. He's all I see and hear. It's nothing deep and lasting, but it's fun, and I think I need that.

"Come on, Ry, you've had enough." Strike sighs behind me, and I glance over to see him fighting to get a drink out of Ryker's hand. "Let's get you home." He tries to help him up, but Ry slaps him away.

"No, I want Fox to take me."

"Damn it, Ry, stop. You aren't being fair. We'll take you," Strike mutters with annoyance in his tone, something I've never heard.

"No, Fox!" Ry slurs.

I wasn't trying to ignore Ry or the others, but I can see how shit-faced he is. He's a mess and clearly fucking drunk despite his one-drink promise. Sighing, I eye him anxiously as he smacks Dash and Strike away again.

"No, I want Fox!" he yells, drawing eyes, and I know we are going to get kicked out before long.

"Shit," I mutter.

"Go." I glance back at Team, and he smiles. "It's fine, go. He's your bandmate. If you ever feel like finishing where this was going, hit me up." He grabs my phone, adds his number, and hands it back. "If not, I had fun flirting with you. You're really easy to talk to."

"You too," I admit as I stand. "Thank you for a good night. I really didn't want to come tonight, but I'm glad I did."

He smiles. "I'm glad you did too."

I smile back, then I turn and hurry to our table as Ry starts yelling again. The bouncers notice. "No, fuck off. I want my Fox!" he yells loudly at Strike as he kicks him, making him grunt.

"I'm sorry, man." Strike sighs deeply as I appear at their side.

"It's fine," I say before I crouch and grab Ry's hands, jerking him up into a sitting position. He blinks at me. "Ryker," I snap.

His yell cuts off, and he grins before tossing his arms around me. "There you are. I knew you'd come. I'm drunk, Foxy, and I want to go home with you. Take me home," he slurs.

I peer at his grinning face. "You're a mess, Ryker. What happened to behaving tonight?"

He pouts. "You didn't want to play with me, but you were playing with him," he mutters. "Do whatever you want. I can drink if I want to," he snaps before he suddenly presses his face into my neck and inhales. I try to ignore him as he wraps himself around me. "I missed you," he whines.

"Alright, time to go." I hoist him into the air and toss him over my shoulder, my hand on his back to keep him in place. "Do not throw up on me, Ry. I mean it," I snap.

Turning to Strike and Dash, I see they already have our coats. "Come on, let's get him home before we get into trouble."

"Good idea. You okay with him?" Strike asks. "I can carry him if you want."

"No, Fox!" Ry yells and almost falls off my shoulder. Grunting, I straighten him and smack his hip.

"Stop moving or I'll dump you," I warn harshly, and he whines as I focus on Strike. "Nah, it's okay. Come on, let's go home."

I wave at Team as I head to the door.

Ryker's hands slide down my back and smack my ass as he giggles.

I fucking hate the way I like it.

He smells like a brewery.

I dump him on his bed, and he groans, his eyelids fluttering, but they remain shut. I should just leave him, but I can't. Crouching down in annoyance, I pull off his shoes and socks before sitting him up. He sighs and buries his face in my chest as I tug his shirt off and toss it toward his hamper. It's a mess in here. There are clothes and makeup everywhere.

"Alright, baby boy, down you go." I help him into bed, tucking the sheets around him before grabbing the makeup wipes on the side table. Pushing back his hair, I carefully rub off eyeliner and mascara before tossing the used wipe into the trash.

My hand lingers on his face, tracing his perfect features, and I allow myself a moment of weakness. He sighs and leans into my touch, and I swallow the pain it causes before leaping up and backing away. I can't let myself become entangled again. I can't give into this. We are too broken.

Turning away, I pick up his clothes and clean his mess, just like I used to in the van, but when I'm lining up his notes on his desk, I freeze when I see the only framed picture in the entire room. I don't know how I didn't notice it before, but it's in a dark frame, the only personal touch in the entire place, and completely clean and dusted.

Picking it up carefully, I scan our faces. It's just him and me. We were young and we had barely just met, my hair my natural bright blond. Ryker and I smile as he leans into me. We look so happy.

How the fuck did we get to this from that?

"Fox," he whines behind me. Setting the framed photo down, I hurry back to his side. "I feel sick."

I roll him to his side and help him sit up, noticing his face is pale. "Why did you drink so much?" I ask.

He's quiet, but his eyes open and he stares at me. "Do you think he's better looking than me?"

"Who?" I ask, confused as I find a bottle of water on his side table and open it.

"That guy from tonight," he mutters, seeming less drunk now. I find some pain pills and place them on the table as I turn back to him.

I ignore his question. I'm not playing this game with him. It isn't fair. The one night I go out and have fun, I'm made to drag his drunk ass home.

"Drink," I tell him, and he turns his face away. "Ryker. Drink," I demand.

"No. Tell me," he counters.

Gripping his chin, I turn his face back to mine. His eyes widen as I pour the water into my mouth and force his open, then I spit it into his and cover his lips with my hand. "Swallow," I demand.

I feel his Adam's apple bob as he swallows, then I nod and release him, capping the water before I grab one of the pills and press it to his lips. He rolls them inwards, and I lose patience. Gritting it between my teeth, I force his mouth open, and he gently bites it from mine and swallows. This time, I pour the water into his mouth, and he swallows it.

"Fox—"

"Don't," I mutter.

He stares at me as I tidy his nightstand. "I'm sorry." His voice is slurred, but it makes me look at him. "I am."

"You're always sorry, but then you always do it again," I mutter.

"I know." He catches my hand, and I look at him, seeing something vulnerable in his gaze as he swallows hard. "I love you."

"Okay, time to sleep." My voice is thick with agony. I wish he could say those words and mean them, but he won't remember tomorrow, and it isn't fucking fair. They are the three words I ache to hear more than anything, and to him, they are just a drunken memory he would rather forget.

How many times has he told me he loves me when he's drunk?

"No, say it back," he demands.

"Ryker, you are being a brat—"

"Good! At least you're looking at me!" he snaps, shoving me away with loose limbs.

"What do you mean?" I frown as I sit him up, but he's swaying.

"You don't look at me anymore. You barely even acknowledge me. It's like I don't exist to you, and I hate it. I fucking hate it!" Tears form in his eyes. "I hate that you spent all night with him. I wanted us to have fun like old times. Why can't we?"

"We just can't," I reply.

"But why?" he demands. "Why do you hate me so much?"

"I wish I hated you!" I snap as I shake him. "We are too far gone, Ryker. Everything is too messed up between us, and you pulling this shit doesn't help. If you want to be in my life, then good, fine—be a better friend, a better bandmate—but not like this."

"You won't ignore me anymore?" he whispers as tears leak down his face, and despite me knowing better, I brush them away. He's always been a sloppy drunk.

"I could never ignore you, even if I wanted to. I'm aware of every single thing you do, and it hurts," I admit. "Now get some sleep. If you want, we can talk again in the morning."

"Okay." He sniffles and settles down. "We'll talk in the morning."

"Sure." I nod even though I know we won't.

He's a liar. He'll be back to running in the morning and acting like nothing happened.

His tear-filled eyes lock on me as he wraps himself around my arm. "Stay with me tonight? Please?"

"Ry—"

"Please, Fox," he whispers. "I can't sleep without you here. I don't want to."

Doesn't that echo my own thoughts? I remind myself that the alcohol addled his brain.

"Okay," I agree despite knowing it isn't in my best interest, and I scoot up the bed, letting him curl into my side. He begins snoring within seconds, wrapped around me tightly, like he's scared I'll run away. In reality, he's the one running as far and as fast as he can from me and our band, wrecking everything we worked for.

I don't understand Ryker anymore. Why is he acting like this all the time?

He isn't the same man I fell in love with, or even the one I joined the band for.

He's different, and I wish I knew what changed him. Was it the fame, the pressure, or something else?

My phone buzzes, and I pull it out with my free arm, reading the text.

> Team: I hope you got home okay. I mean it, rock star. I'm here whenever you need me.

I glance from the text to Ryker, wondering why the fuck I can't just let him go.

SANCTUARY

ELEVEN

RYKER

Fox is gone when I wake up, and I understand how he must feel when I do that—used and annoyed. My head aches like a son of a bitch, though, drowning out everything apart from the annoying ringing of my phone, trying to wake me up.

For a moment, I can't remember why until Po's words come back to me.

Early interview.

Grabbing my cell, I toss it at the wall and drape my arm across my face to block the light, but I know if I stay here, I'll sleep, so I roll to my feet. My skin feels hot and sticky, and my legs are weak. Stupid fucking hangover. Noticing the water on my nightstand, I down it and toss the pills back before stumbling to the shower and turning it on. I shudder when the freezing cold water touches my skin, but it does the trick and wakes me up.

Unfortunately, it also brings back last night's events, and I rest my forehead against the tiled wall in shame. Why the fuck would I act like that? I practically fucking confessed to him, not that he cared. Hitting my head into the wall, I try to beat some sense into myself.

I wasn't jealous. I was just being me, acting out for attention.

That's why I got drunk. That's the only reason. It wasn't because that stupid blond fuck was all over Fox. I was just in a mood.

That's what I tell myself over and over as I dry off and dress before second-guessing myself. If I go down there, I'll have to face Fox. He might continue our conversation from last night or, worse, demand to know why, and I'm not ready for that. I can't hide up here all day though. They are already annoyed with me, and being late for the interview I promised not to be late for won't help my cause.

Plucking up my courage, I head down to the kitchen where I hear them. I stand at the door and look them over.

Act natural, Ryker, act natural.

No weird acts, no showing yourself up.

Natural.

"Good day," I call, and I instantly want the ground to swallow me whole.

Good day?

Good fucking day?

Dash's and Strike's eyebrows rise as they echo my thoughts. "Uh, good day?"

Fox nods, his eyes glued to his phone, and I hesitate, expecting him to demand we finish our talk that I am so not ready for. I don't want him to reject me, not when I already feel this shitty. I might enjoy some pain when I fuck, but not the kind where my heart gets crushed. That doesn't really do it for me.

Choking? Yes. Heartbreak? No.

I might be a masochist, but the love of your life pissing on your feelings is a little too much for me.

I head past them and pour myself a coffee, but Dash and Strike return to their conversation. Fox smiles softly as he thumbs out a text, and my eyes narrow in annoyance. Doesn't he care about why I acted the way I did last night?

He would have before.

I'm pissed that he won't even look at me.

"Who are you texting?" I ask, but it comes out as a sharp

command. Strike and Dash stop talking, but I can't look away from Fox. He doesn't even glance at me, just totally ignores me like I didn't even speak, and I hate it.

I want his eyes on me.

I want all his attention on me.

Narrowing my eyes, I put my mug down and step closer to his back. He's completely oblivious as he types a message, and I see the name Team at the top. Yanking his phone from his grip, I dance out of his reach as he pushes to his feet, his narrowed eyes now on me.

Finally, I can breathe again.

"Give it back, Ryker," he orders, his hand outstretched.

"Nope." He chases me around the table, so I climb on top of it as he grabs me to tug me down. Holding it above my head, I start to read the messages.

"Team? Who's Team? Stupid fucking name. What is he, a sport?" I scoff. "I agree, you looked so strong last night carrying your bandmate out of there." I glance down at Fox, my heart lodged in my throat before I breathe around it. "Is this your friend from last night?" I taunt cruelly as I scroll up. "'Fox, I wish you came home with me.' Wow, he doesn't have much game, but I suppose it doesn't matter who you fuck though. I thought you had better taste." I laugh, and he releases me, but I carry on.

"'We should meet up sometime and finish what we started,'" I scoff even as my heart aches, and my hand clenches the phone firmly enough to crush it.

"Ryker, stop it," Fox demands, but I ignore him, starting to type a message back.

"Ryker, enough!" Strike roars, and my gaze swings to him in shock, my hand dropping. "You are being a cruel asshole."

My mouth drops open as even Dash looks at me in disgust. Fox snatches his phone back, throwing me a hurt glare, and then he storms from the room. I watch him go, knowing I need to go after him, but when I hop down from the table, Strike and Dash block my path, their arms crossed and eyes tight.

"We need to talk," Strike snaps.

"Sure, later." I go to step past him and blow out an irritated breath when they move with me, blocking me. "What? Want me to apologize to him? Fine, I will. I was just having some fun."

"That's your problem. You're always having fun," Strike snaps.

Dash lays a hand on his arm to cool him down as he looks at me sadly. "You don't understand that your fun hurts him. He's your bandmate, your friend, Ryker, so why are you acting like this and treating him like shit?"

"Me? Treating him like shit? Since when?" I retort.

"Since we got the fucking deal. You're either using him and tossing him aside or leading him by the fucking collar. He can't catch a break. No wonder he's confused and pulling away. I don't think you even know what you're doing, but this act? It has to fucking stop before you lose all of us."

"It isn't fair, Ry," Strike says sadly. "You're making him miserable."

"I have no idea what you mean," I hedge.

"Yes, you do," Strike retorts, eyeing me like he sees right through me. Has he always known? Does everyone? "Don't play games with him. Just leave him alone and let him move on."

I stiffen, eyeing them both, wondering what they know.

"What if I don't want to?" I snap, tilting my chin up. "Fox is mine. He's my guitarist—"

"He isn't yours," Strike argues. "You made that clear, which means you need to let him go and let him move on. If this . . . show between you two starts to affect his mental health, then I will put a stop to it, and I mean it. It isn't fair, and it isn't fun for him anymore. It's work, a chore, and it hurts him. Fox is my friend—"

"And I'm not?" I whisper, hurt.

"Not recently," Strike snaps. "You're never here, and when you are, it's to make a mess Fox has to clean up. If you want to be our friend again, then start fucking acting like one and stop hurting us."

Strike storms away, and Dash watches him go before eyeing me dejectedly.

"He's right, Ry. If you keep this up, you'll ruin us. There won't be a band left. We'll crash and burn before we even begin. We can't do this without you, but we need Fox as well, and right now, you're pushing him away over and over, and at some point, he's just not going to come back." He moves past me and shakes his head in disappointment.

I watch them all walk away from me, my heart cracking.

I hear their pain, their pleas . . .

Can't they feel my own agony?

I never wanted to ruin us, which is exactly why I pulled away. It seems I am doomed to fail either way.

TWELVE

FOX

I tug on my shirt, trying to cover more of my skin, but it's no use. The contract stipulates that we have a wardrobe department who chooses all of our clothes, and in this case, that means barely any. I wouldn't usually mind, but there's a crowd waiting for us outside. The interviewer is discussing the latest rock and pop news before we are announced. Every eye will be on us, and they want us to look perfect.

"Here." Ryker steps before me, close enough that I can smell his expensive cologne, and tries to fix my shirt, or lack of one, for me. It's more of a cape with sequins, draped across my shoulders and tied with a bow at my neck. Luckily, the black pants they gave me have a high waist. I'll admit, it looks good, but I feel very exposed.

Ryker smiles at me shyly and brushes some strands of my purposely messy hair away. It's supposed to look wet, whatever that means, but it keeps falling into my eyes and face and probably smudging all the hard work the makeup team did.

They aimed for light and dark. While I'm all in black, looking every inch a rock villain, Ryker is in all white.

His shirt is floral with pearls, and it's tucked into white pants. His hair is pushed back, making him look like a model, and he's barely wearing any eyeliner or makeup, mostly just a highlighter that glitters under the light, making him look ethereal. I can't drag my eyes away from his glowing skin revealed by the sheer parts of the shirt. The fucking glitter on his lips drives me crazy, and I have the insane urge to lick it off to see what it would taste like.

"It's smudged here." Licking his thumb, he reaches up and brushes it under my eye. I pull back a little, and his smile drops as he steps away. "Sorry, I was just trying to help."

I nod and avert my eyes. We haven't spoken since this morning, and I don't particularly want to. I'm still mad at him—not for reading my messages, but because of how he acted. He believed he had a right to be mad, like he doesn't put his dick in every available hole, but the idea of me doing so pisses him off?

Dash and Strike join us. They wear a mix of white and black, blending us together. "You ready?" I ask them.

"As we will ever be." Dash nods, looking between Ryker and me. I'm sure both of them can feel the tension, but I can't seem to stop my simmering anger.

"Okay, one minute," one of the headphones-wearing staff members calls as he appears before us. "When I signal you, walk out, wave at them, and take your seats, okay? Your manager has already handed over the list of questions."

"Sure thing," Strike answers with a wide grin as he tries to change the atmosphere. This is an important night for us, yet we all look like we would rather be anywhere else.

Is my mood really affecting the band that much?

Strike once told me Ryker is the heart of the band, but I'm the head, and what I feel affects them all. I'm starting to realize he's probably right.

"Okay, thirty seconds. Big smiles," the man instructs, and then he starts to count down

"Fox, I'm—" Ryker starts, drawing my gaze to his face just as the man points to us, letting us know it's our turn on stage.

I walk past him, ignoring his words, but I swear I hear the end of his sentence float to me as I step out into the spotlight. "So sorry."

I force a smile, waving and winking at the crowd as they shout for us. When Ryker appears, it becomes so loud, I can barely hear. Heading to the curved sofas, I sit next to Dash, and Strike takes the spot next to him, leaving the space next to me, nearest the crowd, for Ryker. When he sits, we laugh and wait for the crowd to calm down. When it does, the interviewer, Henley, fans himself.

"What an entrance, am I right?" The crowd cheers, and he nods. "I have the great honor of having the up-and-coming rock band Sanctuary joining me tonight. Are we excited?" The applause and shouts last for a while, and I smile tightly through it all.

It isn't their fault. They are here to support us, and we wouldn't be here without them. I remind myself of that over and over to change my mood, not wanting our fans to feel it.

"Alright, alright, before we get started, let's get comfortable," Henley says. "Strike, right? Drum king."

Strike stands and bows as the crowd cheers.

"And then we have Dash, the bass wizard." Dash waves and blows kisses as Henley looks at me.

"And of course, the sex symbol himself, Fox!" The crowd's screams are so loud, I laugh as I stand, smirking and winking at them as they continue shouting. Even when I sit, my name is yelled, and we have to wait.

"And last but certainly not least, the silken singer, Ryker!" The crowd screams even louder as he gives them a little twirl and a wave before sitting. His hand lands on my thigh without him meaning to, and when I glance at it, he snatches it back with a guilty look.

We wait for the crowd to calm again. "Okay, Sanctuary, I think we all fell in love with you online and have been dying to know—"

"Fox, marry me!" My eyes widen as I look at the crowd. Ryker stiffens next to me, and I can't help but be a little petty.

"Come here then!" I yell back.

"He's taken, sorry!" Ryker chuckles, and the audience goes crazy.

My smile loses some of its wattage, but I play along, and when I look at Henley, he's shaking his head. "I totally lost my train of thought. It's clear you have some incredible fans. How has it been for you, stepping into the limelight?"

"Insane in the best way," Ryker answers, crossing his legs. It puts his foot over my thigh, but I don't move away, and neither does he. "We are so excited to be here and to share this night with you."

"That's right. It's a big night. Do you want to tell them why?" Henley teases.

Moving aside slightly since we are cramped, I place my arm on the back of the sofa, accidentally brushing Ryker's neck, and he leans into my touch. It's a small movement, I don't know how they even see it, but the audience erupts again, and I jerk back.

Henley chuckles, and I shake my head. "Y'all are the best."

I laugh. "How about I tell them?"

"Go ahead," Ryker offers.

"Well . . . Sanctuary will officially be supporting Dead Ringers on their upcoming, sold-out world tour." My smile is real this time and wide. It's all I've ever wanted, to travel the world and perform my music for people.

The response is immediate, and we drink it up. I glance over to check on Strike and Dash, who are smiling widely. No one deserves this more than them. They've worked so hard to keep us together. I'm just glad we could experience it as a band, as family, even if we are slightly broken.

"That's amazing news! You guys must be so excited," Henley says.

"Absolutely. Dead Ringers is such an incredible band, and to be able to play for their fans is a dream come true. We are pumped to go on tour with them, and we can't wait to perform, so I hope you'll come support us," Strike replies.

"I'm sure we will. I know I'll be trying to get a ticket now!" Henley laughs.

The interview circles around our songs and our upbringings, and

I add as much as I can, my mood lightening with each joke. Henley is good. He makes me feel comfortable, and the vibes from the crowd are so insane, I couldn't not be happy.

"Okay, how about one last game before we let you guys go? I'm sure you have a lot of packing and rehearsing to do."

"Sure," Dash agrees, and the screen to the right flashes with squares.

"Okay, I'm going to show you some pictures of you guys going viral, and you need to recreate it, okay?" Henley tells us.

Ryker laughs, but it turns into a cough, and I sit forward, grabbing the water bottle and uncapping it for him.

"Thank you," he says as I tip the bottle for him, letting him drink. When he's done, I wipe under his chin and cap it again. As I'm leaning forward to the table, the crowd screams, and I blink, wondering what we did.

"Okay, first picture." It's of us with Dash lying across our knees. He throws himself across us, and we catch him with a laugh until it flashes green. Another image comes up, and this time it's Strike on my back, so I stand and he hops on. Gripping his legs, I grin at the crowd as I spin us, remembering this moment. When it flashes green again, I glance over to see it's Ryker and Dash posing before a mic.

Sitting down, I watch as they copy the pose, and it flashes green before they sit and wait for the last square to turn over.

My heart skips a beat when the photo loads. It's one we posted online ages ago, back before this all became too messy. Ryker is grinning into the camera, and my lips are pressed to his cheek as we pose for the photo. The crowd eats it up, and I glance at Ryker.

"We've done worse," he remarks as he dramatically turns his cheek and pokes it for me. Swallowing my reservations, I order myself to do it.

It means nothing.

I lean in, the crowd and everyone around us fading away like usual when I'm with him. Does he know I framed this photo as well?

Does he know this was the day I fell in love with him?

Ryker turns his face at the last moment, so my lips press to his rather than his cheek. He keeps me there, kissing him, before I jerk away. The crowd is going nuts, and Dash and Strike are howling, but I stare at Ryker in shock.

He's smirking, his eyes alight, but I feel sick all over.

He stole our first real kiss for a reaction from the audience.

Grinding my jaw, I bite back my anger.

I've imagined our first kiss for so long, and having it turned into a joke hurts a lot. It means nothing to him, just an act he puts on for everyone, but to me, it's the person I have been in love with giving me a taste of everything I want and then snatching it away, laughing.

"Oh, wow." Henley fans his face as he watches us. "The chemistry between you two is insane. I have to ask, is it real?"

"Why wouldn't it be?" Ryker jokes, totally indifferent to the fact that I am silently fuming next to him.

I'm quiet for the rest of the interview, and when it's over, I leave the stage as quickly as I can. I'm ready to explode, and if they aren't careful, it will be all over them. I can't ruin our reputation before we even begin, but that was fucked up.

As soon as I pass that curtain, I storm away. I hear my bandmates running after me, but I need to be alone right now. Wiping my mouth, I find the glitter from his lips on my fingers, and that only pisses me off more.

"Fox, what the hell?" Ryker snaps as he grabs my arm and spins me. The staff members quickly scurry away, leaving just us, Dash, and Strike, who watch us anxiously. "What is wrong with you?"

"With me? What is wrong with you?" I yell, and he recoils. "I'm not some fucking prop for you to use, Ryker. I'm a person with feelings, and they can be hurt."

"What are you talking about?" he mutters, looking around. "Let's talk outside."

"No, let's talk here," I snap as I advance on him, glaring down at him. How could I love a man like this? "You can't kiss me on TV for fun. It isn't funny to me, okay? It isn't a joke! When someone you . . .

someone you . . ." Fuck. I clench my teeth, unable to say it. "Steals your first kiss like that, it's fucked up, Ryker, like it's another game, another marketing strategy. Well, it isn't for me, okay? Being kissed means something to me—it should have meant something—but now it's tainted and ruined and wrong."

"Fox . . ." He swallows hard, his eyes wide as he stares at me. "I'm sorry. I just—"

"You're always fucking sorry. I'm sick of it. I'm sick of you using me to sell yourself. We wouldn't even be here if it wasn't for me, but do you care? No. I'm just another thing for you, like an outfit you put on and then discard when it's over, but I'm done. I'm so tired of it all."

Turning away, I rip off the stupid shirt. "Fox, wait!" I hear the panic in his voice, but I avoid his grabbing arms. "Please! Please, I'm sorry! Wait! Let me explain." It's too late.

I stop with my back to them. "I can't do this."

"What?" There is pain in his voice, but I don't care anymore.

"Fox!" Dash and Strike call for me, but I avoid them, striding toward the exit. What I said is true. I can't do this anymore. I thought I could.

I thought it would be okay to be in love with him but never with him, as long as I was still in his life, but I was wrong. I can't be in love with Ryker and in his life. It hurts too much, and in the end, all it does is keep breaking my heart, and I'm done.

It's the last straw.

I head out into the city. I need to get away from them.

My phone hasn't stopped ringing, but I turn it off. I don't know why I'm here, but when the apartment door opens and Team stands in the doorframe, I can't deny that I'm happy to see his face.

I need someone who understands, and he's all I have.

Maybe it's my jumbled emotions or the realization that I'm done, but I just stare at him.

"Do you want to come in?" he asks softly. "Fox, are you—"

Stepping across the threshold, I grab his face. "Don't talk," I order as I press my lips to his. I need to replace Ryker's taste with someone else's. I need to get the sick, used feeling out of me with someone who actually wants me.

I need to taste want, not indifference.

I guide him backwards and kick the door shut behind us. He hits the wall, and my hand slips into his hair as his mouth opens, and my tongue sweeps in, tangling with his. Swallowing his moan, I kiss him harder as his hands slide down my body, grabbing my ass and dragging me closer so there isn't an inch of room between us. I feel every solid inch of his dick, even through his shorts.

"Bedroom?" I pant against his lips.

"That way," he rasps, and our lips crash together as I back him through the apartment. We stumble, and something breaks, but we don't move apart as we eat at each other so hard it hurts. When he falls backwards onto something soft, I come down on top of him.

His hands glide across my back and down into my pants so he can grip my ass through my boxers. The whole time, my mouth destroys his. It's a brutal, hard kiss—a punishment.

That realization startles me. Team keeps kissing me, totally unaware, tugging me to the cradle of his hips, but my desire has gone cold.

I'm punishing him like he's Ryker.

I'm using him like Ryker used me, and it makes me feel so fucking shitty.

I pull back, and his eyelids flutter open. "Fox."

The way he sighs my name only increases my guilt.

I'm not in a relationship, but I feel like I'm cheating.

Flopping back on the bed, I cover my face. "I'm sorry. I can't do this."

When I pull away, I spy glitter on Team's lips, and I feel nauseous. It's from Ryker. If I fuck Team, I would think of Ryker the entire time. It's wrong. I can't replace the person I want with him. It isn't fair to either of them.

He's quiet for a moment. I glance over at him to see him smiling at me. "Okay." He lies next to me, still breathing heavily, but he doesn't push it.

"I'm so fucked up. I'm sorry for messing with you."

"Hey, I got one of the best kisses of my life. I'm not complaining." He turns his head to meet my gaze, and we both burst into laughter. Reaching over, he wipes a finger across my mouth where I'm sure my makeup is smeared. "Want to talk about it?"

"No? Yes?" I throw my hand over my face again. "I'm a mess."

"Everybody is," he replies, and I glance over at him again. "Nobody is perfect. Nobody has it all together. Life is messy, and that's the beauty in it. We're humans, so we make mistakes and try again. We keep trying until we get it right." He arches an eyebrow. "You love him."

My eyes widen as I freeze, and he laughs. "I suspected it when you carried him from the bar. The way you looked at him . . . I'd kill to have someone look at me like that. Does he know?"

I shake my head, and he sighs. "And therein lies the problem. It's called communication, Fox. Why don't you try it? Tell him you love him."

"Then I'll lose him," I murmur.

"So? At least you'd stop hurting yourself and tying yourself in knots, right?" He glances over at me. "Fuck anyone else, fuck losing him. How do you know if you don't even try? It's just an excuse."

"I can't. We signed a deal. He can't be mine," I admit as I stare at the ceiling.

"But you want him to be?" he asks softly, as if leading me to the truth.

"More than anything, but it's all so . . . twisted between us now," I reply. "We keep hurting each other. I keep letting him break my heart over and over, and he's oblivious. I have to watch him come home night after night, smelling of others. I have to let him touch and tease me for cameras like it doesn't make my heart ache. I have to pretend I don't love him for the sake of our band and his dream."

"Hmm, complicated," he remarks, and I grin. "What?" He chuckles. "I don't have all the answers, but if I were him, I'd want to know. You need to figure it out together. If you feel like you can't tell him and that you two can never be together, then you need to find a way to get over him. Unrequited love benefits no one. It only hurts you, and you deserve to be happy, Fox. You deserve to be in love, not feeling like this."

"I don't think I could ever love anyone else," I say as I glance at him. "I know it's stupid, but I'm so tired of love, so tired of hurting. It's left me numb and empty. I don't think I could ever love anyone else the way I love Ryker. I used everything I have on him. There's nothing left."

"Then you need to heal yourself. Fill yourself back up so there is something left before you love anyone else. Your partner deserves that, and you can't love anyone while you're hurting. Love should be healing. It should be a safe harbor to dock in. It should be . . . home. Not this," Team reasons as he reaches over and squeezes my hand. "I might be a stranger to you, but even I can see it, Fox. You try so hard for everyone, but do they do the same? Everything you said has been to protect Ryker, but what about you?"

"There is no me without him," I respond as I glance at him. "That makes me sound crazy, right?"

"A little bit, but not in a bad way. Like I said, I would kill for someone to love me the way you love him. He doesn't realize how lucky he is." He holds my hand as we stare at each other. "Love shouldn't hurt. Either fight for it or let it go. You know it's time. That's why you came here, right? To move on?"

"Yes," I answer.

"And you couldn't?"

I shake my head, and he smiles.

"Then fight for it. Tell him directly. Tell the world. Don't ask for forgiveness, just act. We only get one life, Fox. Do you want to spend it pining and wishing? None of it will matter when death comes, so live for now while you still can. If it ends badly, so fucking what? At least you had a love so bright, you'll always remember it, but don't just linger—make each day count."

"I think whoever gets to be loved by you will be lucky," I murmur.

"I know it." He grins widely. "Too bad I haven't found them yet."

"Do you think there's a chance for us?" I ask after a while.

"I think anything is possible if you want it enough. The question, Fox, is if you will go for it."

"I think . . . someone who loved me wouldn't hurt me like this, and I don't know if I can forgive him enough to try."

"Then you need to figure it out," he says. "Come on, let's have a drink and some food, then you can go back and decide what you will do. This can be your refuge, your attack command center." He smiles at me so sweetly, I want to cry.

It would be easy to love a man like him, but he isn't Ryker.

THIRTEEN

RYKER

I try to call again, even though I know it's useless, and it goes straight to voicemail. I hang up and close my eyes. I'm sitting on the stairs in the dark, waiting. He's been gone all night, and none of us can get a hold of him.

I hate the panic coursing through me.

Is he okay?

He sounded so tired when he said he was done, and my heart won't stop aching. Each breath feels like daggers are being shoved into my chest.

The others went to bed, saying he will come back when he's ready, but I have a sinking feeling. What if he doesn't? What if he meant it? What if Fox is gone just like that?

I know I shouldn't have kissed him, not like that, but it was my only chance to do it. It was the only way I could kiss him, so I turned my head. I wanted to kiss him so badly, and now he won't even answer my calls.

It's all my fault. I never wanted to hurt Fox. He's the last person in the world I would ever want to hurt, but I keep doing it, and I don't know how to stop.

Glancing at my phone, I swallow around the thickness in my throat. The picture on my lock screen has me struggling to hold myself together. Fox and I smile widely, our arms thrown around each other's shoulders.

It was an innocent, friendly gesture to everyone else, but to me, it meant everything. I couldn't stop looking at him that day and every day since.

Does he know how he makes me feel? I've tried my best to stop feeling like this. I thought avoiding him and fucking him out of my system would help, but I was wrong, and the idea that I could have lost him for good . . .

It terrifies me.

I wonder how many times he waited like this for me. When I would stumble back drunk after a one-night stand, he'd simply nod, glad I was safe, and every time I felt like crying.

Did he feel like this? Destined to sit and wait for his lost love, all while knowing he's with another?

Opening my phone, I text him again, but it doesn't even show that it was delivered.

I navigate to social media. We are everywhere, our kiss is viral, and I hate it. It ruined us, but I love that I got to claim him like that.

Maybe it's petty, especially if he's with someone else, but I can't resist.

I pull up one of our private photos, one he doesn't know I have. He's asleep, his head pressed to mine, his chest bare, and I'm leaning on his shoulder in his bed, smiling.

Sorry to disappoint you all. He's mine

I post it without thought, unconcerned about the repercussions. The comments and messages instantly roll in, but I log out and look at the door, hoping it will open.

When it finally does, I almost think it's my imagination. I leap to my feet, staring at him as he silently slips inside before freezing when he sees me. Neither of us speak for a moment. He's in the same outfit, but his hair is messy and his lips are red, and I know . . .

He was with someone else tonight.

I want to throw up, my stomach rolling even as my heart sinks. How could he be with someone else after kissing me?

"Po will be here soon to take us to practice," I force out, my voice choked and tight. I'm barely keeping it together.

He nods, and I swallow hard. "You should shower," I say as tears fill my eyes, then I turn away. He says nothing. He doesn't tell me I'm wrong or that it's all okay. He doesn't come after me.

With my back to him, I hesitate. "You should place a cold compress on your lips. They are swollen," I mutter before I escape upstairs.

I barely make it to my room, slamming the door shut before I sink to my knees and cry. Biting my hand, I press my knees to my chest and try to stifle my sobs.

I can't breathe.

I can't think.

It hurts so much.

I've really lost him, haven't I?

They say love is healing, but they don't tell you how it breaks you as well.

I manage to pull myself together, and my hurt is replaced by anger—not just at him, but at whoever he was with. Don't they know he belongs to me? It's so obvious. Scrolling through social media, I begin to stalk Team. It has to be him. Fox wouldn't fuck a total stranger. It isn't who he is. He likes a connection.

I navigate to his page, but there's nothing. I deep dive, searching and finding a private account. Logging out, I quickly log into Fox's, then I hit follow and wait. He accepts moments later, and I scroll through his posts. It's mostly for his friends and family, stuff celebrities dare not post without being judged or having it used against them, but I open his stories.

It's a film, but there are two sets of feet, and I would know the second pair anywhere.

I know every inch of him even better than myself, and that is Fox.

My anger turns to fury, and before I know it, I have his address from a friend and I'm shoving my shoes on. I hesitate in the hall, staring at Fox's closed door.

Testing his knob, I find it locked, and that's the last shard of my shattered heart. I press my forehead to the wood and struggle to breathe. Turning away, I race down the stairs and out of the door. I drive as fast as I can, and when I find the apartment building, I tap my feet impatiently as the elevator rises.

I'm acting crazy. It's early morning, and he doesn't know me, but I can't stop myself as I hunt down the number I need and slam my fist into the door.

It flies open, and the same man from the club stands there. Team is shirtless, his lips still puffy, as he blinks at me, half asleep. "Ryker?" He rubs his eyes. "I wondered how long it would take you."

"He was here tonight, wasn't he?" I demand.

"And if he was?" he asks, leaning casually against the door.

What does Fox see in him? He's just a pretty face with a terrible attitude. Is that all it takes?

"Stay away from him. I mean it," I growl.

"Why?" He smirks, raising his eyebrow as he tilts his head.

"He's mine." The words slip out before I can change them, but I don't regret them. Fox has been mine since he first joined our band. That won't change. One night with this blond fuck won't take him from me.

There's a flash of satisfaction in his eyes as he uncrosses his arms, and I don't understand. "Let me give you some free advice, Ryker."

"Like I need any from you," I snarl.

"Obviously you do, since Fox was here and not with you," he retorts, cutting me to my core and silencing me. "I thought he was the obsessed one, but I was wrong. He doesn't know, does he? How many people have you warned away from him? How many times have you stolen his chance at happiness, all while being too scared to tell him?"

"Shut up," I bark as he steps closer, his eyes seeing too much.

"You're too scared to tell him that you love him," he finishes, and I swallow hard. "I thought so." He looks me over. "You're a coward, Ryker. Don't try to sugarcoat it. You're scared, but you're going to lose him if you don't do something about it soon." He grips his door as he looks me over. "He deserves better, so sort your shit out before he realizes that too." He slams the door in my face as I gape.

Is he right? Do I love Fox?

Is that what this is?

Fuck!

FOURTEEN

FOX

Ry and I have barely spoken. I have nothing else to say to him, and he's uncharacteristically quiet. Sometimes I worry, but then I remember that's not my place. I don't leave, though, I don't give up, and we start practicing for the tour around the clock, leaving little time for anything else. When I'm not practicing, I'm writing new songs, feeling more inspired than ever before.

I guess heartbreak is good for one thing.

The words flow onto the page. I know he'll have to sing them, and that only seems to spur me on.

Po has tried to talk to us, wanting to know what's wrong, but we ignore him, while Strike and Dash are doing their best to keep us together.

"Here." Strike thrusts a drink at me, and I look up, my back to the studio wall.

"Thanks." I shut my notebook and take a drink as he lowers to his ass next to me. Dash and Ry are talking to Po in the other room, and I watch them for a moment before looking away.

"You aren't leaving, are you?" Strike asks, making my head swing to him.

"No," I reply. "I just can't." I trail off, unsure how to end that sentence.

"Love him anymore," he finishes for me as he glances at Ry. "I get it. What he did was fucked up, but you didn't see him, Fox. He was so scared. I've never seen Ry like that. He wouldn't stop crying and calling you. I'm not saying what he did was right, but maybe he's starting to realize he has feelings for you. The question is, is he too late?"

I don't have an answer for that, and we lapse into silence.

"New songs?" he asks, indicating my notebook.

"Yeah, just some ideas," I reply, and I hand it over. I used to be worried about others reading them, but there's no embarrassment between friends. We've seen the worst and best of each other. Lyrics have this raw capacity to capture your life and inner feelings, and I fear these ones reveal more about me than most, but as he reads them, his eyes widen.

"Fuck, Fox, these are incredible." He looks up at me, licking his lips as he seems to debate something. "You should have him sing one today."

"No, I . . ."

"Yes, he might understand." He hands it back to me. "Your choice, but I think it would be good for both of you." Standing, he heads back over to the others, and I meet Ryker's eyes, noticing he's watching us.

Is Strike right?

My eyes are locked on Ryker. He's read the song I picked. It's in front of him now, ready for him to sing. The ballad is slower than what we are used to, but Po read it and demanded we add it to the set for the tour. Ryker glances at me, and something I can't comprehend flashes in his gaze. I can't turn away, and neither does he.

We run through the melody a couple of times before we dive into it, and then his crooning voice comes out, singing my lyrics about heartbreak.

About the person you love falling into strangers' beds.

There's something therapeutic about the person who hurt you singing the song you wrote about them. When it's over, he looks at me with tears in his eyes, and I finally look away.

We practice it again and again, our eyes locked together as he sings the tale of my broken heart.

The one he broke.

Hands of another, all the while wishing it was me.
I see you falling in and out of love each night.
And I crave that feeling, crave your eyes on me.
Stolen moments that we don't speak of.
Enough to make up a lifetime.
But not enough to call it love.
My broken heart and your stubborn soul.
Please let me go.

The notes trail off. "Amazing!" Po claps. "This set is going to be so incredible. Okay, again from the top. We need this to be perfect. We only have two weeks of practice, and we won't waste a moment."

I finally look away, and when I do, my heart stops aching for the first time since he broke it.

FIFTEEN

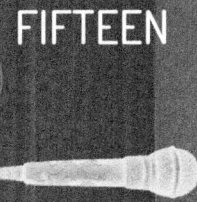

RYKER

All we do is practice. Fox and I barely speak, but we say a thousand words with our eyes. We sleep, eat, and breathe the set until it's considered perfect. His new song has ripped me to pieces. It's so raw. It's a confession, and I don't know how to react because of the end.

He told me to let him go, and I can't do that.

Is Team right? Am I a coward?

Am I too late?

I'm lost and hurt and more confused than ever. No one else notices as we file into the restaurant. We start the tour tomorrow, so Po gave us tonight off and a private meal to celebrate. I sit heavily in my seat, Po on my right, no one on my left.

Fox sits between Dash and Strike opposite us, laughing at a joke they told. He's oblivious to my suffering.

Drinks are served, and while we wait for our food, Po goes live and films us interacting and talking about the upcoming tour, trying to get everyone hyped for it.

I use the camera as an excuse to walk around the table and drape my arms around Fox and Dash as I speak, but Fox shrugs me off, and

I slink back to my seat, feeling like a scolded child. He pulled away, yet he plays it off.

The camera is finally turned off, and I'm in a terrible mood as I play with my knife while the others dig into their food.

He doesn't once look at me during the meal. He laughs and jokes with everyone, eating and talking, but he doesn't look at me at all.

I want to scream to get his attention.

I want him to look into my eyes and tell me everything is fine . . . that nothing has changed. *Please just look at me,* I plead silently, but he doesn't hear me and his gaze doesn't turn to me.

He used to check on me all the time before, when I was the center of his world, but I'm not anymore, and I hate it. I don't feel complete without his eyes on me. He leans into Dash, laughing hard at something he said. That laugh usually makes mine burst from my chest, but tonight mine is tight, too tight to feel anything other than pain and concern.

Something has changed dramatically between us, and I don't know what or even how to fix it. I don't even know what this unspoken thing between us is. We aren't dating. I'm not his, and he isn't mine, yet the space between us hurts so badly.

The idea that I might have lost him for good terrifies me.

I can barely breathe, never mind eat, as my eyes stay locked on him. My whole body is hot as I try to slow my breathing. My eyes start to burn and my stomach clenches in agony, yet no one notices. No one says a thing.

No one sees that I'm dying inside.

Not even him.

I've lost him.

The sudden realization hits me like a truck. All the time we spent dancing around this, resisting and pulling away, has finally caught up to us, and Fox has walked away. He stopped fighting.

He let me go, and it's killing me.

I'm a bastard, I broke what we had, but I need him to fix it—fix me. I'm not myself without him.

The rest of the meal is a blur, and as we walk outside. I'm at the rear, my head lowered. I'm exhausted and so fucking tired of it all. I just want him to hold me and tell me it will be okay, but I don't deserve it.

"Fox, where are you going? The car is this way." Dash laughs, and I jerk my head up to see Fox with his hands in his pockets, turned toward an idling car.

"Ah, I'm going to meet with a friend. I won't be back late," he says.

"Okay, no drinking or partying. Be back in time to leave," Po warns.

"Yes, sir!" Fox jokes as he waves at us. The others turn and hurry back to our car since it's starting to rain, but I watch Fox. I should walk away, but I can't.

"I'll see you tomorrow, right?" I call to him as he heads toward his car. They're the first words I have spoken all night, and when his eyes land on me, I can finally breathe again.

I see flashing lights and glance over to spot paparazzi, but I ignore them as I look back at Fox.

"Of course. It's the start of the tour." He shrugs. "Get home safe, Ryker." He turns away, leaving me staring. I want to run after him. I want to demand he touch me again . . . love me again, but it's cruel.

As I watch him drive away, the first tear begins to fall, and I know I would do anything, give up all this fame, money, and publicity, to go back to the way we were, sleeping in vans and cheap hotels.

I'd do anything to be going home with him.

Instead, I'm left standing there, cameras trained my way as I try to hold back the heartbreak inside.

SIXTEEN

FOX

The tour has begun, and it's busy as we hit the road to the first city and get situated at the venue.

The Dead Ringers are not what I was expecting at all. They are super nice, clearly very private, and down to earth. Oh, don't get me wrong, they hang with us when we reach the first venue in the green room, talking about everything and anything, thanking us for taking a chance on them, but they are just . . . unexpected.

They go to get ready while we head for a sound check. We have a day to get used to this venue, but we want to be totally prepared.

The rest of the day is a blur. There is so much that needs to be done, and the stadium is so imposing that I feel a little out of place. I never thought we would ever play in a place like this. I know the fans are coming for the Dead Ringers, but even if just one person likes us, that's enough for me.

It's everything we have worked for, yet it feels vaguely empty.

As I sit cross-legged in the middle of the T-shaped stage, with rows upon rows of empty seats in front of me, the pit a moving machine of parts and preparing teams, I feel . . . alone, like I have lost something on the way here. I know what it is—him.

Us.

Was it worth it? Was there ever really an us to lose? I don't know, but it makes me feel tired and down. I promised myself I would give up on Ryker and my feelings for him, I promised I could keep our band together and pretend it never happened, but one look at his face when he sings and it gets harder.

Love is a fucking dick. It lives to destroy you over and over again.

I know what the fans and our label want. Hell, I even know what Dead Ringers want on stage tonight, and for the first time ever, I don't know if I can do it.

Every touch just reminds me of what I'll never have, but as they say, the show must go on. This is about more than me. This is about Strike, Dash, and even Ryker. This is their dream. I can't let them down when we are so close. Standing, I run my eyes over the stadium one more time and head back to get ready for the performance of our lives.

Bouncing on my toes, I peek out at the full stadium. The audience members are dancing and singing along with the music that pumps through the speakers as they wait for the gig to start. There isn't one empty seat. A sea of people wait for us and the Dead Ringers.

Nerves fill me, and I wonder if I can be as good as they need me to be. Ry notices, and he grins at us, realizing Strike and Dash are pale and worried too. "Hey, what's with the long faces? Look out there." We follow his pointing hand. "This is for us. Fuck anyone else. Fuck anything else. We did it. We are finally doing everything we always spoke about, and now you're going to chicken out? I don't fucking think so. Who are we?"

We groan, and he waits with his hands on his hips. "I said, who are we?"

"Sanctuary," we reply in soft voices.

"Not good enough," Ryker snaps and cups his ear. "Who are we?"

"Sanctuary!" we yell.

"That's fucking right!" He grins as he looks us over. "Now let's go out there and show them that, show them we were made for this and their trust in us was not misplaced. Tonight, we take our seats among the gods of rock, and we do it together. Hands in, motherfuckers." He places his hand out in a familiar ritual. Dash and Strike grin before adding theirs, and then all eyes turn to me. Taking a deep breath, I set my hand over theirs.

"Together," I murmur.

I'm still confused about a lot of things, but one thing is for sure—I was made to be on stage, and so were they.

"Together," they repeat as our hands bounce, and we throw them back. "Now let's fucking rock!"

The lights dim as we are counted in, and Ryker and I share one last look. We both know what we need to do when we go out there. Even in the dark shadow of the stage, he looks beautiful. He's wearing an open black leather jacket with purple stars down the arms, exposing his incredible chest underneath, and skintight leather pants tucked into boots. His hair is messy, and his makeup is Gothic. He looks fucking amazing, and he knows it.

We all match in some way. Strike has stars over his ass, and Dash has them on his face. Mine are over my nipples, under a sheer shirt tucked into baggy black jeans with chains up the one side, our names dangling from each.

We look like a team, like a band, and I hope we feel like it too.

I hope it brings us back together, like it brought us together in the first place.

Music is the reason we do it.

We are pointed on, then we hurry under the stage and wait. We hear screams as the video Po showed us is played, displaying snippets of us and our past, then the lights cut, a beat starts, and when the lights turn back on, the platform we stand on begins to rise to the stage and higher still, until we are above it.

I swing my guitar around as the voice in my ear counts in, then I shred my fingers across it, letting it echo through the stadium as they cheer and scream for us. I can't see much past the lights, and that helps my nervous energy dissipate. Adrenaline and excitement flood me as the last note plays out, and Ryker takes hold of the mic.

I feel the anticipation in the air as he presses his mouth to it and sings the first sentence of our most viral song.

The crowd screams in response, deafening in its volume, and when the notes fade, Ryker grins as the lights flood us, putting us on display for them. "Hello, rockers and rebels. We are Sanctuary, and tonight, we are going to take you to hell and back," he drawls before he steps back and I step forward, ripping my guitar solo we practiced.

Flames burst out across the stage as Ryker starts to sing. Strike and Dash hurry to their places, and we begin our set.

The platform lowers, and we step off. Ryker dances down the T section as I follow, playing as I go, winking and leaning into the fans as they scream. At the very top, as Ry belts out the high note, we press our backs together, and he leans over me until the last note.

The cheers and chants are insane as Ryker grins. "Alright, that was pretty good, but I think we can do better, don't you? As you might have heard, we are Sanctuary, and we are honored to support the incredible Dead Ringers on tour. How excited are you?" He holds the mic out as we nod and grin at their shouts. "Ah, I see we're just getting warmed up. I said, how excited are you?" He holds it out again, and they scream louder. "Better, that's what we like. I'm Ryker, and I'll be singing for your ears tonight. At the back we have Strike." Strike shreds on the drums. "The ever sexy Dash." He plays a few notes, and Ryker laughs. "Alright, and the god you have been waiting for . . . Fox!"

The crowd screams as I play, and when I finish, Ryker is waving his hand. "Alright, alright, I see you have your favorites. You can look but you can't touch. He's mine," he warns, and the look he gives me makes me swallow, our gazes lingering before he turns to the crowd. "Now, how about another song?"

The beat kicks in, and I walk back as I strum the first low strings. When I reach the top of the stage, I glance at the screens above and to the side of us to see the cameras panning over the crowd. There are signs with our band name on them. I see one with mine, which makes me grin, and there are even signs with both my and Ryker's names together. When Ryker starts singing, they sing along. It astounds me, and I nearly miss my next switch up. We move from that song into the next with only a second for me to switch guitars.

The piano kicks in as I play on the next one, Ryker walking to us as he sings. His eyes are on me, and the lyrics hammer home, trapping me in his gaze.

Sex was our game, love was our winnings, so why the hell do I feel like I'm losing?

Looking into your eyes, I know it's our beginning.

Why can't you follow me down into hell?

When he reaches me, he rubs against me, draping himself on my back as I play my guitar solo, and when he starts to sing again, he moves in front of me, dragging his hand down my chest and lower as he crouches. His eyes stay on me as his hand slides back up, and then he winks and dances away, leaving me shaking my head.

The crowd eats it up, though, and despite my feelings, I play into it, knowing it's what they want. As he screams the next bit, I drop my guitar since I'm not needed, and I reach around him and grab his cock through his pants, dragging him back against me.

He stumbles over the words but leans into me, looking at me as the crowd screams. I lean in, ensuring my voice is low so only he can hear. "Focus on them," I murmur before I release him and swing my guitar back around as I play.

I finish that song on my knees, and Dash drapes himself over me, and then Ryker quickly joins in before Strike does the same, making a puppy pile.

"Alright, alright, we have one more song before it's time for Dead

Ringers!" Ryker shouts. "Let's finish this right, yeah? It's time to go to hell, nonbelievers!"

The crowd screams, surprising us. It's one of our older songs, but as Ryker sings, they join in. The stadium seems to shake as they bounce and dance, their voices reaching ours, and when we get to the chorus, Ryker drops the mic and we just listen to them shout our lyrics back to us.

As Ryker holds the mic to the crowd, I can't help but stare. They scream our lyrics, my lyrics, back at us, and tears form in my eyes. Hearing them sing my heartbreak and songs is more than I could have ever imagined.

Turning away to hide my reaction, I startle when Ryker appears before me and wipes my face.

"This is for you," he whispers. "All of this is for you. It's all you ever wanted."

I meet his searching gaze, words trapped on my tongue.

I want to be yours. That's all I want.

I don't say it, but I nod, and he kisses my cheek. "We did it."

We did, but as he moves away, taking his warmth with him, I wonder if we will still be here in a year, or five or ten, or if it will break us all apart.

SANCTUARY

SEVENTEEN

RYKER

We ride the high from performing as we head off stage. I leap at my bandmates, and they catch me as we laugh and hug. "Did you see that?"

"They knew our songs!"

We talk at the same time, and when we calm down, we are all grinning.

"We really did it," I murmur.

"We did." Strike drags Fox down and kisses him square on the mouth. "Now let's celebrate!"

"The box is this way," a staff member interrupts. "We will escort you."

I glare at Strike, but he's oblivious as we are led into the VIP area so we can watch Dead Ringers perform. I can sense cameras on us, people noticing and spreading the word, so I point at the stage and put my finger to my lips. This is their time, not ours.

The area is pretty small, but we have an amazing view of the stage, and I can't look away from them. Beck Danvers might be new, but she works that stage like an experienced singer, and the others help her, looking as happy as we feel.

When it changes to an upbeat song, Strike grabs Dash and begins to dance him around. I look at Fox, and he looks at me before he grabs me and copies them.

I can't help but laugh as he spins me around as Dash and Strike do the same. The crowd is busy singing along with Beck Danvers, so even though we are surrounded by people, it feels private. His smile is aimed at me as if he has forgotten about everything else for the moment.

It leaves me breathless.

Lost in a sea of fans, I lean back into him, our movements becoming slow until we dance leisurely to the beat.

My head falls back to his shoulder as he wraps his arm around my waist and just holds me. For a stolen minute, everything is normal. We are back to the way we were meant to be. Everything is good, and I'm happier than I've been in a long time.

I feel . . . complete in his arms. I feel like I'm supposed to be here.

All too quickly, it ends as the set finishes, and he lets go. I feel so cold and empty after I watch him leave, following our guards, and I debate reaching for him.

What if he pushes me away?

What if it meant nothing to him?

I follow him, my heart in pieces, feeling more confused than ever.

The green room is abuzz, everyone riding the high of the first night. Drinks are flowing and everyone is dancing, having a good time. I sit at the back, lost in my own thoughts as I nurse a beer. I don't want to get drunk, and I throw anyone who gets too close a *fuck off* look, even the groupies.

I could take one and lose myself in their body, but I don't want to. He is all I can think about. I thought he felt the same way about me, but it looks like he's given up as he flirts and lets the groupies hang all over him.

He was mine, and I was so fucking stupid and dumb, I pushed him away.

Are Dash and Strike right? Have I lost him?

The idea terrifies me, and before long, I call it a night. They return to the bus a few hours later, and I pretend to be asleep. As their snores fill the air, I stare up at the top bunk where Dash is. Fox lies just feet away, and my head turns. He's on his back with his arm under his head, his eyes closed.

He's so close, yet so far away.

Even from here, I can see lipstick marks all over his face and neck. Where else are they? Did he hook up with someone? It kills me, and it's selfish, but I crawl from my bunk and into his, throwing his blanket over me and pressing my face into his neck.

I'm the only one who should stain his skin.

I'm the only one he should smell of.

He lifts his arm and opens his eyes as he turns to me, and for a moment, my heart soars. We are finding our way back to each other—first on stage and then dancing. He's coming back to me.

He frowns. "What are you doing?" he asks quietly, his voice gravelly.

"Sleeping here," I murmur as I move closer.

"Ry . . ." He sighs. "It's hot and small in here. Go back to your bunk."

My heart cracks, so I press closer, throwing my arm and leg over him with a tired whine. "No," I murmur into his skin.

His hand touches mine, and I smile, but he lifts it from his body and moves his legs away as he sits up. I fall into his bed, turning my head to meet his annoyed look. "What are you doing, Ryker?"

"Sleeping—"

"No, what are you doing?" he snaps. "You're climbing into bed with me again like it's nothing."

"We used to sleep together all the time," I whisper, confused.

His eyes sweep over my face. "That was then. We're different now."

I sit up, pain piercing my chest until I struggle to breathe. "Why? Why are we different?"

"We just are. Go back to your bed, Ryker. Don't do this again. Please." He adds the last word softly.

"I-I'm sorry, Fox, if I hurt you—" I start, but he sighs and looks away.

"You're always saying sorry." He looks at me, and his eyes shine with ghosts. "Do you even know what you're apologizing for? Do you even care? Or do you say it just to get your way?"

I flinch. "I mean it. We're friends—"

"Since when?" He throws his blanket back, his expression becoming hard. "Friends don't sleep like this. Friends don't touch like we do. Friends don't kiss like we did. We aren't friends, Ryker, maybe we never were, and I'm—" He looks away. "I'm tired, okay? Go to your bed. We have a long few months ahead of us, so we need to rest when we can."

"Dane," I whisper. It's his real name, the one we shared with each other in drunken slurs. "Don't do this."

His jaw pops. "Ellis." He returns the favor, and just like always, hearing my real name on his lips makes my heart soar, even as his next words cut its wings and bring it back to earth. "Go to bed. It's late."

He waits, and I know he isn't going to budge. Shame heats my cheeks as I climb from his bed and back into mine. I drag the blanket up and over my head as I offer him and everyone else my back, then my eyes fill with tears.

He's never told me no before. He's never pulled away like that and set boundaries. The tears spill, even as I close my eyelids, trying to stop them so he and the others don't hear or see.

I'm in love with Fox.

It's something I denied for so long, but when I sang with him tonight, I realized it.

I love him, and I'm too late.

SANCTUARY

EIGHTEEN

FOX

The next few days are madness, filled with performing and travelling to the next venue. We go through the entire setup and sound check again, and the show that night is wild. The crowds only seem to get crazier and crazier.

We hit up the green room every night, and tonight is no different, but Ryker is. Ever since that first night, he's back to his old ways, drinking and partying hard. I watch him do shots with a cute blonde, then they dance and hang all over each other before I turn to my notebook and continue scribbling. When I look up, he's heading out of the door, her arm through his.

It doesn't take a genius to figure out what they are doing, yet it fucking hurts so much for a moment, I can't breathe. The room narrows around me, closing in until it's all I see.

I watch him go, and I know I am completely done.

I kicked him out of my bed, but now I need to kick him out of my heart. I can't keep doing this. I can't keep hurting myself. I'm bound to this band, but the healthiest thing would be to walk away. I can't though. I'm trapped here with him, so that means I need to cut all this completely off.

Taking my phone, I flee the green room and head deeper into the stadium, entering one of the makeup rooms. It's empty since everyone is on stage or preparing.

Sitting in the swivel chair, I close my eyes and let out a long sigh. I shouldn't have expected any less. Fuck, I'm so stupid. I keep doing this to us, going around and around. I'm so fucking weak when it comes to him, and I hate it.

He isn't mine. I have no right to feel this way.

The door suddenly opens, and a wild-looking Ryker stands there. When his eyes land on me, he slumps.

"You left," he snaps, panting hard. "I couldn't find you—" He swallows. "I thought you left with someone."

His face is red, from alcohol no doubt, but he doesn't seem drunk. "I needed some space," I reply. "I'm fine. Go away, back to your entertainment for the night."

He frowns in confusion before it dawns on him. "Tilly? She's our new makeup artist. She was going to show me her idea for tomorrow."

I scoff, and he shuts the door, slipping the lock into place.

I should kick him out.

Didn't I just say I'm done?

He's here, though, looking so fucking beautiful it hurts. He's here with me, his hands shaking at his sides.

The thing is, I would willingly be torn apart again and again just to have his eyes on me. I'd let him break my heart a million times for even just a moment in his presence.

He isn't mine, but I wish he were. I'm just his bandmate here, his friend, and all I can do is watch as he walks away with blonde after blonde, taking my heart with him. Jealousy and sadness claw at me until I can scarcely breathe.

It hurts to love him.

I'm so tired of it all. I'm so tired of my heart hurting.

Hasn't it been broken too much before?

"Can you leave?" Even my voice sounds tired. "I want some space."

"From me?" he asks softly.

"From everyone," I reply as I turn away and pull out my notebook. My lyrics stare back at me.

"No. I'm not going anywhere," he snaps, and I glance up at him in the mirror. "We're going to fix this once and for all."

My scoff is my only answer.

"Fox, we're friends—"

I spin, leaping to my feet. His words unleash a tidal wave inside me. "Friends? I don't want to be your fucking friend. Can't you see that?" My chest heaves with my words as I meet his wide eyes, but I can't hold it back. It flows up like vomit.

I might regret it later, but I'm so tired of holding everything back. "I never wanted to be your friend, Ryker. I always wanted to be more. I want to be your everything. I want to be the only reason you laugh. I want to be able to kiss you without it being for the cameras. I want to be able to sleep with you in my arms again without it having ulterior motives or PR behind it. I want to be able to love you without it being scripted, but you don't. That's the difference between us. You only want me when the cameras are on, while I always want you, and I'm tired of it. I'm tired of loving you. It hurts. It fucking hurts, so I'm done. I'll be your bandmate, but I can't be more, so don't ask me to be."

We stare at each other, my words hanging in the air. There's shock in his eyes, but also something else.

"Fox—" The way he says my name has me stepping back, his eyes filled with pain as he stares at me. "What are you saying?"

I don't respond for a moment, and he walks over as I turn, the mirror to my left as we stare at each other.

"I'm saying . . . I'm saying I'm done. I'll stop pushing you or trying. You will never want me, and that's okay. It's my own fault. I broke my heart, not you, but I need you to let me go." Turning away, I head to the door, unlocking it with shaking fingers, but his hands slam against it on either side of my head, shutting it with a bang as his warmth hits my back. His breath wafts over my ear, and even now, as my heart breaks, my body reacts.

"Let me go," I beg.

"What if I can't? What if I don't want to let you go?" He rests his head on my back, and I hate the way I weaken. One word from him and I'm ready to give in, but my broken heart reminds me of the pain that awaits if I were to do that.

"Please," I whisper, closing my eyes as I press my forehead to the door and restrain myself from reaching for him. "Please don't make this harder. Please don't give me hope where there is none."

He's quiet for a moment, and I open the door again, but he slams it shut with his hands, plunging us into the quiet darkness of this room.

"I don't want to be your friend either," he states abruptly, and then I'm yanked around, his lips crushing to mine. He pulls away when I don't react, searching my eyes before he carries on. "I never wanted to be your friend either. Fuck the cameras, and fuck what they want. I want this. I want us. I'm not letting you go." He cups my face as his lips press to mine again. I don't respond, so he bites my lip, making me hiss, and then he sweeps his tongue into my mouth, kissing me deeper, and I finally wake up. I push him away, and he stumbles backward, his lips stained with my blood as I lift my hand to my mouth.

"Don't," I whisper as I feel the cut there. "Don't say things you don't mean."

"I meant every single word." He tilts his chin up as he stares at me. "I've always wanted you. I'm sorry I was scared. I'm sorry I was too afraid to admit it or give in. I'm sorry I hurt you while I tried to figure it out. I'm so fucking sorry that loving me has made you this way, but I'm not sorry that you love me. I'm not sorry that you want me. I want you, Fox, more than anything in this world. Why do you think all my hookups are blonde? It was as close as I could get to you. You're all I see and all I need. I can't sleep without your arms around me. I can't sing without your eyes on me. I can't perform without your support. I can't live without you, and I don't want to. I stayed away for so long so I didn't destroy our band with my selfish desires, but if the alternative is losing you forever, then I'll be selfish." He steps up to me, covering the distance.

"I want you, Fox. I love you. I fucking love you so much. I tried to forget you so many times and move on in faceless bodies, and I regret every one. I regret everybody that has ever touched me that wasn't you. They were never you. No one is you. I don't want to be your bandmate or your friend. I want to be your everything. I want to be your obsession. I want to be the only thing you see. I want to be yours."

It's everything I've always wanted to hear. I can barely believe it, so I stare, wondering if it's just my imagination. "Say it again."

His smile is slow. "I want you. I need you. I love you."

"What if this ruins us?" I ask, fisting my hands to restrain myself. My heart pounds with excitement and so much happiness I dare not believe it's real . . . but it is.

He's telling me he loves me and that he wants me the way I want him.

"I don't fucking care. I'm tired of it all too," he murmurs, his eyes filled with fire as he watches me.

I slam into him. His moan fills my mouth as I yank his head back and kiss him. Our bodies press into one as I back him across the room. He hits the dressing table, and I reach down and hoist him up, sitting him on the top as I kiss down to his neck. He cries out, dragging me closer like he can't bear to be even an inch apart.

"Fox, please," he begs, the plea heading right to my hard cock, making it jerk behind these ridiculous pants.

"Please what?" I ask against his skin, unable to leave an inch between us in case that one second gives him room to think and he pushes me away. He said it. He crossed that line, and now he's mine. He isn't getting away from me now.

I'm not a saint. I can't resist anymore.

"I've dreamed of this," he murmurs as I slide my tongue up and press my lips to his.

"Of us?" I ask.

"Yes." He nips my lip. "Of how you would taste, sound, and feel."

"Me too." I groan as I slide my hand down his chest to grip his dick through his pants, feeling it harden under my touch. "You want me to fuck you? Want me to make you mine?"

He nods, his eyes wide.

"They can't have this anymore then, right? It's mine, and I don't share."

"Yes, yes, yes, it's yours." His lips brush over mine. "Yours."

His whimper cuts through the air when I grip him tighter.

Releasing my hold on him, I grab the edges of his stupid jeweled shirt and yank it over his head. He helps me, and then his lips are back on mine as he tugs on my jacket. It hits the floor behind us as he untucks my shirt and yanks on it with a whine.

Smirking, I step back and tug it over my head. His tongue catches on his lip as he watches me, and I arch a brow. "Tell me, baby boy, when you imagined us, was I fucking you?"

His eyes move back to mine, a blush spreading from his face down his chest. I lick his pecs before nipping his pierced nipple, his back arching as he cries out.

"Yes," he finally responds. "Always you fucking me. I-I want you inside me. I want you so fucking badly."

Thank fucking god.

Licking up his chest, I grin as I pull his head back with my hand in his pretty hair. "I wonder what they would say if they knew their perfect bad boy rocker dreams of his guitarist fucking him."

"They'd be jealous." He glances at my lips as he reaches for me again, his body swaying into mine.

"Hmm, just like me every time you went home with someone else and fucked them," I snap, and he winces, sliding his hands down my sides as if to reassure me. "Yet here you are, begging me to fuck you. Did you beg them?"

He shakes his head as I yank him back.

"Good, then beg me to fuck you, Ryker. Beg me like you've never begged anyone else. Beg me to claim you like no one else ever has. You had them, but they never had you, not like I will. Do you understand?"

His eyes are impossibly wide as his next words seal his fate. "Please, Fox. Please fuck me. Please, please, I need you so fucking badly." His words tumble into each other as he pulls me closer, searching my gaze with desperation. "I'm yours. I promise. I don't want anyone else. Just you. Please. Please, if you don't fuck me, I actually might die."

I nip his swollen bottom lip before soothing it with my tongue. "Such pretty words, how can I resist?"

We don't have time to play because someone could find us at any moment, and I need to be inside him too badly to hold back. Next time, I'll take my time with him, teasing him into madness until he begs for me to fill his ass with my come, but right now, we are both too needy for that.

Gripping his chin, I kiss him, hard. "You're going to take all of me, aren't you?"

He nods as I pull my wallet from my back pocket. I brought it in case I hit the vending machines, and I'm thankful I did now. Pulling out a condom, I hand it to him. "Hold that, baby boy."

His eyes narrow. "Why do you have a condom?" he hisses, the fire in his eyes making my dick jerk in my pants. Mad Ryker is a fucking beautiful sight, but jealous Ryker is perfection.

"For you," I answer. "Wishful thinking." That satisfies him, and he nods as I shove my pants down. My cock springs free, and his eyes widen as he looks at me. I nod at the condom and wait. "Put it on." I grip my length for him, and he glances from my cock to my face hesitantly before he bites his lip shyly. "Ryker," I warn.

He pops his lip free and rips the condom open with his teeth before dropping to his knees. Ryker quickly slides it down my length, his hand lingering, and I swell under his touch.

I can't take the innocent way he touches me.

Dragging him up, I undo his pants and shove them down, so his legs are free, and then I lift him back onto the counter so I can get to his pretty ass. I massage it. My obsession with his ass has never gone away.

"Fox." He blinks owlishly at me. "Will it hurt?"

Leaning in, I sweep my lips over his as I reach for the bottle I found on the table when I came in. They use the lube for the leather outfits, but it will work for us as well. Flipping the lid open, I lean back and drizzle it across my cock, stroking my fist through it before I cover my fingers in it. I reach down and circle his ass with them. He tenses, so I kiss him, my other hand reaching down and stroking his length. He's long and slightly curved, a perfect fit in my fist, and as I stroke him roughly, he whines, relaxing into my touch until he pushes back to take my fingers. I slide one inside him, past his muscles, and then I wait. I feel his breath catch, and I stroke him faster until he rocks into me, and then I add a second finger and stretch him. When I feel his cock jerk, I let go, not wanting him to come yet. I want to be inside him when he does.

After pulling my fingers free, I kiss him again. "Do you trust me?" I ask.

"Yes," he responds automatically.

Gripping his legs, I lift him and press my cock to his ass. He tenses again, so I kiss him deeply until he pants and pulls at my shoulders for more, and then I slowly push inside him. It's just a couple of inches, letting him get used to it as he gasps into my mouth, his nails digging into my shoulders.

"Fox," he rasps into my lips. "God, move, don't move. I don't know—"

"I've got you," I tell him as I slide deeper before pulling out and slowly pushing back in, taking him deeper each time as we kiss. He begins pushing down, taking more of me, and finally, I'm seated all the way inside him.

Pressing my forehead to his, I grip him tightly, giving him time to adjust even though it drives me crazy. He's so fucking hot and tight, I want to pound him into oblivion.

He whimpers as I pull out and push back in, and even though it's a pained sound, it does something to me. I pull out and thrust in, and he groans.

"Shit, baby boy, I know you're new at this," I murmur, pressing my head to his as I try to slow down, the urge to hammer into him so strong it physically hurts. "But you feel so fucking good, it's so hard to hold back."

"So don't," he replies, gripping my shoulders.

"I don't want to hurt you," I admit.

"I'm a big boy, Fox. I can take it. I can take whatever you give me." He pushes down to take me deeper. "Fuck, move, please, fuck me harder. This is driving me crazy."

I search his eyes, but I only see truth, desire, and need, so I give us what we both want. Grabbing his hips, I pull out and slam back inside his virgin ass. His cry is loud, but he urges me on, wrapping his legs around my waist as he kicks my ass. I speed up as I lean down and nip every inch of exposed skin I can get, watching his beautiful, perfect abs clench with the movement, his cock jerking against them as his head falls back.

"Oh god, it feels good."

I bite his ear as I speed up, hammering into his tight ass. "You better be calling me your god. You don't call anyone else's name when I'm inside you."

"Fox, Fox." His eyes are wide as he pulls back. "Fuck, fuck, please."

"Do you even know what you're begging for?" I tease as I lean back, looking down to watch as my cock slams into his spread ass. The sight makes me harder, and I move faster.

He shakes his head, and I look up. His eyes are wide and wild, just like I feel, and he's pushing down to take me, meeting me thrust for thrust despite it being his first time.

When I tilt his hips to find that spot inside him, his eyes close, and I hate that he takes them from me.

Sliding my hand up his perfect, sexy body, I grip his throat and pull out of him, making his eyes open as he cries out.

I spin him, keeping my hand on his throat as I force his eyes to meet mine in the mirror as I drive into him from behind. "Look at me when I fuck you."

I keep him bent over as I fuck him from behind, thrusting faster and harder until the wood shakes from the force.

His hand smashes into the mirror, leaving a foggy print on the glass as he pushes back to take me, and when I pull out and slam back in, he cries out loudly, hitting the glass once more and smashing it. Knowing he can't see me, I pull out of his tight, perfect ass and spin him once more. His eyes widen, sweat covering his face and chest.

"Fox," he whines as I lift him, drag his ass off the wood, and impale him on me. I watch as his eyes roll into the back of his head. His beautiful, huge cock pulses.

"I—oh god, I'm going to come. Please, please don't stop," he rambles.

"Not before me, you won't," I order as I reach between us and grip his cock. "You come when I say so," I warn as I pound into him. My own release builds despite me trying to hold it back, wanting this to last forever. My balls draw up, and scalding hot pleasure rolls through me until it takes over.

"Now," I order. "Come for me, baby boy," I demand harshly, and I let go of my grip on his cock as I slam into him.

His yell of pleasure fills the air, followed by my grunt of ecstasy as I come. My back bows, pleasure stealing my voice and my vision as I empty deep inside him, yet it still isn't enough. I push deeper until there isn't an inch of space, and then I slump into him.

My vision clears, even as I shake with aftershocks, and I see him sprawled back on the ruined wood, his eyelids half closed. His face and chest are red and covered in sweat, as well as my hand and bite marks.

Fuck, he looks so goddamn beautiful, and he's all mine.

I lick my dry lips, unable to move just yet. "Good boy," I praise, my voice thick. "You're mine now, Ryker."

NINETEEN

RYKER

F ox presses his sweaty forehead to mine, our eyes locked together, and a smile grows on my lips, matching his. I begin to laugh, but it sounds more like a giggle, so I smack my hand across my lips.

He reaches up and pulls it away before he kisses me softly. My eyes shut automatically, a feeling of safety and pure happiness blasting through me. I've imagined this for a long time, and now he's mine. I can still feel him inside me, the slight pain eclipsed by the bliss of being in his arms.

"So cute," he whispers. "Aren't you, my boy?"

A shudder rolls through me, and my eyes snap open as I lick my swollen lips. "Say it again." My cheeks heat in embarrassment. I sound so whiny and demanding, but Fox simply caresses my cheek as he stares at me like I'm perfect. Nobody looks at me the way he does. I fell in love with his eyes first. They were only for me. Always for me.

"Say what?" he asks.

"Call me that again," I murmur.

"What?" He tilts his head, but there's a teasing glint in his eyes.

"My boy," I snap, louder than I mean to, and his laughter makes me groan.

He finally calms down and leans his forehead into mine again, his eyes pinning me in place as his hands grip my hips and tug me even closer, shoving him deeper inside me. The sensation makes me cry out, and he eats up the sound before his smoky voice fills my ear. "My boy. You are my boy, aren't you? Especially when you're still wrapped around me like this. You're going to feel sore every time you move, reminding you that I claimed you, but you like it, don't you?" His tongue darts out and licks the shell of my ear, and I have to fight the urge to reach for him again. "My boy," he drawls, making me shiver again.

"Can we go again?" I ask, gripping his sides, my dick hardening in agreement.

"Needy boy." He chuckles into my ear before laying a kiss on my neck. "Later. If I stay inside you much longer, we will be here all night and they'll find us, but even then, I won't stop."

"That's fine by me," I say as I move my hips.

His laughter grows as he slowly pulls from my body, making me wince. Stepping back, he runs his eyes over me possessively before he yanks his pants up, leaving them open as I watch him.

I imagined being with him a million different ways. It was our first time together, not something I usually put importance on, but this is Fox. I wish we could have been in our bed like I imagined, but something about it being here is kind of perfect too, and I have the insane urge to cry.

I thought I'd lost him, thought I'd lost the only thing that truly matters to me, but he's here, at my side where he's always been, and I'm not letting him go again.

"Stop those thoughts," he orders as he steps closer and pinches my cheek. "Even if you grow to regret this, I'm not letting you go now."

"Never. I would never regret us," I vow vehemently as I lean into his hand. "I was just thinking about how we should have done this years ago and how much time we wasted."

He shrugs. "Some things take time. We were best friends, bandmates, and roommates. In some ways, we had a closer relationship than most couples before we even took this step. We know everything about each other, and it's kind of beautiful that we didn't complicate it with sex straight away." His hand caresses my cheek before gripping my chin. "But make no mistake, now that we have, we aren't going back. I won't be your best friend, your bandmate, or even just your roommate. I'm going to be your everything."

"Good," I retort, and his grin makes it worthwhile. I know I hurt Fox a lot, and I have a lot to make up for, but at this moment, it's like nothing else matters.

"I'm sorry it took me so long to figure myself out," I whisper.

"You're worth waiting for, baby," he responds. "Now come on before they find us."

Dropping to his knees, he slowly pulls my pants up for me and pats my hips. He gets to his feet and steps back, grabbing my shirt and helping me into it before sliding into his clothes.

"Come on, superstar, let's get back before they come looking for you," he says as he buckles up his pants.

"I'm a rock star, not a superstar," I mutter, sounding like a petulant child.

His smile only grows as he advances on me, and I wait eagerly for his touch, but he simply reaches up and smooths out my hair for me before sliding his hands down and righting my shirt. "Yes, you are, my boy."

Holding my hand, he tugs me to the door and out into the hallway. My cheeks heat with happiness, as if everyone here will know what we just did. I curl my hand tighter into his calloused palm, craving that intimate touch for just one more moment, but as we round the corner into the main hall, he slowly pulls away.

I instantly miss the warmth, but I know why he did it. Our contract says we can't date, and if we are caught, one of us could be kicked out of the band. I don't want that, but each brush of our hands as we walk makes me ache to reach for him. I want to wrap mine in his to show them all I don't care.

That Fox is finally mine.

Instead, our pinkies hook together for one stolen moment before we break apart and head back into the green room, but as he steps into the crowd, his eyes lock on me, and he smirks as I try to sit.

I'm going to feel him all night, even if I can't physically touch him—a reminder that it's real.

I fucking love it.

The bus is filled with the sounds of Strike's and Dash's snores, but I'm wide awake, watching Fox in his bunk opposite me. His eyes are closed. I remember his reaction when I snuck into his bed the other night. I know it will be different now, and I don't know if I need to prove it to myself or if I just can't fucking sleep without his arms around me, but I slip silently from my bed and cross over the short distance to his. Lifting the quilt, I slide in next to him. His head lifts, his eyes opening, as I rest my head onto his bent arm and stare, waiting for his reaction.

"I wondered how long it would take you," he teases, wrapping his other arm around me before he pulls me against his chest, his legs tangling with mine. He lets out a happy sigh, closing his eyes again.

I run my eyes across his handsome face.

"Stop looking at me like that," he says softly.

"Like what?" I whisper.

"Like you want me to fuck you." One of his eyes opens and meets mine. "You're too loud when I'm inside you. The whole bus would wake up. Sleep."

I know I'm pouting. My cock has been hard all night at the memory of the way he felt inside me. I want to come again. More than that, I want to touch him. I want to prove to both of us that I can.

Sliding my hand down his chest, I watch as his eyes open, his head turning as he glares at me. "Ry," he warns.

"What?" I whisper innocently as I slide my hand lower until I feel the waistband of his boxers.

The snores are still loud, so I slip my hand inside and wrap my fist around his hard dick. Satisfaction fills me as I feel the proof of his desire, even if he said no. I jerk him hard, and his teeth sink into his lip as he reaches down to stop me.

I don't want him to.

"I wanted to do this so many times. I even touched you once, pretending I was asleep," I admit as I stroke him, feeling him throb in my fist as I lick and nip his chin. He groans, thrusting his hips into my hand. "You say you can't fuck me here, so then let me play. Let me remember all those nights I lay next to you, imagining this."

"Ry," he groans, biting his forearm as his hips roll, thrusting into my fist. I drink down his reactions as I sit up and tug the quilt down so I can see him. My back blocks anyone's view as his abs constrict, the sight of my hand working him in his boxers making me hard as hell. I slide closer, pressing myself to his leg as I watch him.

I've never felt as powerful as I do in this moment. Nothing compares to the sight of the mighty Fox fighting his need while I touch him. His body is covered in a sheen of sweat as he bites his arm.

It's a sight I memorize, and I know it will remain with me until the day I die.

"Shit, baby." He groans before he covers his mouth.

We still as the snoring stops. One of them turns, and then it starts back up again, and Fox smirks at me. His eyes darken, and then his hand wraps around my throat before he drags me closer. His lips brush across mine with each word he speaks.

"You shouldn't have started this, Ry," he warns just before his lips crash onto mine. I grip his cock harder as I kiss him back. His tongue sweeps into my mouth, tangling with mine, drugging and addictive, until I find myself on my back below him, his hand gripping mine and dragging it from his boxers. He slams both of my wrists above my head and pins them there as he settles in the cradle of my thighs, rubbing against me as he deepens the kiss. All I can taste and feel is him. Desire courses through me until I roll my hips, our cocks pressing together through our thin boxers.

His hand tightens on my wrists to the point of pain, and I jerk back with a gasp, my eyes wide as I stare up at him. He watches me with this dark, greedy look that makes me shudder.

"I didn't bring another condom, so I'm going to take you bare, and I can't fucking wait." He grunts, rubbing himself against me, sending shockwaves of pleasure through my body until his words sink in.

"You said we couldn't," I whisper.

"That was before you wound me up," he grows against my lips. "I'm going to make it work, but you're going to have to stay quiet, baby, because if you wake them, I won't stop, not for anything, and they'll see you getting fucked."

My heart stops, making my chest ache, and then it pounds as he flips me so my face is pressed into his pillow. His scent fills my nose as his hands grip my boxers and yank them down and off, leaving me bare below him. I grind my cock into his bunk as his hands grip my ass, massaging my cheeks until I push back. I turn my head to meet his dark eyes. Our bandmates' snores still fill the air, louder than our ragged breathing, but both of us ignore them.

Reaching past me, he fumbles around in the drawer under his bed before pulling something out, and I shiver when something cold hits my ass. His big hands rub it in before his fingers slide into me. Gripping his pillow, I bite my lip at the slight pain, but I remember how good it felt, and I want that.

"I should take it easy on you, since you're still new to this," he murmurs as he leans over me, thrusting his fingers into my ass as his mouth meets my ear. "But you started this and wound me up, so I'm not feeling very kind." He bites my ear, making me cry out before I swallow it down. "This is going to hurt a bit, but I'm not stopping, you hear me?"

Nodding, I meet his gaze once before his fingers pull out, making me whimper, but then I feel his length press against my ass. My body stiffens before I remind myself to relax, remembering last time.

"Good boy," he praises as he lifts my hips into the air, dragging his dick along my hole until I push back, needing him to do something other than tease me.

As if my words follow his own thoughts, he slowly presses into me. It hurts, but the burn is nothing compared to the one in my heart the last few weeks. I embrace this, pushing back to take more until I feel him buried all the way inside me. I'm so full, it hurts, yet it feels so fucking good, and then he starts to move.

He pulls from my body then pushes back in. I groan into his pillow and press back to take him deeper. He grips my hips, his fingertips digging in until I ache, and then he shows me exactly what he was talking about.

He hammers into my ass, the force pushing me into the bed with a cry. My hands grip the pillow as pain pierces me, but it's quickly eclipsed by blissful pleasure as he takes me faster and harder.

There are no words—just us and our bodies.

My entire world narrows to him—his smell, touch, and sounds.

He remakes me into his possession, and it's all I want.

This world thinks I belong to them, but they are wrong. I am his.

He presses my face into the bedding as he powers into me from above, the bunk squeaking with his frantic movements. I groan and cry into the pillow, pushing back to take more.

I don't even care if Dash and Strike wake up. I wouldn't let him stop now, not for anything.

I want to come so badly.

I'm close. My cock leaks all over his bed, my balls drawing up, and my spine seems to bow as pleasure spirals through me. When he tilts my hips back and his cock hits a spot inside of me that has my eyes crossing, all thoughts flee in the face of such ecstasy.

It explodes out of me, my muffled yell directed into his pillow as I jerk, my release spilling out of me. His grunt is loud behind me as he buries himself so deep, I feel him in my stomach as he comes, filling me.

"Fox," I whisper, and he gently pulls his cock from me. It aches, but he must know because he leans down and kisses my ass before gathering me into his arms.

We're both breathing heavily, and our skin is sticky, but neither of us seem to care as we bask in the afterglow and let our bodies recover until exhaustion consumes me.

He holds me tighter so I can't escape, laying a gentle kiss on my shoulder. "Sleep now, baby."

SANCTUARY

TWENTY

FOX

I wake up before Ry and find myself watching him. He's facing away from me, his hand trapping my arm against his chest, and there isn't an inch of room between us. Usually, he would sneak out of my bed before dawn, but he's still here, and it's in this moment that I realize he meant what he said.

It doesn't make up for the past, but I wouldn't change anything if I get this. I don't know how long I watch him before I hear the others start to wake up. The moment Ry stirs, he stiffens slightly before relaxing, his eyes still closed.

I expect him to be embarrassed when Strike and Dash swing their legs over and catch us at the same time. Their hair is in disarray, but it's their eyes that make me smile—they bug from their heads as they freeze. They've seen us cuddle before, but this is different, and we all know it.

As usual, Ryker surprises me. He wraps my arm tighter around him with a yawn. "Morning," he says to them before turning and nuzzling my shoulder.

Dash and Strike both raise an eyebrow in question, and I shrug before kissing Ryker's head. Strike lets out a squeal before coughing and covering it, and they both throw me thumbs-up before they go to the bathroom, giving us privacy.

"It's time to get up, baby boy," I say as softly as I can, scanning him lovingly.

"Five more minutes," he whines as he buries his head in my chest, gripping me tightly.

How can I deny him anything?

"Okay, five more minutes," I promise as I kiss the top of his head and hold him tighter.

We lounge while the others get ready, and then I force Ry to get up. He's half asleep as I help him shuffle to the bathroom, his hair stuck up at all angles. He's so fucking cute. Turning him to the mirror, I grab his toothbrush and load it up for him. "Here." I offer it to him, but he doesn't take it. Rolling my eyes, I turn him, open his mouth, and brush his teeth for him. He wakes up as I do and blushes, making me grin. "Can you wash your own face, or do you need me to do that too?" I tease.

"I can do it," he grumbles as he turns to the sink. I shove my boxers down and crank up the shower. It's not the hottest, but it does the trick, and when I climb into the glass cubicle, he gasps.

"Fox!" he yells.

"What?" I turn in confusion.

He rushes to the bathroom door and slams it shut, and I raise a brow as I slick my hair back. "The door was open," he snaps.

"Baby, every single person on this bus has seen my dick a million times. We lived in a van," I scoff.

"Yes, but that was before," he mutters, his bottom lip protruding out in this adorable little pout that makes me want to fill them with something else.

"Before?" I lean out of the shower and wait for his answer.

Sighing, he shuts off the sink and crosses his arms. "Before you became my boyfriend. Now they shouldn't see it, okay? So shut doors."

"Possessive little thing, aren't you?" I smile, though, loving how protective he is. "Want to shower with me?"

"No, you just want to feel me up." He grabs his skincare products and starts on that. Shutting the shower door, I meet his eyes in the mirror as I soap up my body, slowly going over my abs, knowing how much he likes them, then I grip my cock.

His eyes widen in the mirror as he freezes, watching me intently as I work my dick. "Are you sure you don't want to?"

He slams his skincare on the side of the sink, turns, and points at me. "My ass still hurts. Leave me alone, you animal." He flees the bathroom, slamming the door as my laughter chases him.

My smile doesn't disappear the whole time I shower and dress, and when I head out, they are all sitting at the small square table, with cereal and toast spread across the black surface. Sliding into the booth next to my boy, I sling my arm over the back of his seat, massaging his shoulder as I grab a bowl and start to eat.

I notice he doesn't have any juice, so I get up and pour his apple juice before he can ask, knowing he needs it in the morning. His fingers touch mine as he takes it, and his eyes meet mine and then drop to my lips before he looks away. This blush staining his cheeks might be my new favorite thing.

Ryker is always beautiful, but knowing that tint is for me alone? Yeah, he's fucking stunning.

"Give me a bite," I tease as I lean in. His gaze returns to me as he bites down on his toast. "Ry," I whine.

Sighing, he offers me the other end, but I turn his hand and purposely take a bite of the same bit he did, and when I lean back, I wink. "Delicious."

A scoff makes me turn, and I arch a brow as Strike props his head on his fist, still holding his spoon as he looks between us. "You know, I'm glad you two finally gave in."

A satisfied smile curves my lips as I lean back and sip the coffee Ry must have poured for me. "Gave in?" Ry asks, glancing at me and then Strike.

"And fucked?" Strike says. "Wait, sorry, made love."

I hide my smile behind my mug as Ry gapes, and when his voice comes, it's almost a squeak. "I thought you were asleep."

"I'm a deep sleeper, not dead." Strike laughs as he scoops up more cereal and takes a bite. I hold back my laugh since Ry looks so red, he might explode.

Dash lifts his head, still half asleep, his hair stuck up all over, and I'm pretty sure there's a candy wrapper stuck to his shoulder. "Wait, these two were fucking and I missed it?" he asks, confused.

"You're a perv," Strike scoffs as I shake my head at them. As they speak, Ry's face turns redder and redder. It's so adorable.

"Hey, the Wi-Fi here is shit. No good porn options," Dash grumbles.

"You watch men on men porn?" Strike asks curiously.

"Sometimes. I like to change it up every now and again, and it's hot. I'll show you this one video."

"Please stop," Ryker demands.

"Sorry, I'll show you later," Dash whispers to Strike. "Anyway, congrats you two. It's about time you banged it out. You have more sexual tension than me and food, and that's saying a lot since I would fuck a slice of cheese."

"Remind me never to eat the cheese here," Ry mutters as he looks between them. "You aren't bothered by this?"

"Ryker, in the nicest possible way, you're a moron. This has been a long time coming." He smiles at us. "Just don't hurt Fox again, okay? I want you both to be happy."

"I won't," Ry replies instantly as he looks at me. "Not ever again."

I can't hide my smile this time, so I steal a kiss, and his eyes widen.

"Do it again," Dash calls, but Strike just hits him.

"Then we're good. Don't worry, we won't tell anyone. I remember the contract," Strike says. Ry looks surprised again, and Strike smiles knowingly. "We are family, Ry. I don't give a shit what anyone else thinks or says as long as you two are happy. Just, um, maybe close your curtains so Dash can't watch you."

"Aww, you just said we are family. Sharing is caring," Dash says, making us laugh, but he winks at us. "Your secret's safe with us, don't worry. We'll keep you two safe. Just no fucking in my bed, okay? It's a man's sacred space."

"Trust me, we know what goes on in your bunk. It's the last place we will fuck," I promise.

Ry just sighs and slides down, leaning his head on my shoulder. "I guess we don't need to hide it then."

"We don't hide anything from family," I tell him as I kiss his head, unable to resist. "But out there, we are back to normal."

"I don't know if I like that," he admits, "but you're right."

"It won't be forever. Now let's get ready for the sound check. We're going to have an amazing performance tonight," I say.

Strike nods. "Too right."

"And then you two will have an epic night fucking!" Dash calls, making us laugh.

Ry lowers his head in embarrassment, but he's smiling as well.

After all, isn't it a family's job to embarrass you at all times?

He's being a brat, and he knows it, teasing me relentlessly as we perform our sound check.

Licking my lips, I lift my gaze from my guitar as I track him around the stage, knowing he's heading for me again. He's in a crop top that shows off his abs every time he moves, and his loose jeans display his boxers. He looks so fucking good, and he knows it. His taunting eyes pin me in his sights once more as he heads over. He doesn't need to do this at sound check since no one is watching.

He just wants to wind me up. He dances closer, his lips pressed to the mic as he sings, and when he stops in front of me, he looks at me through his lashes as he turns and rolls his hips, grinding against me to the song. His hand slides across my skin as he moves around my back, and he sneaks his fingers under my guitar then caresses my cock before he dances away again.

I glare at him, warning him that he is going to pay for this, but he doesn't seem to care as they change the track. We wait for the count in as he gears up and starts singing the next song. This one doesn't require me to come in just yet, so I walk over and grab a bottle of water to take a drink, but it's suddenly snatched from my hand. I look to the side as Ry grabs my bottle and downs half of it, spilling it on his white shirt, turning it see-through, before he moves back to the middle of the stage. Downing the rest of the water, I crush the bottle and put it back into the box with the others, then I stride over to Ry because two can play this game.

Leaving my guitar behind me, I stop at his back and slide my hands over his hips, then I drag his damp shirt up, caressing his abs as I blow on his neck. He shivers and spins, his eyes wide, and I smirk as I step back as my cue hits.

Spinning my guitar around, I play the first note as I move over to Strike and lean into him as we perform.

By the time the sound check is over, we are both wound up, and I'm ready to tan his ass red for taunting me like that on stage. He was bad before, but now he's on a whole other level.

As we walk off the stage, we hand our equipment back to the team to prepare for tonight, and once they are out of sight, I turn to Ry, take two long strides, bend down, and scoop him over my shoulder. His startled yelp splits the air as I turn and wave at Strike and Dash then march toward our bus.

Strike and Dash laugh, waving at us. "Have fun!" Dash calls.

"Hey, guys, have you seen Ryker and Fox?" I hear Po asking, so I speed up.

"Uh . . . nope. I think they went to the merch stand," Strike answers, covering for us.

We barely make it to the bus before he's smacking my back. "Fox," he rasps, sounding embarrassed. "I'm sorry."

"Shut up," I growl, slapping his ass as I hurry up the steps. I hit the button to close the door then lock it before I slide him down my body. He swallows hard as he stumbles back a step, his hands coming up as if to warn me off.

He steps back, so I advance on him. "I'm sorry. I shouldn't have teased you like that—" He gasps as I wrap my hand around his throat and pull him closer.

"No, you shouldn't have," I warn, my voice dark. "If you want to be a brat, then I'm going to treat you like one."

Pushing him to his knees, I keep one hand on his head while I unbuckle my jeans with the other and shove them down.

"Fox, I'm sorry." His eyes are wide as I arch an eyebrow.

"Then you're going to show me," I order. "You need to sing later, baby, but you need to be punished for winding me up, don't you? I'm going to bruise your pretty throat so when you sing, it will hurt, and you'll remember what happens when you piss off your boyfriend and make him jealous."

He breathes heavily, and his tongue darts out to wet his lips as he glances from my cock to my face.

"Open your mouth," I order, knowing he's nervous and unsure. He needs me to take control, which is fine with me. I've wanted to put this brat on his knees for years.

His mouth drops open, and I drag my cock along his lips. "Taste me," I demand.

He licks his lips and groans, then I tap his mouth with my cock. "Open again," I command, and he does as he's told. This time, I don't hold back. I press into his mouth, feeding him my entire length until I'm down his throat.

His eyes widen, and he slaps my thighs as he gags, so I grip his hair and jerk him tighter against me. "Don't you dare choke. Breathe through your nose. You're going to suck all of me down. You are going to take all of it." I keep myself there as he panics, but then he slowly calms down, and I pull out as he inhales. I surge back in, hitting the back of his throat, making him choke again. Tears slide down his face, and I kind of fucking love the sight of them.

I want to take a picture, but I know how risky that would be for us, so instead I just memorize the sight of him on his knees for me as I fuck his mouth hard and fast. I don't hold back at all, forcing him to take me over and over, even as he gags and struggles. Eventually, he gives up and just lets me fuck his mouth, and it's the most beautiful surrender.

"Look at you. You look so good on your knees for me. If only your fans could see you now, sucking your boyfriend's cock. They'd be so fucking jealous that I get to touch you, but you're all mine, aren't you?" I thrust deeper, and his eyes tighten, but he doesn't protest.

His nails dig into my thighs as I use his mouth, my groan filling the air as I watch his drool drip down his throat as I fuck him, taking my pleasure. Seeing him like this, where I've always wanted him, sends me over the edge.

My release slams through me so hard, my back bows from the pressure as my balls draw up, and I explode in his mouth.

He blinks rapidly, tears coating his lashes as he tries to pull away while I fill his mouth.

"Swallow," I order, grabbing his throat. His Adam's apple bobs as he swallows my cum. "Good boy."

Pulling from his mouth, I tuck myself away as I kneel and massage his throat as he pants.

I kiss his raw lips. "Next time you tease me, it will be your ass." Standing, I help him to his feet just as we hear something outside the bus.

"Yes, what amazing weather!" Strike yells from somewhere nearby.

"Why are you yelling?" Po questions.

"It would be a shame if we were to head into that bus right there that is ours in search of our bandmates," Dash adds loudly.

"What is with you two? Did you accidentally drink that CBD drink again?" Po scoffs.

"Oh, our bus, it's right here. I hope Fox and Ryker are in there resting like you thought."

"We need to talk about the legal drugs you take," Po responds from outside the door, so I push Ry into the bench seat and slide in next to him, leaning back as I grab my iPad and open it like I was scribbling lyrics just as the door opens.

"I wonder why it was locked." Po sighs as he climbs up and inside, spotting us.

"Hey, you're here!" Po says as he heads over and sits down opposite us. "I just wanted to run through any issues you might be having. Are you okay, Ry? Your lips are really swollen."

"Oh, I tried a new gloss," he rasps, his voice hoarse.

"Shit, are you losing your voice?" Po darts over to the small kitchen and starts making him some warm tea as I smile. Strike and Dash are panting, and they look relieved as they lean into each other, undoubtedly worried we were about to get caught. Po sets the mug before Ry, who's blushing hard. "Drink this and go rest. We need you in good shape for tonight."

"Yes, Ry, make sure to rest," I say as I focus on my scribbles, but I can't hide my smile.

"All of you, rest before tonight's show. I know you normally hang with the others, but you look tired. I want happy, refreshed faces later. The tour is just beginning, so don't get sick on me yet," Po warns as he points between us. "I'll order you all some food. Rest. That's an order." He leaves, and Strike dramatically flops to the floor where Ry was kneeling.

"That was fucking close," he grouses. "I was so stressed."

"Tell me about it," Dash agrees. "You two need to behave."

"Us two? We didn't do anything," I reply innocently.

"Sure you didn't." Strike groans.

"Okay, we did something right where you're lying," I tease, and he yelps as he rolls to his feet while Dash just watches curiously. He turns his head, moving his hands, and Strike sighs.

"What are you doing?" he mutters.

"Trying to figure out the position," he admits as he scratches his head. "Were his legs open like this—" I smack him with the pen, and he whines.

"You really are a perv," I mutter as I turn to Ry. "Drink your tea."

Nodding, he sips it as I smile.

SANCTUARY

TWENTY-ONE

RYKER

Tonight's performance is just like any other, or so I tell myself. It doesn't matter that Fox and I are officially dating. It doesn't change anything . . . . Okay, it changes everything. I'm more nervous, as if everyone who is watching will know we fucked just by looking at us. It means I'm stiff for the first song, and he must notice because during the second, he breaks the routine and heads over, leaning into me, and when the drum solo begins, he whispers in my ear.

"Relax." He smacks my ass as he dances away, and it does the trick. I get into it in the third song, having fun once more, dancing and playing with the crowd. This is for them as much as it's for us. They came to see us and Dead Ringers, but we need to give every show our all.

Even if my throat aches like a son of a bitch, the show must go on.

By the fourth song, I've decided I no longer give a fuck, and I let go and do what I normally do. No one can prove we're together anyway. Besides, we always flirt and dance. I make my way across the stage to Fox and kneel, then I run my hand up his thigh as I come in on my notes. Looking at the crowd, I slide my hand higher until I grip his cock, and then I wag my finger at the crowd as I get to my feet, dragging my mouth up his leg when the chorus breaks. Darting my tongue out, I drag it along his exposed abs, and the crowd goes wild.

I turn as I lift my mic and start to sing again. Dancing over to Strike, I lean into him as he grins at me, and when the drums kick in, I move to the front of the stage, throwing my arm out as I hit the high note.

I feel him before he touches me. His warmth radiates against my back. Since he's not playing, he slides his hand between my legs and up, gripping my dick for the world to see, his head in the crook of my neck as I lean back and sing. My cock grows hard under his touch, but then he slowly pulls away and swings his guitar around, walking to the edge of the stage. My eyes track him as he leans into the audience as he plays.

He's magnificent. I can't take my eyes off him and neither can the crowd. They scream his name, fighting to get closer, and I want to laugh at how easily I could touch him, so when the song is over and he grabs a drink, I lean into my mic.

"I see y'all thirsty barricaders reaching for him." I wag my finger as they scream louder. "Sorry, he's mine. No touching. Only I can."

"Ryker, let me marry Fox!" someone yells, and I cup my ear so they shout louder.

"Ah." Turning, I glance at Fox. "No, sorry. What do you say?"

Fox laughs as he strides over, sliding his arm around my shoulders as he leans into my mic so his face is next to me. "Sorry, but Ry is possessive." He winks at the crowd.

"Fox, Fox, Fox!" they chant, and he waits, trying to distinguish their voices. When he can't, he heads over to the edge and crouches. "Slow down, what are you saying?" he asks as Strike and Dash take a little break.

I head over and lean against his shoulder as I listen. He wraps his arm around me, anchoring me without even looking, and I wink as they react. His hand strokes my leather pants, and they go wild. "Oh, I can hear you now. No, sorry. Ryker is mine, so you need to behave.

You can look, but you can't touch. Isn't that right, my boy?" He glances up at me, and my eyes widen at the endearment, but satisfaction fills me with him claiming me so openly.

"That's right, so how about we give them another show? Are you ready to swear to our gods? Are you ready . . . to go to church?" I shout into the mic, and the crowd goes wild.

Fox stands and kisses my cheek before he heads back to his spot on stage. Their screams only grow louder, and I chuckle into the mic as I walk to my place. The lights cut out, and the spotlight hits me, an organ playing as I croon into the mic.

The others slowly chime in with their instruments before the drop, and the crowd screams, my voice filling the stadium as I tilt into the mic.

The organ only increases as red crosses flash across the screen. Falling to my knees, I continue to sing, and when the last note tapers off, Fox is above me with his hand on my chin, tilting it up, and he leans down as the stage goes black.

His eyes meet mine in the dim light, and despite where we are, he steals a kiss before walking away as the lights come back on. Panting, I lick my lips as I climb to my feet, my mic in hand, but all I can think about is him.

"I don't know about you, but I think I missed that. Did you?" I call into the mic as I walk over to Fox. When he turns at my voice, I grab the back of his neck and yank him down.

I plant a quick kiss on his lips, and he jerks backward, his eyes wide even as the crowd goes wild. "Wasn't for them," I tell him through a pant. "That was for me." I turn and head to the edge of the stage. "Thank you for rocking with us! Now get ready for the show of your lives with Dead Ringers!"

Their stomps shake the stadium, and we hurry backstage as the lights go down.

We are all sweaty and panting but happy as hell. I don't think I've seen my band this elated in a long time. Now that everything is fixed between Fox and me, it's like we are back to the way we were, and I love it. Dash throws his arm over my shoulders and kisses my cheek. "It's good to have you back, brother."

Strike grabs my other side. "Just don't hurt him, okay?" he asks.

I find Fox grabbing all of our water bottles, and at my look, he arches a brow in question. "I don't plan to. I plan to love him as long as he lets me."

"Aw!" They both fake gag and swoon as Fox hands over our bottles, his eyes for me.

"Let's go watch the set in the green room," he murmurs, and I nod, hurrying to his side as Strike and Dash mock me. I wave at Po, who's busy talking to crew members, and he waves back as we duck into the green room. It's empty right now, and I sprawl across Fox. He massages my neck, his free hand sliding across my thigh as we turn our attention to the screen just as Dead Ringers comes on stage.

Their music is addictive, but not as addictive as the man at my side. My eyes linger on him as his lithe fingers tap my thigh to the beat, his head bobbing slightly. His hair is slicked back with sweat and his makeup is smudged, but he's never looked so beautiful.

I struggle to catch my breath, barely believing that he's finally mine and I can touch him without needing a reason.

As if sensing my gaze, he swings those bright orbs to me, the corners of his eyes crinkling as he smiles. "Aren't you watching?"

"I'm watching something infinitely more important," I murmur.

He kisses my cheek as Dash and Strike fight over the beer they hold. "You did good tonight, baby," he praises, and I swing my hungry gaze to him. It drops to his lips as everything else fades around us. "I can see those dirty thoughts of yours."

"Do you think we have time for a quickie?" I ask, and he laughs loudly.

"Oh shit!" Dash yells, and we jerk apart, our eyes going to the screen to see what he did.

"What happened?" I ask as I watch Beck Danvers flee the stage.

"Not a clue," Dash whispers as he looks at us. "She'll be back, right?" We all remain silent as the rest of Dead Ringers look on in shock and confusion. "Right?"

Beck Danvers is gone, and so is the tour.

Po paces before us, worried even though he won't admit it. This isn't good. This isn't good at all. Without Beck, there's no Dead Ringers, and without them, there's no tour and no us. It's our dream, our chance, and it's slipping away.

Fox drops a pillow on our thighs, which are pressed together, and under it, he grips my hand. "It will be okay," he murmurs to me.

I don't have the same faith. What if this is it? What if everything we worked for is just gone?

We've been in our own bubble for most of this tour, so happy to be involved that we didn't even notice anything was wrong in their band.

"What happened?" Fox asks when Po hangs up.

"Nothing to worry about, just some slight issues. She will be back. I'm sure of it," he lies flawlessly, but his eyes are twitching.

"You're lying. You don't know if she will. What happens to us if this tour is cancelled?" Fox asks sternly, speaking for us all since we stare at Po like lost puppies searching for answers.

"It's just on hold for now," Po answers. "Don't worry, we'll figure it out. Go back and rest early, okay? We'll have a plan tomorrow and know what's happening. You did great tonight, guys." He departs, and we are left with more questions than answers.

With no other choice, we head back to our bus, but we are all quiet. It was the best show of our lives, and it might be the last. This is out of our hands, and I hate that. Dash and Strike go to bed, both looking beat and stressed, but I can't sleep. I climb the ladder at the back of the bus and lie on the roof. I stare up at the stars when I feel him lie next to me. Despite everything, I smile. I knew he would come.

"You remember when we used to do this every night in the van? Dash and Strike would be snoring, but we would watch the sky for hours together, talking about everything and anything. Neither of us wanted to sleep," I recollect as he reaches over and takes my hand. He places it on his chest and plays with my fingers, and the connection makes me sigh happily and turn my head to see him.

He's staring at the sky, his wet hair held back by a cute, fluffy headband I bought him when he kept complaining about how long it was getting.

Fuck, I love this man.

I love every version of him, but I think this is my favorite. It's a side of him only I get.

"It was my favorite part of every day," I whisper shyly, and his head turns so his eyes meet mine. "Even if I didn't understand why I craved it, I would count down the hours until it was just us and the sky. You were always the best part of my day, Fox, and I missed it so much. I used to go outside and look up at the stars when we drifted, hoping you were as well and thinking of me like I was you."

"Ry . . ." He sighs, kissing my fingers as I watch him.

"I made so many mistakes. I ran, and I hurt you, yet you're still here with me. Promise me you won't go anywhere. I won't hurt you ever again. I won't ever be scared again, but please, Fox, please don't stop watching the sky with me. Please don't take that from me again," I implore, knowing I sound desperate, but my world is now up in flames, everything uncertain, and he's my safe harbor.

"Never," he promises as he kisses my hand again. "We'll do this until we are too old to climb up here, and then I'll get us blankets so we can do it on the ground instead. We've both made mistakes, baby, and both hurt each other, so stop dwelling on it. The past is the past for a reason, and it got us here together, didn't it?" His eyes are so soft, I drown in them, and something in my chest loosens. All the guilt and pain I felt flee at his confession.

I was too much of a coward back then to take what I wanted, but I never will be again. I'll be brave for him.

"Do you remember our first kiss?" I ask. It was on a night like this, the world silent around us.

"Hmm, it was on stage, wasn't it?" he asks as he turns to face me, our hands trapped between us as if he has no intention of relinquishing his hold on me.

"No, it wasn't," I admit slyly, dropping my gaze to his lips. "It was before that, way before all of this. It was in our van. We were broke and tired, and you were in front of me, looking so perfect I couldn't resist."

He frowns, thinking for a moment, and I know the second he remembers what I mean because his mouth parts in shock. "I thought you were asleep," he whispers.

My smile is small and guilty as I move closer. "You were staring at me, and I was hoping you would kiss me, but you didn't so I kissed you. I pretended I was asleep to get away with it, not ready for what it meant, but even then, I knew if I didn't kiss you in that moment, I would die. I'm sorry it took me so long, baby. I got lost along the way, but it's always been you. Every bed I left was me running toward you. I promise I will never hurt you again. I love you, Fox. All I know and all I have ever known is that I'm lost without you. Without you, there's no me, and every love song I have ever sung has been for you." I wipe away a tear that falls from his beautiful eyes, remembering how many I put there before. "I don't know if I believe in fate or destiny or anything like that, but I believe we found each other in this fucked-up world for a reason, and I'm never letting go again." I press my lips to his, keeping my eyes open this time, loving him fully.

I move closer, echoing what I did that night as I watched him through slitted eyelids.

This time, he doesn't try to move away.

No, he reaches for me, cupping my cheek. Our lips tastes like his tears as he kisses me softly, like I'm precious. When he pulls away this time, he holds me close, his legs thrown over mine as if he's worried I'll disappear. I know I put that fear there, and I'll spend the rest of our lives making sure he never feels it again.

"We named our band Sanctuary," I whisper, and his eyelids open, "because we were all lost and searching for a home. I found mine, and it's you."

He smiles, and it's like the sun shining through a storm. "You have a way with words, baby. I guess that makes sense."

"No, you always wrote them for others, but I'll write them for you," I promise as I kiss him again. "I know you're worried about what's going on, but whatever happens, we'll be okay because we have each other," I tell him as I look into his eyes. "We've done it before, and we can do it again, but I'd happily lose it all as long as I have you. You're my life, Fox, not music or this band or even this dream. I can live without being a singer, but I can't live without you."

"Then don't," he responds. "You're right. We'll face it together."

A throat clears, and we both roll our heads back to see Dash and Strike. "Sorry to interrupt. We couldn't sleep, too worried. Can we join?" Strike asks hesitantly.

Fox and I share a look, and then we both hold out our hands. They come over, Strike taking Fox's, Dash taking mine, and they huddle around us, just like those nights in our van. Fox smiles at me, and I know I'm right.

No matter what, we'll be okay because we have each other.

We might have lost our chance, but we found our family again, and that is worth more than fame ever could be.

SANCTUARY

TWENTY-TWO

FOX

Despite our nervousness, we do manage to get some sleep, but when morning arrives and there is no more news than before, we all feel the stress.

"Why don't you two get out of here? We'll be on the road later, and it's going to be crazy for a few months. Go have a date or something," Strike suggests. "We'll call if there is any news."

I know he's doing it to stop me from pacing, but as I stare at Ryker, who perks up at the idea, I find I like it a lot. "Do you want to go on a date with me?"

"Absolutely," he replies, pink tinging his cheeks. "Let me get dressed." My eyebrows rise as he darts past me, smiling despite the situation.

He's so fucking cute.

"Better go get ready. Your boyfriend is waiting," Strike teases. Flipping him off, I go to the bathroom and find Ryker there, fussing with his hair. I lean into the door and watch him for a moment before he notices me.

"What?" he asks. "It's our first date. Can't I be excited?"

He looks down, and I hate the way his smile dims. I step inside, wrap my arms around him, and prop my chin on his shoulder. "You'll never be as excited as I am, but whatever you do, you'll look handsome."

That makes him smile, and he keeps fussing with his hair. "Go get dressed," he says, elbowing me.

Pressing my lips to his cheek, I dart away as he slaps me, and I get dressed and ready before him. When he comes out, he looks good enough to eat, wearing an oversized sweater and loose pants with a jacket over the top. "I thought we could try to go incognito," he says before his eyes widen. "Not that I'm ashamed or anything. I just thought that way it's us—"

"Adorable," I call as he rambles. "Come on, baby."

I hold out my hand, and he hurries to take it. I flip off Strike and Dash, who mimic us, and we sneak out of the bus. Avoiding security is easy, and I hold the gate for him, letting him duck out first, and then we are out on the street. Our whoops of laughter echo around as we run from the venue as fast as we can. Usually, we can leave if we want to, but Po wouldn't let us right now.

No, this is our stolen time, and I love it.

"Where are we going?" he asks when we stop.

"Anywhere." I look around since we don't really know much about the area. We should probably stay close. "I should have made a plan," I admit with a frown.

"Fuck plans. Let's just go where we want." He pulls me after him, and we eventually find a main street. We window shop for a while and just enjoy walking together, holding hands without a care. We are just two men on a date, and it's so fucking perfect. I keep my sunglasses and my mask on just in case, so nobody ruins this for us.

We find some small boutiques and take pictures, trying on fur coats and funny hats until our camera is full of them. In the last shop, I find this perfect little signet ring, so I secretly buy it, and once we are outside, I turn to Ryker.

"Here." I thrust the bag at him. His eyebrow rises, and he peeks inside, pulling out the box in confusion. I wait with my hands in my pockets, feeling nervous.

When he opens it, he stares for a while, and I grow anxious. "I know it isn't like your designer stuff—"

"I love it," he whispers, sliding it onto his fingers, trying to find the right one before he puts it on his ring finger. It fits perfectly. The gold is bright against his skin, the flat top displaying two interlaced hearts. "It will be for us, so we know . . . unless you replace it with a diamond," he teases.

Laughing, I drag him closer and hug him. "One day," I say, knowing I will. When we are allowed to be together and there won't be consequences, there will be a ring on his finger and he will be mine.

We haven't been together long, but it doesn't matter. I knew Ryker was the one the moment I met him.

"Come on, let's find somewhere to eat," I say, realizing we have just been standing together far longer than is normal.

We wander aimlessly, searching for something that feels right. We don't want fancy food—we want home-cooked meals like we used to eat before everything started.

We eventually find a retro bar to eat at, and there's a live band on stage despite the early afternoon time. We sing along as we eat, our smiles so wide they feel like our faces might break, and when a slow song comes on, I offer him my hand.

He takes it, and I tug him over to the small wooden dance floor. We are the only people on it, but I don't care. His head rests against my chest and his hands are in mine as we rock to the song.

"I wish we could be like this forever," he murmurs.

"Me too," I say as I rest my chin on his head. "But it just means the time we do get is even more special."

"Do you think one day we can be together without hiding?" he asks, propping his chin on my chest.

"Yes." I rub his back comfortingly. "I have to believe we will be, but for now, this is enough for me. Is it enough for you?"

"As long as I have you," he replies, a smile growing on his lips. "I still want that diamond though."

"Brat," I tease as I spin him around, his laughter filling the air. The song changes to an upbeat one, and we dance for a while, uncaring who is watching.

After eating, we just walk, enjoying our quiet time together. We take photos that are just meant for us and don't worry about anyone watching, but as the sun starts to set, I know we have to get back. Both of us drag our feet, and at the gate, we share a look.

I kiss the back of his hand before I let go. "It's still us," I promise, and he nods as he slides inside. We head back over to the bus, our hands swinging so closely together they nearly touch, but not quite. We don't want to take the risk.

When we round the front of the vehicle, we freeze.

Po is waiting for us, and he doesn't look happy. "Pack your stuff. We are going home for a while."

"What happened?" Ryker asks.

"Beck Danvers was attacked and badly hurt. They are postponing the tour." He forces a smile. "Don't worry, it will start again. It's just a small break." He claps his hands. "No dejected looks. We'll take this time for more music, okay?"

That makes us groan, but as I look at Po, I see his worry, and I wonder how bad it was.

Is that why she left?

We arrive home the next day and unpack. None of us know when or if the tour will start up again or even how Beck is. It haunts us, leaving us all listless, so we decide to have a movie night.

We huddle around each other in the living room and turn on the TV to see the news. The name Dead Ringers stops me from changing it over to a movie.

We watch the news report in shock as it shows a motel room and reports that Beck Danvers survived a murderer. There isn't much else, but they keep running through the facts, and horror washes through me.

We all sent Beck and the others messages and flowers, but it's all over the news, and none of us can believe our eyes.

No wonder the tour is paused. They have more important things to deal with. Despite my own concern, I hope she is okay. Surviving something like that can't be easy.

"It's crazy." Ryker sighs, leaning into my shoulder. "Who could do something like that?"

"Psychopaths," I murmur as I kiss his head and focus on the news just as the doorbell rings.

"That will be pizza," Strike says. "Foxy, get it for us. I'm comfy."

"No," I mutter, and Ryker looks up.

"Please, baby?" he asks sweetly.

"Fine." I heave myself up, ignoring their ribbing at how easily I gave in to Ryker. Opening the front door, I focus on getting my cash from my pocket and handing it over. "Keep the tip—" My head comes up, and I freeze.

It isn't a pizza delivery person.

No, it's Theo, my ex.

RYKER

"Fox has been a while," Dash mumbles. I glance at the hallway, realizing he's right.

"I'll go see." Hopping from the sofa, I slide into the hall, grinning as I skid. Fox's back is to me, and his arm is across the door, the other holding it tightly. He looks tense, so I hurry over, poking his side to get him to laugh.

"What's taking so long?" I whine, popping up and seeing the guy on the doorstep. Definitely not delivery.

I sober up, running my eyes down him. He's taller than I am and muscular. His black hair is partially shaved, and his face is square and handsome, with a black mustache above plump lips.

He's very attractive and different from me.

I look between Fox and him, and it's obvious what they are to each other. Nobody looks at someone like that unless there's history—romantic history.

"Fox?" I cover his arm bracketing the doorframe. He snaps his head around, and I turn to the guy to see his eyes locked on my hand touching Fox. "Who's this?"

Before Fox can introduce him, he sticks his hand out, a cocky smirk in place. "Name's Theodore. I'm Fox's first love." The smile he aims my way is not nice, and he returns his gaze to Fox as if he's dismissing me. "Not even going to let me in after I came all this way to see you?"

"Why are you here?" Fox finally speaks, his voice tight.

"We need to talk," Theodore responds, that cocky smile in place. "I didn't think you'd answer my calls or texts—"

"You were right," Fox snaps, sounding crueler than I've ever heard him. "Nor should you just show up in my life. I made that clear after you made your choice."

"Dane." I jerk at the use of Fox's real name, and Fox's nostrils flare. "Five minutes, please, for old times' sake."

Fox stares him down before stepping back, his jaw clenching. "Five minutes. Follow me." He looks at me, and his expression softens. "I'll be right back, okay?"

Nodding, I watch him go. Theo winks at me as he passes, following Fox through the hallway to the kitchen, then out back. He shuts the door after him, and I kick the front door shut, silently wandering after them. I linger in the kitchen to watch them through the window.

Fox's arms are crossed, and he looks pissed, but Theodore doesn't seem to care as he steps closer, smiling brightly.

"Who's that? I don't remember anyone delivering pizza like that before," Strike scoffs from my side.

"I don't know. He knows Fox, said he was his first love," I grumble as I watch them. Theodore is talking, and Fox is staring at him. There's this connection between them that wouldn't take a genius to figure out.

"I hate him," I mutter.

"Of course you do." Dash laughs as he swings his arm around my shoulders. "He's a rival."

"No, he isn't. Fox is mine," I snap.

"Sure thing." Strike hugs my other side. "He is hot though. Fox has good taste. I wonder how long ago they dated and why they broke up. Has Fox ever mentioned him?" He looks at me.

"Not once." That is weird in itself. Fox tells me everything, even before we started dating. I suppose I never asked about his love life, not wanting to know.

We all stand there watching until Fox opens the door, and then we scramble away to look like we weren't eavesdropping. I grab a mug and pretend to fill it. Strike lies on the table, playing with some fruit, and Dash dives into the fridge.

Fox just blinks at us, looking around. "You guys are so weird," he mutters as Theodore appears at his side. Fox spares us another glance and begins to head through the kitchen, but Theodore stops.

"So this is your band." Fox turns back, and it's clear he isn't happy, but he remains silent. "I guess you finally got everything you wanted, huh? I'm proud of you. I always knew you would make it."

"Sure you did," Fox scoffs.

Theodore's smile fades for a moment before he looks at me. "You must be Ryker. I've seen you on TV with Fox. Thanks for taking care of him for me."

"It wasn't for you," I snap.

"Of course," he replies slyly. "I'm just glad you aren't alone in this," he tells Fox. "I know how hard you worked to become the best you could be. How many hours did we spend at music shops and lessons?"

I freeze, my gaze swinging to Fox. Just how long have they known each other?

"Theo," Fox warns. "Enough, I don't want a trip down memory lane. It's called the past for a reason."

"Not everything," Theo retorts, and he looks at me. "I guess some things do change though. He's not your usual taste. He's . . . very raw."

My heart pounds and anger fills me. Dash and Strike step in front of me before I can smash my fist into his perfect face.

"Enough," Fox barks. "Do not speak to Ryker or any of my family like that. You've said what you wanted to, now leave. I've made it very clear that I don't want you in my life. You made your choice, Theo, so live with it."

"And if I don't want to?" he counters, stopping before Fox. "What if I want what we had back? What if I made a mistake?"

"Too bad," Fox replies, his voice cruel. "Now leave."

"Think about what I said, okay?" He looks at me. "When you get tired of slumming it, come back to me."

My eyes widen, and then he's gone, the door shutting softly behind him. Fox scrubs at his face then spares us a look before heading outside, and I shove Dash and Strike out of the way, going out after him.

Irrational jealousy and fear control me.

I yank his arm, turning him around. "Not now, baby, please," he murmurs.

"Yes, now!" I snap. "Who the fuck was that?"

He looks at me, and I wait, furious. "My ex," he answers.

"And why was he here? Why did you let him in and talk to him?" I ask. I'm acting crazy, but what did he mean about going back to him?

Is Fox going to leave me?

The idea makes it hard to breathe, and I implore him with my eyes to make this feeling go away.

"He wanted to talk about something, but it wasn't important. He's gone, and he won't be back," he promises.

I'm angry, really angry and jealous as hell, which is something I hate. "He seems to think he will be, that you'll be back together."

"You know that's not true. I'm dating you," he soothes, stepping closer, reaching for me, but I shove his hands away.

"How can I say anything?" I hiss. "I'm not even officially your boyfriend, everyone knows that, and I didn't even know who he was! Evidently, I don't matter."

"Ry . . ." Fox sighs.

"How long did you date?" I ask. "When did you break up? Why? What did he tell you?" When he stays silent, I scoff bitterly. "You won't even tell me? That lets me know exactly where I stand in your life. I'm good enough to fuck, but not good enough to trust, huh?"

"Ryker," Fox snaps. "That isn't fair, and you know it isn't true. I trust you more than I've ever trusted anyone."

I'm quiet then, my heart aching. It hurts as I stare at him. I don't know why. I guess I always thought I was Fox's first love, but hearing it from that bastard? It ripped me to pieces and made me unsure in our relationship, and now I'm taking it out on him.

"This is what he wants, for us to fight," Fox says sadly as he stares at me. "Can you just hold me? Seeing him fucked me up."

His words make all my anger disappear. Fox never asks me for anything, and seeing how troubled he is makes everything else seem stupid. Despite my own pain and uncertainty, I wrap my arms around him, and he rests his head against my chest. "I'm sorry," I murmur. "I shouldn't have reacted like that. He just pissed me off."

"He has that effect on people," he grumbles, holding me tighter before he pulls away, cupping my face. "Next time, don't let him talk to you like that, okay? You're all that matters. I mean it, Ryker. He's nothing to me anymore. You're my everything. I'm sorry if that hurt you. Ask your questions, and I'll answer. I promise." He takes my hand and leads me over to sit, and I debate if I really want to know.

Is it better to be oblivious? That bastard might use it against me though.

I saw that look in his eyes. He doesn't plan on going anywhere.

"Tell me everything," I say.

We sit side by side, and Fox takes a deep breath. "I don't want to hurt you."

"It hurts me more not knowing, like he's worthy of knowing it and I'm not," I admit.

"That's not true. He is my past, Ryker, before I even met you. I don't want you to question anything, but I'll tell you. We met when we were teenagers, when he moved into my class at school. His dad owned a music shop, so I spent time there, learning to play. We grew close, and we started to date. He was my first everything." That hurts like hell, but I try to cover it. It's my own insecurity. He can't help who he loved before, but I'll admit it hurts knowing that Fox is my first love but I'm not his.

"I thought I'd marry him. I thought he was my forever, Ryker. I loved him a lot. I won't lie about that." He takes my hand and presses it to his chest. "But this is yours. I vow it. There is nothing left of him in there anymore. He made sure of it."

"What happened?" I ask.

"He cheated on me. When I found out, I even forgave him. I was so young and desperate for him to love me. We graduated and were living in his shitty, one-bedroom apartment as I tried to support us, and I couldn't bear the idea of losing him. He was all I had, Ryker—no family or friends, just him—but he did it again and again, and when I confronted him, he admitted he didn't love me anymore and that he couldn't stay with a 'futureless loser fighting every day for his meals.' He moved in with the guy he cheated on me with that very same day—some older, Wall Street motherfucker. It hurt a lot. He fucked me up with mind games and cheating, and then I turned back to music, more determined than ever to make it. I met you two years later."

"Oh." It's all I can say as I process his words. His ex sounds like an asshole. How could he do that to Fox? If you don't love someone, just leave. Why the hell did he need to cheat and break his heart and trust?

Gripping my face, he stares into my wide eyes. "But I never loved him the way I love you. I needed to lose him to find you, and I'm so fucking glad I did. This thing between us is forever. This is what I was missing. This is real love. Don't ever doubt that. I loved him as a kid, but I love you as a man. I'm sorry you aren't my first love, but I swear, Ry, you will be my last."

"I better be," I grumble as I lean into his side, holding his hand. "I hate him," I admit childishly.

"Good. Don't ever let me see you insecure and cowed like that again. The Ryker I love is crazy and bold and not afraid to say anything." He kisses my head. "Don't change because of him. I don't plan to. He doesn't matter, and our past doesn't matter. Only this does." He lifts my chin. "I love you, baby, so much."

"I love you too." I sigh as he kisses me softly until there's a crash.

We both turn to see a smashed plant pot, Dash holding the tree that was in it, his wide eyes visible through the foliage. Strike is at his side, and it's very clear they were eavesdropping.

"I guess you have a family now. We are just a bit insane," I comment, a smile tilting my lips.

I still hate that I met his ex, but it isn't his fault. It's my own issue, not his.

"I do, and I've never been happier. I wish I had all of you back then, but now will do." He kisses my head again. "Don't let him ruin our night. Let's go watch movies with those two dumbasses, and then I'll make it up to you all night."

Desire floods me, and I crane my head back, a flirty smile curving my lips. "You better."

"It's a deal," he says as he kisses me, chasing away all those petty, insecure feelings.

Nothing has changed between us, and that makes me feel safe.

TWENTY-THREE

FOX

He sleeps like a baby, his face so happy and open in slumber. It's turned toward me, and his legs and arms are tangled with mine as if he's worried I'll disappear. Ever since the night we confessed our love to each other, we haven't spent time apart. It's like old times, only better because now there is nothing else lying between us, just the truth.

Ryker is mine, and I've never been happier. It's everything I wanted, yet seeing Theo brought back a whole lot of shit.

I guess it's never nice seeing an ex you ended on bad terms with, but when someone broke your heart so badly? Yeah, it wasn't just a shock. It was horrible to see him again. He smiled at me like he had any right—never mind that he wanted to talk to me about being back in my life.

As if he had any right.

He was my entire world, and I would have done anything for him. He ruined it. He destroyed what we had, and now he wants to come back? Not a fucking chance. The worst is how insecure it made Ryker. I've never seen him like that, and I hated it.

I've moved on, and I'm happy. I love Ryker, my friends, and my job, so why is he back now, of all times? It's like he senses my happiness and wants to ruin it.

He's the reason I find it so hard to trust, why I almost gave up on my dreams. I wasn't enough for him, didn't have enough money, power, or connections. Glancing down at Ryker, I wonder if he would still want me if I wasn't this . . . rock god, as they call me, but then I remember he did. He wanted me when we had nothing, when we were crowded in a van, barely scraping by. It didn't matter to him. All that mattered was who I was and what I wanted.

We both shared the same dream, and it created a bond like no other. Loving Ryker healed the trauma Theo caused.

Cheating on someone doesn't just end the relationship for most people. It's the effects that are the worst—second-guessing everything and everyone in your life, never being able to fully trust another person, no matter if they have done something wrong or not.

The worst, though, is blaming yourself.

If I were a better boyfriend, would he have still cheated?

"Baby?" Ryker lifts his head, blinking sleepily. "What's wrong?"

"Nothing, go back to sleep," I murmur as I kiss his head. It isn't fair to be thinking of this when Ryker is right here, but I can't seem to help it. My mind keeps going around and around in circles.

"You're overthinking," he grumbles as he moves closer, humming happily. "Want me to blow you to stop that?"

A surprised laugh escapes me, and when he lifts his twinkling eyes, I know that's why he did it. He pokes my head with his finger. "Stop this, okay? You need to sleep."

"I know," I murmur. "I just . . . Seeing him brought a lot back."

"Good or bad?" he asks, and there is no judgment there.

"Bad," I reply as I pull him closer. "He's always had the ability to do this to me and make me feel . . . weak."

"You aren't that person anymore," Ry says. "So don't let him. The only person who should ever be able to hurt you like that is someone you love. Do you still love him?" It's an innocent question, but his body tenses against mine.

"No. Not even a little," I promise as I tip his head back so he sees the truth in my eyes. I never want him to worry about that. "He's my past, Ryker, nothing more."

"Then don't give him one more minute of your future," he responds as he moves even closer. "He isn't worth it. Besides, if he never hurt you, then you never would have found me."

That makes me smile as I rub his back. "That's true," I muse. "How happy I would have been—" I laugh when he hits me. "And lonely," I finish with a wink.

"Better," he grumbles, and we lapse into silence for a bit, both lost in our own thoughts, but what Ryker said is true. I can't give Theo control over me again. I wasted enough of my time on him in the past. He doesn't get my future, nor will I ever hurt Ry by making him think Theo has any say in my life now.

That fear remains, though, one that has never gone away.

"Please don't break my heart," I croak.

He leans in and kisses me softly, tasting my pain. "Never. It's mine to keep, and I plan on doing just that. Sleep now, okay? I won't ever let him hurt you again."

Nodding, I slide down and rest my head on his chest, listening to the steady thump of his heart as his arms wrap around me.

"I've got you. I won't ever let anyone hurt you. Sleep now, baby."

I do, thanks to him.

"Holy fuck, did you see?" Dash slides into the room, hitting the table in his haste. I blink at him as I sip my coffee, perched on the counter. Ryker is cooking at my side.

"Did you accidently put Strike's face on porn again and post it?" I ask.

"No!"

"Did you post your junk again?" Ryker asks, grinning at me.

"No, listen—"

"Did you message another F1 driver and call him Daddy?"

"Yes, but that's not the point!" He thrusts his phone at me, his eyes wide. Sighing, I take it then stiffen when I see what he's showing me. It's a post tagging me on Instagram. I never really check it, but Dash must have seen it from the likes and comments because it's blowing up.

It's of Theo and me. There are four photos gridded together—one of me kissing his cheek, the second of us smiling with our arms wrapped around each other, the third of us kissing, and the fourth, we are pressed together. It's from years ago, on my birthday if I remember correctly, but it's definitely me, and his caption . . .

My forever.

I hide the screen against my chest, swinging my gaze to Ryker as he bites some bacon. "What is it?" he asks, and when I don't speak, he swallows, looking between us. "Fox, what is it?"

"Listen, I need you to remain calm—"

"Show me," he orders, holding out his hand. Wincing, I give it over. He's silent for a moment before he turns and throws the phone into the sink.

"Hey, that was mine," Dash grumbles.

Without looking, Ryker pulls his wallet out and throws a wad of bills at Dash. "Buy a new one." As we watch, he grabs the meat tenderizer and very calmly smashes the phone to bits. When he's done, he's panting as he looks at us. "Does anyone have a problem with that?"

"Nope, not even a little," Dash squeaks, throwing me a look as if to say *it's all you*, then he runs away as fast as he can.

"Baby," I coo.

"Don't baby me right now," he snaps, leaning into the sink.

Sighing, I slide down and wrap my arms around him, resting my chin on his shoulder. "You know that was from years ago."

"I know," he grumbles. "But why is he posting it? What is his problem? What did you talk about yesterday?" he demands, turning in my arms, his eyes narrowed.

"He wanted to be part of my life again, and I told him no," I answer truthfully. "I shouldn't have taken him outside to talk, but I didn't want him to upset you. Next time—"

"There will be no next time," Ryker snaps as he points in my face. "Or I will cut off your penis and feed it to you."

"Baby," I whine, trying to bite back my smile. "You like what it does too much," I murmur as I back him up.

"Don't, I'm mad," he warns.

"And so fucking cute," I retort as I run my lips up his neck until I press them to his. "I love it when you're possessive. It makes me hard as hell."

"Pervert," he sighs, but he relaxes in my arms, and when I kiss him again, he kisses me back. "I hate him."

"I know," I murmur. "I'll deal with it."

"Not alone, you won't," he says as he wraps his arms around my neck. "You don't meet that bastard alone ever."

"Whatever you say, baby," I promise just as my phone rings in my pocket. I pull it out and wince when I see Po's name. Answering, I put it on speaker as I keep Ryker trapped in my arms, so he doesn't destroy any more poor defenseless devices.

"Have you seen social media?" he greets, his voice tense. "It is blowing up. People are speculating that he's your boyfriend and that you've been lying to everyone so far. It's going crazy. I'm going to release an official statement, but if this man keeps posting, it will ruin everything we have worked for. I need you to deal with it."

"I know. I'm sorry—"

"It's not your fault, Fox, but just take care of it, okay? We can't have anything ruin your band's brand right now, especially with the postponed tour." Po sighs. "I don't mean to be snippy with you, but the label is breathing down my neck. If you need my help, let me know, okay?"

"I will, but I can deal with him. I promise," I mutter.

"Good. I've already untagged you and made sure you aren't following each other. I have to ask, Fox, should I prepare for a scandal?" he asks softly.

I glance at Ryker. He should, but not in the way he thinks. "No. Theo is my ex from years ago. I don't know why he's back now."

"It's normal, sadly. They come around when you have power and money, wanting a piece of it. Okay, let me know if you need our help. I'll do damage control on my end." He hangs up.

Sighing, I lean into Ryker. "I hate him right now."

"He clearly wants your attention, so let's not give it to him." He holds out his hand. "Give me your phone."

I do as he asks without pause, and he scrolls through it for a moment before hitting call and putting it on speaker. I wince when I see who he's calling.

Theo answers on the second ring. "I wondered how long it would take for you to call me."

Ryker raises an eyebrow at me, and I wince. "Why did you post it?"

"I wanted your attention. I got it, didn't I?" he replies, something rustling in the background.

"Take the post down," I demand.

"I will after you meet me. I'll text you the address. See you in two hours." He hangs up, and I look at Ryker.

"I'm coming with you," he snaps as he hands my phone back. "I don't trust him."

"But you trust me?" I ask.

"Of course I do," he replies as he kisses my cheek and steps past me, still holding the meat tenderizer, so I grab it and put it back.

"No weapons, okay?"

"Fine." He points at me. "But if he fucks with you, I'm going to beat that stupidly handsome face, and I'll enjoy it."

"You're scaring me, Ry," I grumble, scrubbing at my head.

"Good, remember that," he warns as he turns and stomps off, leaving me staring after him. My head drops back. Everything is such a mess, and I can't imagine this is going to go well.

"Good luck." I glance at the door to see Dash and Strike standing there. They give me two thumbs-up, and I wince.

"You'll need it," Dash comments with a laugh.

TWENTY-FOUR

RYKER

We turn up to the address he texted Fox in three hours, not two. He doesn't get to order us around, and I wanted him to wait, so I fucked Fox's brains out while we were getting ready, making sure to leave marks all over his neck for his petty fucking ex to see.

It's a fancy-looking house on the east side of the city. I wonder if it's a rental, but I suppose it doesn't matter as we walk up the stone steps. I knock loudly on the door, and it opens a few seconds later. Theo looks irritated.

"I said two hours," he snaps.

"And you don't get to order me around," Fox responds, his voice tight and angry.

He finally looks from Fox to me, his eyes narrowing further. He's wearing nothing but some low-slung, gray sweatpants, showing off an impressive chest. His muscles are clearly sculpted to look good, not for use. I can't imagine this man has worked out a day in his life.

"I didn't realize you were bringing backup," Theo sneers as he looks me over.

"And I didn't realize people still used steroids," I retort sweetly as

I barge past him, hitting him with the door as I step inside. "Let's get this over with. We're busy." I glance back at him. "Unlike some people. Fox, come." He ducks past Theo and follows me into the living room. I sit on the sofa, blocking one side so Fox can sit on the other. He does so silently as Theo slams the door and follows us in, sitting opposite us. He crosses his arms, posing so his muscles flex, and eyes me for a moment before looking at Fox.

His gaze lands on Fox's exposed neck, then he glances at me, and I smirk as I rest my hand on Fox's leg and arch a brow, daring him to try me. I kept quiet yesterday, but I won't today.

Fox is mine, not his, and it's time he understood that.

"Nice neck," he comments as he leans forward, his eyes heating as he eyes Fox hungrily. "You always did like it rough, but I remember you were the one who liked to mark me, not the other way around."

"Enough, Theo," Fox snaps, not rising to his bait. "Take the post down."

"Let's talk first," Theo says as he leans back.

"No." Fox stands, taking my hand. "Either you take it down or I go."

"Alright, alright!" Theo huffs when he realizes Fox is serious. Pulling his phone from his pocket, he focuses on it for a moment before tossing it to the sofa. "It's done. I could have posted a lot worse, you know."

Pulling my phone out, I check it to make sure, and only then does Fox sink into the sofa. "Why are you doing this?" he asks, and he sounds so hurt, I hate it.

Theo senses it and pounces. "Because I can, and because I always get what I want. I want you, so get rid of my replacement and come back to me."

"You've got to be kidding me," Fox growls. "I told you no yesterday, but let me make it very clear. I'm dating Ryker, and I love him. I am going to spend the rest of my life with him. I have no intention of ever coming back to you. Even if I wasn't with Ryker, I wouldn't, so stay out of my life."

"No," he replies with an arched brow. "I want you back."

"Why?" Fox throws his hands up in frustration. "You have everything you want here, no doubt thanks to that idiot you cheated on me with, so why me? Why now?"

"I made a mistake," Theo admits, staring at Fox with longing, and despite his bravado, I realize he truly means it. "I didn't know how good I had it with you."

"Putting your dick in someone else is not a mistake. Forgetting to text back is a mistake, but fucking someone else is a choice. You made that choice, and I chose to walk away. Respect that, or at the very least, accept it," Fox replies coldly.

Theo isn't going to back down, though, and I refuse to let Fox stand alone. He's mine, and it's time Theo understands what that means.

"Now that you've spoken, let me tell you something. You might think you have ammo here or a chance, but you're wrong. I'm friends with every rich, powerful man in this country. If you come for my boyfriend or my band again, you are going to find out what power tastes like. You crave that, right? Power and wealth? That's why you fucked that guy when you were dating Fox. Well, I'll happily show you. Just keep testing me." I stand. "Here's what is going to happen. You will post a statement apologizing and admitting you two have not been in contact in years, and then you will disappear. I never want to see you in his life ever again," I warn, my voice cold as I glare at the man Fox used to love.

"Does he speak for you?" Theo snaps, looking at Fox.

"Absolutely," Fox answers as he stands as well.

"I'm his first love." He looks at me, and I laugh.

"Yeah, well, I'm going to be his last." I run my eyes over him cruelly. "You made the mistake of letting him go. I never will."

"Let's go," Fox murmurs, clutching my hand before he looks at

Theo. "Stay out of my life, Theo. Despite everything, I hope you're happy, I really do, but I will never be part of it again."

I'm so proud of him, I squeeze his hand as we reach the door.

"That's too bad." He sighs, crossing his legs as he looks at us. "I guess I have no choice then."

"About what?" Fox mutters.

"Exposing your relationship. You aren't allowed to date, right? I'm sure if your label finds out, you'll be dropped for breaching your contract." His smile grows as we stare at him, shocked and scared. "Ah, so my intel was right. Interesting."

He looks at his nails idly. "I always get what I want. I warned you."

"I didn't realize how much of a cruel streak you had," Fox sneers.

His smile is bitter as he looks at us. "That's because you never wanted to see the true me, only the person you wanted me to be. I could never compare to the image you built in your mind. I was never kind enough, never funny enough, so I hid it so you would still love me." Standing, he eyes Fox once more. "But it doesn't matter. You can hate me, but we both know you'll come back to me because unlike me, you are a good guy, and you would never risk your band's future. I know what you're like. You're so by the book and straightlaced, you would never put anyone else in harm's way, especially for you. I have the money and lifestyle I wanted, it simply took a few years, and now I want you. End it and come back to me, or I will be forced to act. You know I never bluff."

Standing, he pats my shoulder as he walks past. "First rule in this game, rock star, is that you have to have something to bargain with, and you have nothing." He looks at Fox. "You know where to find me when you're done playing with him."

We watch him go, both of us silent, and when we share a look, there is fear in our eyes.

"Do you think he'll do it?" Strike asks softly. We are sitting around the dining table, discussing what happened. Fox looks anxious and ashamed. Gripping his hand under the table, I squeeze it to let him know I'm here.

"I don't think he was lying," I admit, which I hate.

"Me either," Fox says. He's been so quiet. "If he found that out about our contract, it means he's been digging. You only put that much work in if you are willing to follow through." He scrubs his face, looking so lost it makes my heart ache for him.

"Shit," Dash exclaims, banging on the table. "That fucker is willing to ruin your future and everything you have worked for just because he can't have you?"

"We should kill him," Strike says, and we look at him. "It was just a suggestion."

Smiling, I lean into Fox as he stares at the table. "I'm sorry, guys. This is my mess, but it's affecting you."

"Shut up," Strike demands, his voice harsh, and we jerk around. "We are a family, so your mess is our mess. You aren't inconveniencing us, so don't apologize. When Dash got drunk and crashed, who helped him? When Ry made all those mistakes, who helped clean them up? We help each other. That's what we do. You aren't at fault."

"He's right," I murmur as softly as I can. "You had no idea he would do this. Nobody did. You can't blame yourself for simply loving someone in the past."

"But what do we do?" He looks so lost as he stares into my eyes. "Tell me and I'll do it. Every option I think of ends the same way. I'll lose you or I'll lose this band. I can't do either. I don't want anyone to get hurt."

"Remember what I promised you?" I ask, unconcerned that the others are watching. "We are in this together now, no matter what. I love you, Fox, and I love this band. I will not let you lose either of us. I will protect you. No matter what, we aren't giving in." I look at Strike and Dash then Fox. "Whatever the consequences, we stay together."

"Together." Strike and Dash nod.

"But what if—" Fox starts.

I kiss him to silence him as I grip his cheek. "Let him come for us. As long as we have each other, it doesn't matter. Okay?"

"Okay." His eyes close as he presses into my touch. "I love you guys."

"I love you too," Strike replies before he coughs. "Just not in the way Ry does." That makes us break apart, and Strike grins. "What? He's a big boy. My poor ass couldn't handle that."

Laughter explodes from us, and even Fox chuckles.

Let him try to ruin us. I don't care. This is all I need, right here. Fuck everyone else.

SANCTUARY

TWENTY-FIVE

FOX

Despite my outward bravado, I'm worried. Theo never lies, so if he says he will expose us, then he will, and it isn't me I'm concerned about. It's Ry. He only just realized he likes men and that he loves me. He has a past they will use against him, and our band could suffer. I hate the idea of anyone else being hurt because of someone I once gave everything to.

It's why I'm still awake. Ry snores next to me in my bed as I sit at my desk, scribbling absentmindedly in my lyric notebook.

The vibration of my phone makes me sigh. Picking it up, I expect to see more Instagram notifications, but I freeze at the words staring at me.

> THATPRICK: VIDEO ATTACHMENT

My heart freezes in my chest. I know before I even open it that it won't be good. With shaking fingers, I open the file, and a low moan fills the air as the camera turns. My blood runs cold as I watch what he sent.

It's of him and me fucking.

He's moaning and pushing back into me while I fuck him from behind in our old apartment. He opens his eyes and looks at the camera, his smile cruel.

He knew it was there.

He recorded us without me knowing.

Horror washes through me as I watch myself bend him over and fuck him harder, all while telling him I love him.

Another text comes through, shutting down the video, and for that, I'm thankful.

> THATPRICK: Come see me right now or I'll post this. Not even your label's lawyers could stop this when it's out there.
>
> THATPRICK: And leave your toy behind. You have one hour.

Sickness rolls through me, along with violation. He took something that was between us and is using it as a threat. Running to the bathroom, I throw up, his texts lingering in my mind.

Would he do it?

Would he really lower himself to ruin both his and my reputation, just to get back at me and prove a point?

I don't know, and that scares me, but what terrifies me more is Ry seeing that. Knowing I was with him and seeing it are two very different things. He would be forced to see it over and over because the internet never forgets, especially not sex. Yes, the label's lawyers could suppress it, but he's right. It would still be out there.

Rinsing my mouth out, I press my forehead to the bathroom wall and glance at the clock on my phone.

It's fifteen minutes before midnight.

The background picture haunts me. It's of Ry and me, our hands joined. If I tell him, he'll go in guns blazing, and Theo might release it. With no other choice, I haul myself up, still nauseous as I grab a coat and then stand above him. Taking a deep breath, I lean down and kiss his head. "I'll be back, okay? I promise."

I hate every step I take away from him, but despite everything we said, this is my mess. I won't let Theo hurt Ry. Not for anything.

I slip out of the house and onto my bike, and I do as I'm told.

It's the single hardest thing I've ever done, driving away from Ryker, but I do it because I love him.

I arrive before the hour is up. The lights are off inside, but as I raise my shaking hand to knock, the door opens, revealing Theo on the other side. A cruel smile tugs up his lips, and he steps back without a word.

I linger in the entryway, still feeling sick. My hands itch to grab my keys and get the hell out of here, damn the consequences, but that video would destroy my reputation, our band, and probably my relationship with Ry.

"I don't like to be kept waiting," he snaps, and as I watch, he tugs his phone out of his pocket, showing me the screen. The video is ready to upload to his accounts, and that sick feeling only grows. I can handle whatever he's up to. I have to. I can't let this get out and ruin everything we have worked for. Taking a deep breath, I step inside and shut the door behind me. His satisfied smile enrages me as he pockets his phone and turns, sweeping by as he heads into the living room. "Come on then."

With no other choice, I follow him, but I stop at the doorway. The change in the space since this morning shocks me. The lights are all off except for a small lamp, candles are lit around the entire room, and pillows are piled before the roaring fire. A charcuterie board is displayed on a side table with decanted red wine, which he pours himself a glass of before he turns to me and takes a sip.

"What do you want, Theo?" I demand. "I came like you ordered, now delete the video from every device you have it on." When he simply stares, my fists clench at my sides. "You realize how fucked up this is, right? You're blackmailing me with an illegally made sex tape—"

"You think anyone will care? They'll see it, and that's all that matters. At the height of your career, it's all they will remember you for." Stepping closer, he touches my shirt briefly. "Besides, I remember you being very . . . actively involved that night."

Smacking his hand away, I cross my arms. "I didn't know you were recording."

His shrug is lazy, and it pisses me off further as he turns to the wine. "Grab me another glass, will you?"

"I'm not drinking. I'm only here for you to delete the video."

He rolls his eyes as he looks at me. "One drink and I'll delete the video. You have my word."

I try to find the trap, but I can't see it, so I head over to the bar in the corner, grab a clean glass, and thrust it at him. As soon as he takes it, I step back as far away from him as I can. He pours the wine with his back to me, and when he turns and holds it out, I look from him to the glass. Rolling his eyes, he grabs his own and drinks from it, then offers me that instead.

I hesitantly accept it. "One drink?" I ask. "Then you'll delete it?"

"I promise." He nods at my glass. "We can talk, and then you can rush back to your new toy. I won't even stop you. Let's have a truce for tonight."

I debate his words, but honestly, I'm sick and angry, and I just want to be back in bed with my baby so he can make this all better and I can pretend I never loved this monster.

With that in mind, I flip his script and play him at his own game.

I turn the glass so my lips don't touch where his were, and then I gulp the entire thing before wiping my mouth. I hate red wine, and he knows that. The bitter taste always makes me sick.

"There, one drink. Now delete it," I order, putting the glass down on the side table as he watches me. "Theo," I warn when he does nothing.

"Well played." Pulling out his phone, he turns to show me as he deletes the pending post.

"In your storage too," I order.

Muttering under his breath, he hands me his phone. "You do it then." Sparing him an annoyed look, I navigate to his videos and delete any I see with me in them, then just to be sure, I check his texts and his email, but I don't see anything else. "That's it? Where else?"

"Only in my mind," he grumbles as he grabs his phone. "You have to admit it was a good fucking night."

"It was the only time you were happy," I snap, "because you were using me to get what you wanted."

He pouts. "It wasn't all bad."

"No, it wasn't, and if you hadn't ruined it, I would probably still be with you. You did that, not me, but I have to thank you for breaking my heart. If you didn't, I never would have joined Sanctuary and met Ryker, and I never would have met the person I was supposed to spend the rest of my life with. I never thought I would say this, but thank you, Theo, for breaking my heart so I could find the people I was meant to be with in the first place. Now I'm going to leave, and if you contact me again, I will involve my agency. I don't care about the consequences."

My body is hot, probably due to my anger and that stupid red wine—another reason I want to get the hell out of here.

"It's a shame you feel that way," he drawls as I wait for his response, my phone buzzing in my pocket. I don't dare pull it out and answer it, not with Theo here. Who knows what he will do? "I was going to be nice, but that was cruel of you, Fox. You really think I don't have that video backed up?"

"You bastard," I hiss. "Delete it now. We had a deal."

"Hmm, we did, but I want a new one." He puts his glass down as he watches me. "How are you feeling, by the way?"

"What do you mean?" I mutter, but my voice sounds odd.

Blinking, I fall back a step. My head feels fuzzy, like I drank too much, my hearing is weird, and I feel hot all over. "Delete it," I demand, but it's more of a slur.

His smile is cruel as he looks up at me through his lashes and takes a sip of the glass I gave him. "You should have kept this glass," he says, and as I watch, he pulls a vial from his pocket, shaking it to show me. "You always were too trusting."

I fall back another step. My body isn't working right, and my legs feel heavy. Turning, I try to reach the door, but he blocks my path and pushes me back to the sofa.

I fall without meaning to, unable to stop myself, and sink into the deep cushions as I struggle to fight off whatever he gave me. "You drugged me," I accuse.

"I did." He chuckles as he undoes his robe to reveal nothing but some tiny boxers, and then he swings his bare legs over mine, straddling me. "I knew you wouldn't give in otherwise—you're too noble. This way, we can have some fun like we used to."

"What did you give me?" I reach forward to push him away, but my hands won't lift and my voice is odd. My head falls to the side, too heavy to keep up as the room spins.

He drags my head back around, and all I can do is blink at him.

I realize I'm paralyzed.

"Something to make you relax. Don't worry, you'll still feel everything we'll do. They promised me your body will still work, but this way I can have my fun without you fighting me. You were always stronger than me, after all, which was something I used to enjoy, but I find it annoying now that you won't give me what I want." He sweeps his tongue along my lips, making my stomach roll, and a tear squeezes from my eye. "You should have taken me up on my offer while I was being nice. I always get what I want, Fox. You know that." His lips press to mine in a swift kiss, and my stomach churns harder as I scream in my mind, demanding my body to move, but it won't listen.

I can't get away.

His hands slide down my chest as he smiles at me, my cock limp under his touch. "Don't worry, I have something for this if we can't make it work." His mouth brushes against my ear. "I'm going to play with you all night, and I'm going to make a whole other video. In the morning, if you report me or you don't break up with that pretty boy, then I'm going to show the world both. He'll think you cheated. He'll break up with you, your band will be ruined, and you'll have nowhere to go but to me. It's perfect, don't you think?" He bites my ear, and I feel the sharp pain stab through my heavy body. "You always said I was smart and could do anything I put my mind to. I guess you were right."

He leans back, rolling his hips across my thighs, his hard dick peeking from his boxers. I gag, my mouth falling open at the implication of his words.

He can't . . .

He can't . . .

He's going to.

"Let's have some fun, Fox, just like old times."

TWENTY-SIX

RYKER

My eyes open as I pat the bed, finding Fox's side empty. Sitting up, I peer around his dark room. "Fox?" I call, leaning to the side as I rub my face to see if he's in the bathroom, but the door is open and the light is off. "Fox?" Throwing the covers back, I slip from the bed and open the door. The house is silent, and everyone is asleep. Heading back to my phone, I see there are no messages or notifications, and that's when I start to worry.

Fox wouldn't leave me alone like this without letting me know. Biting my lip, I call him, but it doesn't go through. I text him as well, but it doesn't even show as read. I slump in his desk chair, confused and concerned. Running my eyes over his notebooks, I consider waking the others, but then my gaze lands on his iPad.

I turn it on, knowing it's linked to his phone. He's never hidden it or his phone from me. In fact, the passcode is my birthday, so I put it in and log into his texts. Mine are unread at the top, which only makes me worry more, but the one below it makes me go cold all over.

THATPRICK

There can only be one person Fox would name that, so I navigate to that text, open the thread, and read. I know I shouldn't click on the video from the frozen image it's showing, but I open it anyway.

Moans fill the air, graphic and loud, and I can't blink or look away as Fox drives into Theo, who smiles at the camera. Sickness hits me as well as jealousy and anger.

Throwing the iPad away, I cover my face and breathe through the pain.

I know they dated, and I know they fucked, but seeing it is a whole other thing. I remind myself that's not important. Only Fox is. If Theo is threatening to release that, then Fox would go to him like he demanded—not just for himself, but for me.

Everything Fox does is always for me. He wouldn't want me to get hurt.

What is Theo planning? Nothing good, that's for sure, and Fox walked in there alone. I'm going to kick his ass later for not waking me, but right now, I need to find him and bring him home.

Picking up my phone, I hit his number, terror clutching my heart, but he doesn't answer. I keep calling as I pull on my boots and coat, but it won't go through. Once outside, I open the app that shows all our locations—something management demanded we get, which I'm thankful for now—and one look at his confirms my fear.

He went.

I barely remember the journey to Theo's house. Luckily, the roads are empty, so it doesn't take long, but as I stare up at the closed front door, I hesitate. My heart demands I turn around, and my brain tells me I won't like what I'll find inside, but this is Fox. For a moment, pain pierces my chest before I push it away. Fox wouldn't leave me unless he had no choice, which means something happened. I have to trust in that and in him. He would never do anything to hurt me.

I can't leave him alone, even if he's chosen Theo. Even if he went back to him, I'll beg him to come back to me.

I don't bother knocking, instead taking the last step, opening the door, and storming inside. I look for him as I rush to the living room, only to stop in the doorway. The candlelight casts everything in a romantic glow, but there's no romance or happiness in my chest at the scene before me as I find the man I love below his first love.

My heart cracks and shatters in my chest as Theo leans back, his lips swollen. There are marks all over Fox's chest, his shirt is gaping open, and his pants are unbuttoned. I'm about to turn and run when I realize what's wrong with this picture.

Fox doesn't appear happy, and he isn't reacting in guilt or calling my name.

He looks . . . wrong.

Tears slide silently down his cheeks as he meets my gaze, my heart breaking at the desperation and hopelessness in those depths.

"Ryker." His voice is slurred. "Help—" His voice cuts off, but his eyes bulge at me.

Despite the agony in my chest, I run my gaze over them once more before glancing around the room. I find two wine glasses, and there is a vial next to them. My eyes land on Theo.

"Did you drug him?" I ask.

His bored gaze meets mine as he tilts his head. "The door's there. Leave. I was just getting to the good part."

"Did you drug him?" I roar as I stride over, grabbing his hair as I drag him up and off Fox, who whines, tears cascading down his face.

Theo swings, but I slam my fist into his bare gut, and he bends forward. It's then I realize he's naked, a robe and boxers discarded on the floor, and his cock is hard. I've never hated someone so much as I do in this moment. Sickness courses through me at the sight of Fox looking vulnerable and heartbroken. His hand lifts then drops as if he has no energy, and I slam my fist into Theo's stomach again, making him gasp before I jerk his head back.

"Did you?" I scream in his face.

His smile is wicked. "He would have enjoyed it. We both know that. He came here of his own accord. It's his own fault—" I slam my fist into his gut again, and this time I let him drop to the floor. He crumples to the carpet with a groan, and I slam my boot into his side, fury washing through me.

He drugged Fox.

He was going to rape him.

Fuck!

If I hadn't arrived in time . . . Horror consumes me, and I take it out on him, kicking him over and over as he curls up, laughing as I beat him. When I step away, chest heaving, he rolls onto his back and smiles up at me. "Do you want to see the prequel? The video is still on my phone. You'll see just how much he enjoys our games—"

I drive my boot into his face, and his head snaps to the side from the force, his yell escaping his split lips as he coughs up blood. Dragging him up, I hammer my fist into his face. My knuckles split and break, but I don't stop. I keep seeing that smug look and Fox's hopelessness and horror, and I can't hold back.

He hurt my love.

He tried to take him from me.

He touched him without permission.

"Ry . . ." Fox's choked voice is what stops me from killing the bastard. Taking a deep breath, I drop him to the floor. Theo wheezes through his bleeding mouth and broken nose. Grabbing his robe from the side, I tie his hands and feet together, and then I shove his boxers into his mouth to silence his words before I hurry over to Fox, who is struggling to sit up. I don't know what he was given or how long it takes to wear off, but I'm worried more about what he's going through mentally right now.

I help him sit up, and he leans into me, heavy and uncoordinated. I need to get him to a hospital and get him some help.

"I've got you, baby. I've got you," I promise as I help him up. His body seems to be coming back online, but his hands fumble with his shirt and pants, tears sliding down his face as he sobs.

Pulling off my jacket, I drape it around him and zip it up before softly fastening his jeans, and then I lead him outside, ignoring Theo's muffled yells. Once out in the fresh air, I sit him down on the steps, struggling under his bulk, and grip his cheeks. "It's okay, baby. I'm here. I'm here, okay? Nothing will happen to you, I promise."

"I . . . Sorry." He sobs as he leans into me, wrapping his arms tightly around my back and chest, his strength finally returning. "I never should have come. I'm sorry. I'm so sorry. I love you."

"Shh." I kiss his head as I hold him, the cold air cooling my red cheeks. "You have nothing to apologize for." Lifting his head, I lean in so he looks at me. "I mean it, Fox, nothing. What he did is beyond fucked up, but it isn't your fault. I know you were only trying to protect me and the band, and I'm not mad, okay? I'm so fucking sorry, baby, that he did that to you."

He cries against my chest, and I pull my phone out and dial 911, all while rubbing his back. "I've got you," I murmur. "I love you, and I'm right here. You're safe. He can't touch you again."

It's true. I will never let Theo hurt him again.

Police swarm the house, and Fox is put into the back of an ambulance. I don't leave his side, my hand in his despite them needing room, but he won't let go and neither will I. His wild, desperate eyes remain locked on me as they fuss over him.

"Sir, I'm sorry." I look to the side to see a police officer there. "We will need you to come with us for a statement. The other party is extremely injured." He looks anxious just saying it, and I narrow my eyes.

"I go where Fox goes," I tell him.

"Sir, please, I don't want to have to arrest you—"

"Try it," I retort. "See all those people out there?" I jerk my head to the side, where they had to set up a police barricade. There are people there with cameras aimed at us. I heard our names shouted, so they know we're here. "You think they won't have something to say about you arresting me?"

"Ryker." Fox looks worried as he sits up. "Don't leave me, please."

"Shh, I'm not going anywhere," I promise as I kiss his cheek. "One second, okay?"

He clings to my hand, and I kiss it before tugging mine away, crouching at the end of the ambulance. "He's been through a lot tonight," I tell the officer. "I won't leave him alone. He's the victim here."

"Sir," he begins, just as another officer arrives and whispers something to the first cop. His eyes widen as he looks at me. "I'm very sorry, sir. Please go ahead. We'll find you both later to talk. Get him some help."

"Wait." I grab his arm as he turns to leave. "What happened?"

He bites his lip and glances at Fox before quietly answering, "They found a camera inside. It was all caught on film."

My heart freezes—not at me assaulting Theo being on camera, but because of what he did to Fox. I know it's good, since it will prove Theo drugged Fox, but the idea of Fox being seen like that? "Nobody sees that who isn't necessary," I warn.

"Of course not," he promises. "I'll deliver it myself." He hesitates. "I'm a big fan of yours. I promise I won't let this get out. You should call your management so they can help deal with this." He leaves, and I know he's right.

I shoot off some texts as I take Fox's hand again. "What is it?" he asks, concerned. "Are you being arrested?"

"Shh, it's all okay. Just rest," I assure him as I sit at his side, and the ambulance finally takes off toward the hospital.

It all moves quickly from there. We are taken to the back entrance, and once there, Fox is ushered into a private room and the next steps are explained. He clings to me the entire time, until they politely ask me to leave. I only do that when he nods and releases me, but I don't go far, standing just outside of the door. My knuckles are bloody, and they ache as I wring my hands nervously before me.

The paramedic from the ambulance stops in front of me. "You should get your hands checked out," he tells me.

"Later," I mumble distractedly, listening in case Fox calls my name.

"He'll be okay. He's very lucky to have you. He has no physical injuries," the paramedic says softly. "Mentally, though . . . that will be another thing altogether, but with someone who loves him as much as you do, he'll be okay."

"Thank you," I say as I look at Fox when the paramedic steps into the room.

They are going to take labs, his clothes, and pictures as evidence, and I hate that I can't be in there with him.

My name is yelled, and I turn around to see Strike and Dash rushing toward me, still in pajamas. Tears fill my eyes when I see them. They smack into me, and I lean into them, letting myself be weak for a moment before I pull away.

They talk over each other as they fire off questions. "We got your texts. Where's Fox? Is he okay?"

"He's in there getting some tests done. He's going to be okay." I don't know if I'm telling them or me. "Did you bring him some clothes?"

"Of course." Strike lifts a bag, eyeing me. "What happened?"

I debate what to tell them, but they need to know. "Theo drugged and assaulted him."

They are quiet for a moment, and then it seems to sink in, and the horror in their gazes gives way to the same anger I feel.

"I'll fucking kill him!" Dash roars as he turns, and I expect Strike to hold him back, but Strike nods, rolling his sleeves back.

"I'll help."

"He's been arrested," I tell them. "We can't do anything right now. Besides, I beat him to within an inch of his life."

"Good," Strike snaps before he softens. "Fox?"

"He . . . I've never seen him look like that," I reply, tears in my eyes. "He looked so lost, so vulnerable."

"He'll be okay. Fox is strong," Dash says, but he looks worried. "So what now?"

Po appears at our side. "I've been in contact with the police. Rumors are already circulating on social media. Someone took a picture of Ryker shielding Fox as he was led into an ambulance. We will have to address it at some point, but for now, our priority is Fox."

Dash and Strike nod, and I spare them a glance. "I need to talk to Po. Can you wait outside the door? If he yells for me, come get me right away."

"Of course." They hurry over and stand guard outside the door, and I couldn't love my bandmates more than I do in this moment.

Taking Po's arm, I lead him away so no one can overhear what I'm about to say. "We need to protect Fox."

"Of course," he starts, but I shake my head and interrupt.

"No. I mean it, Po. If you spoke to the police, then you know what happened. I don't care what it takes," I warn. "I want him in jail, and I want a restraining order against him. I don't want him anywhere near Fox again. Do you understand me? You will do this or I will walk away and take him with me. You're our manager, it's your job to protect us, so do it." I turn away, only to turn back. "Another thing. Fox will be given as much time off as he needs. He will be given consideration and any help he requests. We will add new layers of protection for him, and you will be understanding and give him whatever he asks for. He has given everything for this band and your label. It's your turn to do the same for him or you will lose Sanctuary, and we both know we are your big ticket right now."

We've spent a long time worrying about the label dropping us, but the truth I realized over the short tour is that they need us. With or without them, we will succeed. It's time they stepped up.

"Of course, Ryker." Po wrings his hands, looking far too upset. "I should have dealt with him in the first place. I'm so sorry. I will have the best lawyers on our side and get a press release—"

"No, you will wait until Fox decides what he wants to disclose," I snap.

"We need to announce—"

"No," I growl. "When and what he wants. Nothing before. This is his life and his story. You will not decide that for him, and neither will I."

"If we are pressing charges, then it will be hard to keep it quiet," Po cautions.

"Find a way if that's what he wants. Take all my earnings, I don't give a fuck. You give him that. Understood?"

He nods, looking shocked, and I swallow my anger. "I'll do anything to keep Fox safe. If it's a choice between his mental well-being and our band, then I will always pick him first."

"Is he okay?" he asks.

"I don't know," I reply, my voice finally cracking, but he needs me to be strong right now.

He nods, his phone ringing in his pocket. "I'll handle everything while you focus on him, okay?" I have to trust him to keep his word, so I head back to Strike and Dash, and we wait for Fox to come out.

It's another hour or so before the door opens, and a very friendly nurse pokes her head out. "Ryker, he's asking for you."

I grab the bag of clothes and step inside. He's behind a curtain in a hospital gown, and staff are bustling about on the other side.

"Okay, Fox, remember what we discussed, okay?" the nurse asks softly. "Ryker's here."

He looks up, his eyes wide, and in that moment, he looks so small and vulnerable. "Hi, baby," I murmur softly. "Are you doing okay?"

He nods, but his lips tremble, and I don't even bother with any more words. I wrap him in my arms, and he sinks into my embrace. His head presses against my chest as I hear the nurse and doctor leave the room, giving us space. "You did so well, baby," I murmur as I kiss his head. "So fucking good. We can go home now. Strike and Dash are here. We'll go home, and it will just be us, okay?"

He nods, but his tears wet my shirt as his hand clutches my back.

"He didn't . . ." His voice is soft, and I strain to hear him. "He didn't fuck me. This is stupid. You got to me in time—"

"He drugged you and touched you without your permission," I snap before reining in my anger. "It doesn't matter how far it went, Fox. What matters is that it happened, period."

He nods, and I stroke his hair. "I won't let him get away with it. I'll keep you safe, and no one will ever touch you again," I vow. I'd give up anything to keep him safe.

We sit like this, neither of us breaking apart, as his tears seem to fall more steadily, his back shaking.

I try to blink back my tears as I hold him in my arms. It's his pain, but feeling him unravel breaks my own heart. The first tear falls silently down my cheek as he falls to pieces in my arms.

"That's it, baby. Let it out," I rasp. "Get it all out. I'm right here. You aren't alone. We are all right here. It's okay. It's okay."

I know whatever comes next won't be easy, but I'll be by his side the entire time.

SANCTUARY

TWENTY-SEVEN

FOX

We are allowed to leave after I dress. The police wanted to talk to us, but Ryker said Po is handling it and not to worry. We walk out of the back door and duck straight into a van, and just as the sun rises, we reach our house. There are reporters outside as we pull up to our door, so Dash and Strike unroll their coats and get out first, holding them up and nodding at us.

Ry takes my hand and helps me out, and my bandmates wrap us in their jackets as we head inside, out of view of their prying eyes. I'm grateful.

Everyone has been so nice. The doctor and nurse who did my tests earlier were so kind and respectful, which made me feel comfortable. They kept telling me it was okay and that I could take breaks, and they comforted me when I wanted to cry.

I hesitate in the dark hallway, unsure what to do now. It was just one night, but my whole world seems to have flipped upside down. Ryker's hand is still in mine, but I can feel everyone watching me.

I'm unable to meet Strike's and Dash's eyes, uncertain what I'll see there.

"Baby," Ryker murmurs, drawing my gaze.

The soft way he touches me and talks to me makes me feel like breaking all over again.

"Do you want to shower or bathe or eat anything? Or sleep? What do you need, baby? Tell us," he implores.

"To shower," I reply. "I can still feel him—" I swallow. "A shower."

"You guys go wash. We'll make some food and drinks and set up some beds down here. We'll sleep together tonight, okay?" Strike goes to hit my arm before pulling his hand back at the last second. "Fox," he says, and I meet his gaze. "We are right here, brother. You don't ever need to be hesitant with us. We're family, and we love you. We just want you to be safe and happy, okay?"

When I look into his eyes, I don't see pity or shame. I see nothing but concern, so I nod.

"Come on, baby, let's shower." Ryker leads me upstairs. He even climbs into the shower with me, and when I start scrubbing my skin, needing to get the lingering touch of his hands and mouth off me, Ryker takes over. He washes me gently, kissing the red, raw skin. I stand still, letting him take care of me, my heart still pounding from earlier.

I've never been as scared as I was tonight. I couldn't move or fight him off. For all my strength, for all my size, I was helpless. If Ryker hadn't shown up when he did, it would have been a lot worse than it was, but even still . . . I remember his hands touching me like I was his to do with as he pleased. I remember the fear coursing through me as he caressed and kissed me, ready to use my body like it was his right. For all my terror and disgust, my body reacted, and shame filled me.

The moment Ryker walked in and I saw the heartbreak in his eyes, that shame and fear tripled. Even now, I'm terrified he's going to disappear.

"Talk to me, baby. What can I do?" he asks when he finishes washing me. "What do you need?"

"Just you," I reply, and it's true. I just want him with me. I don't want him to disappear.

"I'm right here. I'm not going anywhere," he promises as he searches my gaze, his hair slicked from the water. The look in his eyes makes the words flow out.

"I should have done something more, fought harder," I whisper, but Ryker covers my mouth.

"Don't even speak that bullshit," he snaps before his voice softens. "What you endured is not your fault, no matter what happened or what you're feeling. I need you to understand that. He's a fucked-up monster who did this to you. Nothing else matters. What he did was horrendous, and you are a victim, baby, and we are so sorry you went through this." He cups my face, searching my gaze. "You know that, don't you? It wasn't your fault, Fox. None of it was. You did so fucking good, baby. You're so strong and brave, and I'm so proud of you."

Something about those words makes me want to cry again, but I'm sick of crying. As Ryker stares at me like he can heal every part of me with his love, I know I won't be alone in dealing with this. I expected the way he looked at me to change, but if anything, the love in his eyes is only stronger.

"You still love me? You still want me?" I whisper.

"Always," he replies, gripping my cheeks so I pay attention to him. "Nothing could ever make me love or want you less, Fox. If anything, I love you more. You're so fucking brave, baby. Stop blaming yourself, okay? Stop worrying about how I'll react. Look at me. I'm right here. I'm not going anywhere. I'll be at your side forever."

Nodding, I close my eyes and let my body relax under his ministrations as he tries to wipe away Theo's touch. I know what others might say—why does it matter, we had sex before. We are exes. My body reacted. It was just fun.

The truth is I didn't want it.

I didn't want him, and he didn't care.

It's fucked up, and that's what it boils down to.

He tried to rape me. He tried to take away my choice, and I'll never forgive him for that or for the way he makes me feel now.

"Come on, baby." Ryker turns the water off and helps me out. He gently dries me, placing kisses over the marks Theo made that I can't bear to look at. I still feel weak from the drugs, and the doctor said that's normal, but it doesn't explain the agony in my heart as I look at Ryker.

When he's done, he brings me some sweatpants and helps me into them, and then he lifts a shirt over my head. I let him do whatever he wants, and when the shirt settles, tighter than my others, I glance down and realize it's his. As I breathe in his familiar scent, I relax further. Sitting me down on the toilet, he puts my socks on my feet before grabbing the hair dryer and kneeling between my legs. He dries my hair and braids it back before smiling at me.

"Perfect, as always," he remarks then kisses me softly, replacing the hurt with love. "Come on." Taking my hand, he leads me downstairs, and we find the living room is transformed.

I don't know where they found all this stuff in the short time we were upstairs, but there's a canvas tent, which I'm pretty sure we put up outside, the sofas have been moved, and blankets, pillows, and duvets overflow it. String lights hang everywhere, keeping the space bright and cheerful. The table is filled with junk food and sealed bottles of juice and water. The TV has an old action film I love paused on the screen, and Strike and Dash wait in pajamas, smiling at us.

"Come on." Strike pats the duvet. "You need to rest."

"I don't know if I'll be able to sleep," I murmur.

"So don't." Dash shrugs. "We'll watch movies until you can."

Ryker waits, letting me decide, and I hold his hand as I climb into the pit they created. Ryker follows me and wraps us in a duvet as I lean into the cushions, watching the TV as they hit play and settle around us. Dash and Strike recline behind us as if to protect my back, and that makes my eyes well with tears once more.

"Thank you," I say sometime later. My eyelids are heavy, and despite everything that has transpired, I'm tired.

"You never have to thank us, brother," Strike replies softly. "This is what family is for."

It's then I realize just how much they truly are my family. My own didn't really want me, and when the world turned against me and someone I used to love hurt me, they came for me . . . protected me.

As my eyes close, I know I'm going to be okay surrounded by people who care.

TWENTY-EIGHT

RYKER

We don't leave our pit for two days.

We watch movies, talk shit, listen to music, and eat junk food. Fox slowly comes back to life, but every night, he wakes with a gasp and clutches me like he's worried I've disappeared. I'm always there to promise him I won't and that I never will.

Po has kept his word. No police have come.

We all turned our phones off, and we know there are reporters outside, but we block the world out, creating a safe space for him.

I know we'll have to leave eventually, but not until he's ready.

"How about *Princess Diaries*?" Strike suggests.

"No, we just finished the first *Ms. Congeniality*, so we should watch the second!" Dash argues.

Fox is wrapped around me, his head on my shoulder as I lean back into him, smiling as I watch them quarrel. "But she finds out she's a princess—"

"She finds Dolly—"

"This is what I needed," Fox interrupts, and I blink, turning to see him. "Just you guys, thank you."

"Stop saying thank you," I murmur as I kiss his cheek. "Besides, do you really want these idiots to think you find them funny? Please, they won't ever stop."

He smiles, and it's the first full one I've seen since everything happened. My heart stutters at the sight of it. When his sparkling eyes land on me, it only grows. "I love you."

"I love you too," I murmur. "So much."

My cock stirs to life as he tugs me closer, but I ignore it as I cuddle back into him. "I'm ready," Fox states after squeezing me, drawing their attention. "Po will want to talk to us, and so will the police. I'm ready."

"Are you sure?" I ask. I don't want him rushing into this because he feels like he has to.

"I am." He hugs me closer. "It's time. I want to get this over with. I don't want him to have another second of my time. He broke my heart before, and I refuse to let him have another day of my future again."

I'm worried, but I have to trust that he knows what he can handle. "If you're sure . . ."

"I am."

I nod at Strike, and he leaves, coming back with our phones. With a look at us, he lays them down and turns them on.

The screens show our screensavers, and within seconds, they start to blow up. There are so many notifications, we all gape. It doesn't stop for minutes, and when I finally pick up my phone, I ignore everything else and hit Po's number.

He answers on the first ring. "Are you guys okay?" he asks.

"We're okay. Fox is here, and he wants to talk to the police and you," I tell him.

"Are you sure he's ready?" Po asks softly. "If he isn't, I can push them off. I haven't released a statement yet, and everyone is going crazy, but I don't care. We'll keep them at bay as long as he needs."

That only seems to make Fox more sure, and he nods. "I'm sure, Po," he says. "Can they come today? I don't want to go out yet."

"I'll make sure they come to you guys, and I'll arrive with them." He hesitates. "Fox, I'm so sorry about what happened to you. Just know we have your back, okay? Whatever you need, I mean it. That's what I'm here for. Just take care of yourself."

"Thanks, Po," he responds with a tight smile. "I'll be okay, I think. I just want this over with."

"Understood. Any time in particular?"

"Two hours?" I ask. That will give us time to get ready.

"Sounds good, see you then." Po hangs up, and I lean back, closing my other notifications. I don't care what the world is saying. My entire world is right here, and that's all that matters.

Po arrives in two hours on the dot with two officers in tow. The detectives are dressed in casual clothes, and they seem nice. There's a man and a woman, and we escort them to the kitchen where Fox is. I take a seat at his side, holding his hand as Strike and Dash sit in the other chairs. Po offers them a coffee and then takes a seat with us.

"It's nice to meet you. I am Detective Reiss," the older male says. He must be in his late forties, and he has a handsome face and graying brown hair. "This is my partner, Detective Williams. We are in charge of your case, and I want you to know we are taking it very seriously. We have patrols outside, clearing away the press, and Mr. Patterson is still at our station, so you're safe." The fact that he takes the time to say that makes me like him instantly, and Fox must feel the same way because he nods.

"Okay, Fox, we won't take too much time, and whatever you feel you can share is fine. If you aren't ready, that's okay as well," Williams says as she places a recorder on the table. "If you need a break, let us know, okay? We're here for you, no one else, and I want you to know we are on your side. We are here to help you get justice. We also have your blood test results, and it shows the drugs he used on you. We tracked down his dealer and got his witness statement from when he sold it to Mr. Patterson. With your statement, we are going to formally charge him if that's what you want."

Some people probably wouldn't want that due to the attention it would bring, but whatever Fox decides, I will support him.

"I want to press charges," Fox says, his chin lifted. "I would also like to announce it publicly. I don't want our fans to think we are hiding things. They are the reason we are where we are, and they deserve the truth."

"Fox, that isn't important," Po begins.

"We can release a statement. I'm not ashamed of what happened to me," he argues. "Besides, it happens to so many others, so shouldn't I lead by example?"

"You don't have to do anything but feel how you feel," I assure him.

"No, I am in a position to highlight issues like this, so I will." He nods at me. "It's my choice. I'm not ashamed, Ryker. What happened to me happens to other people. If I can help at all, then I will." He turns to the detectives. "Should I start at the beginning?"

For the next hour, Fox talks and answers questions. The detectives are nice. They listen and take the evidence Fox offers from his phone. They are respectful and informed, and when Fox leans back, looking tired, they shut their recorders off.

"That will be all for today, Fox. Thank you for all your help. I think we have everything we need. In the meantime, if you want to speak to us or would like any updates or anything, here is my number." Detective Reiss slides a card over. "Please make sure to rest and take care of yourself. I can see you have an amazing support system."

"I do." He looks at me and smiles. "Thank you for coming here."

"Of course." Detective Reiss hesitates. "For what it's worth, Fox, what you are doing is very admirable. I knew there was a reason I liked your music." He winks, making us smile. "We will see ourselves out."

We watch them go, and Fox leans into me. "Tired?" I ask, and he nods.

"About the statement . . . let me know when you want to do it," Po begins hesitantly.

"Now," Fox replies. "Can we record it here now? I want this all out. I don't want it hanging over me. The longer I hide it, the more he wins. He wanted to blackmail me to keep this all secret, thinking I would be ashamed, but I'm not. I refuse to be. He is the one who should feel ashamed, and I want to make sure he does."

"If you're certain," Po replies, and Fox nods. "Okay, do you want me to get a makeup team—"

"No. I refuse to hide behind it. I'll announce it as myself, right here in our home with my family."

Po nods once again, and he hustles around. Fox sits up taller, holding my hand, and Strike and Dash move to his side. When Po is ready, he looks at Fox.

"Say whatever you want to. I can cut or edit it later. We should have a script, but I don't want to tell you what to say on this, okay? Just leave the charges out for now until we have all the evidence," Po advises. "Ready whenever you are."

Nodding, Fox takes a deep breath, gripping my hand. "Hi, everyone. I'm Fox, Sanctuary's guitarist. I'm sure you are all wondering what's happened recently, so I'm here to give a quick statement. Our label will release a more in-depth one later, once we have all the facts, but I thought it was important to update you so you aren't in the dark. I want to thank everyone for giving me some space these last few days as I come to terms with what happened. Two days ago, I was sexually assaulted," he says starkly, and I'm astonished by his bravery. "It was by someone I knew, someone I once trusted. I was drugged and . . ." He swallows. I want to hold him and shield him from the world, but I can't, and I hate it.

"It's currently under police investigation, and I was very lucky Ryker found me in time and managed to save me. I have no plans to keep this secret or conceal what happened. By doing that, it gives the perpetrator a shield to hide behind. I will not be ashamed of what happened to me. I will be pressing charges, and as we speak, evidence is being gathered. What happened to me is not okay. Nobody should have to go through what I did, but I know I'm not the only one who has been through something like this, and I want to tell you how brave you are and how proud I am of everyone who has fought and is still fighting afterwards. I'm also asking for some privacy so I can come to terms with what happened and spend time with my family while I heal. I know how lucky I am. I'm surrounded by people who love me and are willing to fight for me, and I'm forever grateful. Thank you all for your understanding and love, and to the person out there that did this—if you ever see this, I want you to know that I don't forgive you, and I never will. You took away my choice, and I won't allow you to get away with it. Thank you." He nods, and when Po turns the camera off, Fox slumps.

"You did so well," I promise as I kiss his head, and Strike and Dash rub his shoulders. "We're so proud of you, Fox."

"He's right, you're doing amazing, but you don't have to be strong all the time, okay?" Po says. "I mean it. I'm in your corner. Whatever you need."

"Thank you," Fox responds, and I can tell he means it. He looks at me and smiles softly. "I just need time, I think, and for everyone to treat me the same."

"What? You mean we can stop being nice to you?" Dash groans. "About time."

We all laugh, and it's nice to see Fox joining in.

SANCTUARY

TWENTY-NINE

FOX

Two weeks later...

The outpouring of love from fans and even other celebrities has been insane. I've finally checked my socials, and the support has been such a major boost for me to keep going. Messages of encouragement fill every inch of my phone, and I've even received messages from men who have been through the same or similar events and have either never told anyone or were ignored. Each one breaks my heart, and I spend every night responding to them, offering to help in every way I can.

Their lives are just as important as mine. I have money and support to get justice, but so should they.

Ryker has been by my side the entire time, and the police officially released their statement last week along with Theo's name. I expected some backlash, and maybe there is some, but I don't see it. I have no doubt Po and the others are protecting me from it. It's giving me room to heal, and I'm grateful for that.

We hope it won't have to go to trial, but if it does, I will be ready to fight for my truth.

I must sound so sure to everyone, but I wake up every night in a cold sweat, unable to move, afraid I'm back there. Ryker is always there to kiss me and hold me through it. We haven't done more than that. I think he senses I'm not ready for more, and I didn't think I could love this man more than I already did, but I do. He's become so protective of me, so possessive, yet he still treats me the same. He doesn't look at me differently or sugarcoat things.

We are still Fox and Ryker, and while the rest of the world looks at me as a victim now, I'm grateful he just sees me as I am.

"Fox, help me!" Ryker yells as I sit in my chair at the kitchen table and watch as he darts around it, Strike chasing him while Dash cheers them on. Whatever they were cooking is burning, and the music from the radio is cranked up as they yell and run. Ryker almost slips, so I catch him and right him, pulling his socks up. "There, now carry on." I smack his ass, and he yelps as Strike leaps for him.

"Betrayer!" Ry yells at me.

Smiling, I lift my mug and continue to watch them. They are crazy, but I wouldn't change them for the world. There was a time when we were lost to each other, and I used to wish we were back in the van, but as I look at our kitchen and listen to their laughter, I know we're only stronger than we were then. Things change, people change, and lives do as well. I'm grateful for our past, but I'm excited for our future and spending as much time as we can just like this.

Ryker picks up a spatula and turns with an evil smile. Strike yelps and dives over the table and into my lap, wrapping himself around me like a monkey. "I claim sanctuary!"

"Hey, that's my boyfriend! Get off him!" Ryker yells as he hurries around, hitting him on the back with a spatula. "Bad friend! Off!"

"Fox, help me," Strike whines. "He was my friend first!"

"Yeah, well, he's my boyfriend. Off," Ryker demands.

Rolling my eyes, I stand and lift Strike with me, who yelps and clings on. "Shit, you're strong. You've been working out so you can throw him around—" I drop him on his ass, and he stares up at me in shock. "Not cool."

Grabbing Ryker's hand with the spatula, I tilt his wrist and push it back. "Like this, it will hurt more," I instruct before I kiss him. "Go ahead."

Ry grins evilly and starts hitting Strike with it as I head upstairs. Once in my room, I pick up my guitar and continue with the new song I have been working on. Their laughter drifts up to me until Ry slams into our room, shutting the door and locking it. "Hey, baby," he comments casually as someone screams his name downstairs.

"Hey." I shake my head with a smile as I strum, and he walks over, sitting cross-legged before me on the floor, watching and listening. I stop to scribble new notes and then retry the beginning section again.

"I like it. It's slower than your normal ones," he says.

"It's a love song," I reply shyly. "I guess it's our song. We can't announce that we are officially together, but we can sing this, and we'll know."

I look up when he doesn't respond. He suddenly dives at me. I manage to put my guitar safely away before he tackles me backward, kissing my face. "I love you, you romantic bastard."

Laughing, I roll us and kiss his cheeks like he did me. "Good, because you're stuck with me," I tease as I lift my head. The atmosphere shifts as I stare into his eyes.

I can feel every hard inch of his body against mine, and my cock hardens at his touch. That hasn't changed, even though we haven't been intimate. I think he's worried about how I would react, and honestly, I was too, but as I kiss him, all I feel is Ryker.

It's just us and the love we have for each other.

Theo and his actions have no room here.

"Fox," he whimpers when I pull back. "We shouldn't—"

"I want you," I tell him as I nip his lip. "I'm okay. I want to fuck my boyfriend."

He pulls back, searching my gaze, and I see the moment he relaxes. "Then fuck me," he dares. "Show me just how much you love me."

"Oh, I plan to," I warn as I crush my lips to his and strip him of his clothes with his help. He pants into my mouth as he reaches for my shirt, so I tug it off. The marks Theo left have faded, but as Ry looks up at me, I know he remembers them. He lays gentle kisses along my entire chest where they were. A moan escapes my lips as I hold him, clutching him as his hands slide down my sides to my pants, and he unbuckles them. Pushing him back to the floor, surrounded by pages of my lyrics, I stand and shove my pants down so I'm naked before him.

Any hesitation or worries I have disappear as his gaze drinks in every inch of me. His chest heaves, and his hard dick leaks for me.

Dropping to my knees, I crawl up his body, and our lips meet again as I grab his hips and lift him. He wraps his legs around me, and I rock my hips, dragging my cock over his pretty ass as he gasps, his length trapped between us.

"Fox," he begs. "Please, I need you so badly."

All it takes is a few words from him, and all my strength goes out the window. I line my cock up and slowly push into his greedy ass. The tight heat wraps around me, and he groans, relaxing and pushing down to take me deeper. I watch him as his eyes roll back in his head, and his teeth dig into his lip as I pull out and push in until he takes all of me. When I'm fully seated, we are both panting, our foreheads pressed together. My hands shake as I press them to the floor next to his head and start to move.

I take it slow, with long, sure thrusts as we kiss. This isn't fucking, this is making love, and I show him that as I reclaim my body and what was almost stolen from me.

As our bodies meet, our lips chase each other. Theo can't ruin this for me. It's my body, not his. He will never have a claim over it. It belongs to me and Ryker.

He gasps my name as I kiss every inch of his face and skin I can reach as we come together. Pleasure explodes through me, and I groan my release against his neck as I fill his perfect ass, and I feel him spurting across our chests as he cries out my name.

RESIST

The sound reclaims my aching heart like nothing else could.

THIRTY

RYKER

I t isn't going to trial, and I don't think I've ever been so relieved —not because I am ashamed, but because I was terrified of Fox having to confront someone he loved and trusted and recall what he did to him. Fox is strong and not afraid to stand his ground regarding what Theo did, but he's already having nightmares. Theo will face prison time, but our job is done. He will never hurt Fox again, and the outpouring of love and support is incredible.

So many men have written to Fox, asking for his strength and help, and it's really affected him. We spent days reading letters sent to him as a band, and more than once, we had to take a break to cry and rage in anger.

It's sparked something in Fox, and we are all glad to help him. He's taken it upon himself to become the champion for those who have been silenced. He's been speaking with local charities on how he can help, and we've all donated our time, money, and voices. We're planning a charity show next week to help raise more money and awareness, but I couldn't be prouder of my boyfriend and friends. Strike and Dash have stepped up big time and have been volunteering, as well as making content online to help those in need. Despite all the good we are doing, it's heavy and tiring, and Fox is burning out. He's been through so much recently, and I want to give him a day of happiness with no other thoughts.

Early the next morning, I steal him away. Strike and Dash cover for us, and we wear hats and masks and venture out into the city.

We go undercover, avoiding fans and paparazzi as we wander through a mall before stopping for dinner. Later, we stop at an arcade and play games for hours. It's nothing major or special, a mundane day, but this slice of normal is heaven and indescribable.

I smile at Fox as he cheers, spinning away from the shooting game he beat me on again. Laughing, I let him whirl me around, and when he puts me back on my feet, he tugs my mask down. My eyes widen as he tilts his head to avoid our hats hitting and presses his lips to mine. He holds my hips, tugging me flush against his body as he deepens the kiss. I begin to lean into him, and only then does he pull away. His eyes are bright with happiness and love, and his lips are tilted in a warm, familiar smile.

"Thank you for today," he murmurs. "I needed it."

"I know you did. Admit it, I'm the best boyfriend ever," I tease.

Laughing, he turns me and drapes his arm around my chest, resting his chin on my shoulder. "You are," he agrees, sounding serious. "I don't know what I'd do without you, Ry."

"You'll never find out," I promise as I interlace our fingers over my chest. "Now, I want a rematch. Loser is bottom tonight."

That gets him moving as I grin.

"It's too early," I whine as my phone starts to ring again. I pick it up and hit answer. "This better be good."

"Um, Fox?" Po asks, confused.

Pulling the phone away, I realize I picked up Fox's phone. I roll over and smack him to wake him up. "Fox, phone." I toss it on his chest as he grumbles and grabs it blindly, shoving it against his ear before putting it on speaker.

"It's actually good you're, uh . . . both there. Could you guys come into the label this morning please?" He sounds odd, but it's probably because it's barely light out.

"Sure, I'll let Strike and Dash know," I grumble.

"No, just you two please. See you soon." He hangs up, and Fox and I share a confused look before he dives at me, making me laugh.

"No, don't!" I groan as he pulls the comforter down and presses his lips to my chest. "Fox."

"We're awake, so we might as well make the most of it," he murmurs against my skin.

I grip his hair and tug him up. "My ass is still sore from you last night," I whine.

"I'll be gentle this time, I promise." He smirks, knowing he'll get his way.

By the time we make it out of the door, the sun is up, my body is covered in bite marks, and every time I glance at Fox, I blush.

The label is pretty empty at this time, which is surprising, but I have an unsettling feeling, especially when we are escorted to a meeting room where Po, some managers, and a few directors sit across from us. I don't know most of their names other than Mrs. Noel and Miss Wilson, but sitting in the middle is the CEO, Mr. Atlas. Sharing a look with Fox, I take a seat and wait. I'm used to being in trouble, but I've been well behaved since Fox and I started dating. I wonder if this has to do with what happened with Fox and Theo. It's the only thing I can think of.

"Do you recognize this?" Po winces as he turns the iPad and shows us some images.

I lean in, and my heart stops. Fox and I are on the screen. It's from yesterday, when our masks were down as we kissed and hugged by the arcade machine. They were taken from a distance, but it's undeniably us. Our private moment was stolen and sold. My eyes dart up to Po's and back down, and he sighs.

"They were published early this morning online. The news has already picked up on it and are calling you two the new 'it' couple of the century. Fans are confused and picking sides. We've had two brands already contact us to drop deals because they don't want to be associated with any scandals."

"Scandals?" I scoff, pushing the iPad back as Fox stays silent. "We fake being together all the time to sell your music, remember?"

"But this isn't fake," Mr. Atlas snarls. "This is real and has undercut everything we have been working for. We told you no more bad news, and this is bad news. Flirting for cameras is fine, but two of our biggest stars dating and sneaking around? You specifically signed a contract that says you can't date. It puts us in a bind. What were you thinking?"

I look between them, getting angry. "I was thinking I love him," I snap, hating how silly they are making us seem, diminishing our relationship.

"Ry," Po begins, but I glare at him as I grab Fox's hand. His eyes meet mine, and he nods, holding mine tightly.

"I was thinking I fell in love with my best friend and I wanted to be with him. You're going to sit there and tell me it's wrong that we are in love?" I refuse to deny it any longer. Why should I? I won't hide it. I refuse to hurt Fox like that.

"Which is fine, when you aren't under contract," Po admits. "You read the contract."

"We didn't know then," Fox argues. "It just happened. Isn't this a good thing? You're always selling our supposed relationship, and now it's real."

"People don't want real. They want fantasy," Mr. Atlas sneers. "They don't want *this*." He pushes the iPad back at us. "We are losing numbers, not to mention breaching contracts."

Sickness rolls through my stomach as I stare at their cold, impassive faces. Even Po looks down at the table, refusing to meet our eyes, and I spare Fox a look to see his concern as I grip his hand, in desperate need of connection and support.

"Here is what we are going to do. You are going to stick to the PR plan we have come up with. You will distance yourselves from each other until these rumors die down. Ryker, I want you seen with your usual entourage of beautiful women, the more the better—"

"No," I interrupt, my voice sharp. Even the idea of putting on that show makes me feel sick.

"Excuse me?" he responds, a threat in his tone.

"I won't do that to my boyfriend," I protest.

"You are breaching your contract!" he roars.

"I don't care!" I yell, and he sits back, stunned. "Do whatever you want. I won't betray Fox in any way, not even for show. Let them all know it's real. I'm tired of hiding it anyway. If it means walking away from this or losing the love of my life, then I will choose him every time. I'm tired of trying to be what this world wants of me. This is who I am." I jut my chin out, daring them to fire us.

"If you won't comply with our demands, then you leave us with no choice." He leans forward, drawing my gaze. "We are suspending you until we decide what to do about your contract. Please go back to the house. We will be in touch in the next few days about your future with the company."

Fox's hand slips from mine, and I glance at him in panic to see him sitting back, his eyes wide with shock.

"You can leave now." The cruel demand makes me swallow, and Fox lurches to his feet. He nods at them and turns to leave. I spare them a glare and hurry after him, catching up to Fox at the elevator door just as it opens and he steps inside.

"It will be okay," I tell him softly when I reach the elevator. I reach for his hand, but he jerks away. "Fox, I promise it will be okay. I'll figure this out."

He nods, but he isn't looking at me.

Panic winds through my chest. After everything we have fought against, will this be what breaks us?

THIRTY-ONE

FOX

I could barely look at Strike and Dash when we told them. It's all my fault. I reached for Ryker and pushed him to accept this. I wanted more from him, and now look what it got us. My best friends could lose everything they have worked so hard for. Dash and Strike deserve their dream. They are incredible artists and even better people, and Ry . . . He was born to sing and perform. It's what he loves, and today he chose me over his destiny.

I won't let him sacrifice his dream just for me.

I love him too much for that.

We decide to go to bed early, since none of us are really in a talking mood. Usually, when the door closes, Ry and I can't keep our hands off each other, but tonight, we fall into the bed, silent and lost. He scoots closer and rests his head on my chest, and I can finally draw in a full breath.

It's strange. I feel a mix of happy and sad. Happy because he defended me earlier, and sad that this might be over. He might lose this dream because he loves me.

"I'm so sorry, baby. I couldn't do it. I couldn't do what they wanted, not if it meant hurting you, not even for our band," he whispers, his voice soft.

I lift my head to meet his gaze. He looks so worried, so lost. I wrap my arms around him and drag him closer as I kiss the top of his head. "I'm so happy you feel that way, but I'm also so sorry that loving me has caused this."

"I'm not." His voice is muffled. "I wouldn't change a thing. As long as I have you, nothing else matters."

Fuck, my heart cracks apart, and I know what I'm going to do is the right thing. It has to be. He needs me to look after him—they all do. It's my job to keep us together, so I'll do whatever it takes.

"I feel the same way," I murmur as I kiss his head again. "Sleep, it will all be better in the morning."

"Promise?" He sounds so young, I shudder.

"I promise," I answer. I wait until he's asleep—a shitty move, I know, but he would never let me do this otherwise.

I tuck him in up to his chin and steal a kiss before pulling on my jeans, jacket, and boots. I sneak out of the silent house. The good memories seem long past as I cross the living room, remembering us curled up there, happier than ever, just last week. Now it's empty and cold, and I need to fix it.

Once outside, I hit dial. "It's me. We need to talk."

"This better be good. I was in bed," Mr. Atlas grouses, and Po nods at me. He isn't sure what I'm going to do, but he trusted me enough to get everyone back here—well, two of them at least, since it's like eleven.

"I know our relationship is the problem. If I leave the band, will you support them and push them further?" I ask.

"Fox," Po protests, his eyes widening in horror, so I hold up my hand.

"I will not end my relationship with Ry, so this is the only other alternative. I won't let my friends suffer because I'm too selfish to let the man I love go. As long as you promise me that they will be taken care of and taken off suspension, I will end my contract in the morning when the office is open. I will also sign an NDA, whatever you want."

"Sir, Fox is just upset. Let me take him back," Po begins.

"Wait, this could work," Atlas murmurs as he leans back, considering my offer. "You would give up your shot at fame?"

"Yes," I answer without hesitation. "As long as they are safe and get their dream, then I'll do whatever." He tilts his head, and I lean in, sensing his weakness. "But you will not stop me from seeing Ryker, and you will not push him to act out for the cameras or pretend to be single. We won't advertise our relationship, but we won't hide it either. That's the deal or you're back to square one with the rumors and us unwilling to back down. This way, we all win."

"But you—" Po snaps. "Fox, have you thought about this? Playing guitar was all you ever wanted. You told me that. You said you would do whatever it took—"

"That was before," I murmur as I smile sadly at him. "I love him, and if this means he and my friends can keep their dream alive, then I'll do anything."

"They won't like it." Atlas shrugs.

"I can handle them. Do we have a deal?" I ask.

"Come back tomorrow and we'll finalize the details, but yes, that will work." He stands, and I shake his hand. He looks tired, and it's then I notice the sadness in his eyes.

"We aren't bad people, Fox, but in this industry, you don't always get what you want. Artists don't get to be happy *and* famous—they can't have both. I know you hate us and don't understand right now, but what we are doing is for the band's benefit. It's what it takes to get to the top."

I shake his hand tighter. "I know, but there were other ways to deal with this," I admit. "I appreciate everything you have done for us, and I know you have our best interests in mind. I hope it stays that way." I nod at them and head out.

Po catches me outside of the building, spinning me around. "Fox, it isn't too late to back down on this. We can think of other ways—"

"I've tried. This is the only way. We both know they will never let us be together, and Ryker is so stubborn, he won't back down. Sanctuary will be disbanded, and I'll lose them all anyway. At least this way I can still be in their lives and see them achieve everything they ever wanted."

"And for you?" he presses.

"I'll have Ryker." I shrug. "He's more than enough."

"Shit." He scrubs his face. "Go home and talk to them. If you're still sure tomorrow, then fine, but if not, I'll have your back, okay?"

Nodding, I shove my hands in my pockets and hesitate. "Thanks, Po, for everything."

"You make it sound like goodbye." He smacks my side. "You can't get rid of me that easily. Go home, Fox, and talk to them."

Nodding goodbye, I duck my head against the chill and hurry to the road. A taxi comes by a few minutes later, and on the way home, I stare out at the city, wondering what life will be like after. It isn't going to be easy, since they will be busy and touring and I won't be with them, but as long as I can still text and call, then I can wait. I can also still help them with their lyrics and support them. It will hurt seeing them climb to the top with our songs, but I'll do it for them.

After tonight, nothing will ever be the same. I'm walking away from my dream, yet despite the sadness I feel, I know it's right.

When I get home, the kitchen light is on. Frowning, I kick off my boots and head that way, my eyes widening when I see all of them sitting at the kitchen table. Ryker's face is drawn, and he's clutching a mug.

"I woke to find you gone. I panicked, thinking something bad happened again." He takes a deep breath, and I see his hands are shaking. "I called Po. He told me you were on your way home and we needed to talk, so I woke them up."

Strike and Dash look fully awake and just as worried. Blowing out a breath, I shrug out of my jacket, hang it on the back of the chair, and sink into it opposite Ryker. "I'm sorry I worried you, baby. I just needed to do this alone."

"Why? Where were you?" he demands, angry now. "Do you know how scared I was? It was just like that night. I was so fucking worried."

"I'm really sorry." Reaching over, I unclasp his hands from the mug and kiss them. "I never meant to worry you. I just knew if you were awake, you would stop me."

"Stop you from what?" Strike demands, meeting my gaze. "What's going on, Fox? Is it about the suspension?"

"Did you manage to get it lifted?" Dash looks so hopeful that I can't help but smile, and I keep Ryker's hand in mine as I lean back.

"I did," I admit.

"How?" Strike asks.

Ryker looks terrified, and he grips my hand like he's worried I'm going to slip away. "Did you come back to break up with me? For the band?"

I blink incredulously, and my heart shatters when I see tears brimming in his eyes, turning them glassy and broken. Shoving my chair back, I quickly close the distance between us and sink to my knees next to his chair, dragging him down into my arms as I rub his back.

"Never," I vow. "You're stuck with me. Don't ever think that."

He shakes in my arms, and I hear him struggling to breathe. I let him calm down, and when he does, I wipe under his eyes. His smile is small and shaky but there. "Then how did you get them to listen?"

"I offered them an alternative, something they could make work," I reply slowly as I grip his hands. It's my turn to hold on tight now, terrified that he will walk away from me when he hears this. Licking my lips, I glance at the others and take a deep breath. "I am going to leave the band."

The room falls silent, and I can hear my heart hammering in my ears with terror. "If I leave the band, they will lift the suspension and continue pushing us—you—to the top. Ryker and I won't have to break up, I made sure of it, and we won't have to hide. It's the only way."

"No," Strike snaps. "Fox, what the fuck?"

"I'll always be at your side. I'm not letting you go, but I love you enough to walk away from the band. You guys don't need me. You're the talent." I glance at Ryker, and he recoils in horror.

"I'm not the talent! We all are. Without you, there is no Sanctuary. We do this together or not at all," he scoffs.

"We could lose everything we've worked for," I start, hoping they will understand.

"I don't care!" Ry yells.

Ryker is staring at me like I'm a stranger. "This is the only way, baby. I realized something today when they told us. I can give this up. I could never touch a guitar again and I'd still have a good life as long as you were in it, but I could never give you up, so if the choice is between me walking away from the band and walking away from you, then I choose this band. This way, you get your dream, and I get you." I smile as I kiss the back of his hands as he gapes.

"Fox, your dream—"

"It's an easy choice. It was always you. It's always going to be you. I'm not going back to being just your bandmate. I can be your number one fan. I'll be your support, but my life means nothing without you, Ryker. This way, I get you, and you get your dream," I explain gently.

"You're a fucking idiot." The venom from Dash makes us all turn to look. He's on his feet, his face angry, but there are tears in his eyes. "You think we want this without you?" His lip quivers, and Strike wraps his arm around him. "We're a family, or do we mean so little to you?"

My heart sinks. "You know you mean everything to me."

"Then don't do this!" he yells. "Don't make us go on without you. I won't do it."

"Dash is right. We aren't doing this without you. Ryker, tell him," Strike demands.

My gaze swings back to Ryker, and I smile sadly. "It's okay, baby. You don't have to feel guilty. We are okay—"

"Guilty? I'm mad as fucking hell."

My eyes widen.

"What the fuck made you think we would ever let you go? I don't care if you are doing it for me, for us, or whatever martyr shit you're pulling. You don't get to decide this on your own. You just don't."

"He's right. It isn't even just down to you two," Strike murmurs.

"This is our band, our family, and he's right. This is our dream. Without you, it isn't. We either do this together or not at all. I'd rather be broke and unknown and happy than lose you. You know you're our heart. We aren't doing it without you." Ry's voice is loud and unrelenting as he shakes my hands. "Do you hear me? If you try to leave us, I'll walk away too. We are a band, a family, so no, you aren't leaving the band or me or any of us. I don't care what they do to us. We'll stick it through together."

"Ry—"

"He's right," Dash mutters. "It isn't your choice. If you leave, I'll leave too."

"Dash," I protest frantically.

"I will as well." Strike smiles. "Maybe I'll go back to flipping burgers."

"Stop it," I beg. "I'm doing this for you."

"We didn't ask you to, baby." Ryker sighs as he cups my jaw. "This isn't for you to solve alone. It's a problem for all of us. I love you, but you can't protect us from everything. Whatever will be, will be. All that matters is that we are together. I've had a taste of fame and fortune, and it means nothing without my family."

Looking to the ceiling, I try to blink away my tears, but they slide down my cheeks, and I choke on a stifled sob. "I just want to make sure you guys are happy," I admit.

"We know." Ryker slides down to his knees and grabs my face.

"We know, baby. You are always protecting us, but you can't protect us from everything. We are happy to see this through, but together, okay?"

"I don't want you to lose your dream for me," I croak.

"Without you it means nothing anyway," he says. "The only reason I'm comfortable up there on that stage is because of you. We'll do this together no matter what. Promise me, promise us you'll stay and see it through."

My eyes close as I sink into him.

"Promise us," Dash demands. "No heroic shit, it isn't your style. You're making us all look bad, you know," he mutters, but he's serious.

"Besides, who would make sure we aren't late? Who would write our songs and wash our underwear? Nah, you aren't going anywhere," Strike adds.

"Promise me," Ryker orders as I look at him.

"I promise." It slips free, but it's the truth, and he sags in relief, embracing me.

Arms wrap around me as Dash and Strike kneel and hold me. "We'll do this together," Strike whispers, "or not at all."

"Together," Dash agrees.

"Always together," Ryker says, and I know they are waiting for me.

"Together, no matter what it means," I promise, and their relief is palpable. I would have given it all up for Ryker, Strike, and Dash, but the fact that they don't want me to? Yeah, I'll admit that I can breathe for the first time since we got that call.

"Fucking idiot, trying to leave us." I jerk as someone slaps my head. "Bad Fox, very bad Fox. You're grounded."

I laugh, and their chuckles add to mine until we just laugh and lean into each other, ready to face whatever tomorrow brings together.

SANCTUARY

THIRTY-TWO

RYKER

I'm still mad as hell that he tried to sacrifice himself for us, but I also couldn't love him more. It doesn't mean I'll let him get away with it though. As soon as our bedroom door closes, I lean against it. He stands in the middle, looking sheepish and a little shy for once. Scrubbing the back of his head, he blows out a breath as he looks around nervously. "Ry—"

"Don't," I snap, and his eyes land on me, wide and worried. "You don't speak until I say you can."

He blinks as I push away from the door and walk his way, ripping my shirt off as I go and dropping it to the floor. It drives him crazy when I leave my clothes lying around since he's a neat freak, and I see his eye twitch before he drinks in my exposed chest, my clothes forgotten.

Stopping in front of him, I block his hand as he reaches for me. "You tried to leave me tonight. No, I don't want to hear it. Dash was right. You were bad, and you need to be punished."

His eyes heat as he watches me, his lips parting as he glances at my lips. "You want to punish me, baby boy?"

Gripping his throat, I watch his eyes widen as I tighten my fingers hard enough to leave bruises, but the desire in his expression flames brighter. "I said not to speak," I snap. "If you do it again, I'll sleep somewhere else." When he says nothing, I grin. "Good boy." I stare at his lips. "I can think of a way for you to make it up to me." I press my palm to the top of his head and push until he has no choice but to sink to his knees.

His smirk grows as he realizes what I want. It's rare to see him on his knees for me, as usually it's the other way around. I love when he takes charge and uses me. It's something I never had before, but right now, I want him to remember that he belongs to me. I want to show him he isn't going anywhere.

There is no Ryker without Fox.

There never has been and never will be. Without him, I would simply cease to exist.

I want him to let go so all those worries and thoughts flee and it's just us.

Neither of us know how tomorrow will go. We could lose everything we have worked years for, but I don't care because he loves me and I love him, and no matter what, we will have each other.

"Fuck, baby, look at you. You're so goddamn beautiful," he praises.

"I didn't say you could speak."

He smirks, and I shiver as he wordlessly opens his mouth and waits for me, obedient and submissive.

Gripping his hair, I yank his head back. "You want to taste me?"

He nods, and I run my other hand across his face, stroking my thumb over his open lips before shoving my fingers into his mouth. He sucks them as I watch, and when I pop them free, his tongue darts out and laps at them as I pull away.

"Push my pants down," I demand.

He grips the waistband of my sweatpants and slowly pushes them down until they pool at my feet. Stepping out of them, I kick them away, now only in my boxers. He waits, his eyes narrowing as I drag it on until he understands I'm in charge. "Take me out."

He slides his hand into my boxers, grips my rock-hard cock, and pulls me from them, stroking my length as he groans. I let him touch me for a moment, sliding my hips forward as pleasure hammers through me before I step back out of his grip. "I didn't say you could do that."

His eyes narrow further, his nostrils flaring. My desire is so strong, yet I want him to understand, so I grip my length and stroke it fast as I look at him.

He waits with his hands on his thighs until I can't take it anymore, and I step forward, pressing my dick to his mouth.

"Suck me," I order.

He eagerly wraps his lips around my length, tugging me closer until I slide all the way down to the back of his throat. The sensation makes me groan, my eyes closing for a moment before I force them open and watch him. He holds my stare as his head bobs, then he pulls me all the way from his mouth before sucking and licking my tip.

I grip his hair, dragging him forward, and he chuckles before swallowing me. I use his mouth, fucking it hard and fast. My grunts are loud, but the wet sucking of his mouth is louder as pleasure consumes me. I speed up, slamming down his throat, yet he doesn't complain. He watches me with such loving eyes, it undoes me, and when he reaches down and cradles my balls, squeezing and massaging them, I can't hold back, but I still need him to understand.

He's mine.

Pulling from his hot mouth, I stroke myself, pumping out my release, and it splashes across his chin and chest. He sticks his tongue out, catching it as I come, and when I stumble and fall, he grabs me.

"I played by your rules, baby," he murmurs, his voice hoarse. My cum still drips down his chin, but he doesn't care, and neither do I as he leans in and kisses me hard, standing with me in his arms before dropping me to my feet. "Now it's time to play by mine."

"Fox—"

He spins me around and slams me into the closest wall. The strength in his hands has my cock hardening once more as I remember how it feels when all that passion and desire is aimed at me. I just dared the wild animal and played with him.

I can't fucking wait to pay for it.

My hands hit the wall with a slap as he shoves my boxers the rest of the way down and squeezes my ass. "I'd let you fuck my ass to feel better, but we both know you'd enjoy it a lot more if I fucked you, baby. I made a mistake, and I'll make it up to you. I'll fill your pretty ass and give you more orgasms than you can count until you forgive me."

Fuck, I missed his dirty mouth. His filthy promises drive me insane as he kicks my legs open. "Fox," I beg.

"That's right, baby, say my name." His voice is mean and hoarse as his dick presses against my ass, so thick and hard I shudder. He's had me every single way by now, but every time feels like the first, and I can't get enough. I'm just as crazy for him as he is for me.

I've never wanted another person so badly, like I might die if he doesn't fuck me.

He knees my legs wider apart, and I feel him pressing against me. Anticipation has me smashing my face into the wall. "Am I still being punished? Maybe I shouldn't fuck you—"

"Don't you fucking dare," I snap. "You better get inside me right fucking—" I moan as he buries himself inside me with one smooth thrust, stretching me to the point of pain, yet I love it. He holds me and places kisses along my shoulders and neck as I whine.

He begins to move, his teeth digging into the back of my neck as he pulls out and thrusts in. My hard cock is trapped between me and the wall, the pressure making me gasp as pleasure spirals through me. His bite deepens for a moment before he kisses it better.

He speeds up, but the closet next to us gets in the way. Snarling, he grabs me and throws me into the door, and then he's on me again. He slams into me, and I stand on my tiptoes from the force. My fingers scrabble at the uneven surface, holding on as he fucks me hard and fast.

I bang into the door, my cry loud and unchecked. Dash and Strike are used to it by now, but my face still reddens in embarrassment at how little control I have around him. I used to struggle to come without imagining his face, and I never made a sound, but now I'm like a fucking porn star, crying out as I push back, demanding more.

His hands slap into the wood above mine before they slide down and he interlaces his fingers with mine. "I love how you still blush for me, even when I'm balls deep in your ass. You act like you haven't crawled and begged for my cock before."

"Fox," I whisper shyly, and he chuckles. It was one time—okay, two, but fuck.

"I love it," he croons. "I love how you look amazed each time, as if you can't believe how much you love it. It drives me wild, and those little moans you make?" The door rattles from the force of his next thrust as he proves just how much he loves it. "Fucking bliss."

"Please," I beg as my pleasure grows. He tilts my hips back and hits that spot inside me that has me seeing stars.

"Come for me, baby," he orders. "Let me feel it." I come, yelling into the wood, and he follows me with a grunt, filling my ass with his cum before slipping out of me. Our hands are still together as we lean into the door, panting and shaking.

"You don't get to leave us," I remind him.

"Never," he says, kissing my sweaty neck. "But feel free to punish me anytime."

Sitting opposite the same men from yesterday, I feel more confident now that Dash and Strike are with us—a united front. Fox and I spent the rest of the night in bed, pushing each other to the brink before we had to get ready and come to this meeting. My ass is sore, and I'm exhausted, but I don't care as I look at Fox. He understands that he belongs with us now, no matter what.

"As we discussed last night, Fox, here is the NDA for you to sign," Mr. Atlas says. Po looks sad, glancing between us, and I gaze up at Fox, waiting.

"I have changed my mind." Fox glances at us and then sits taller. "I'll be staying in the band. We are happy to keep the suspension, pending your decision, but I'm not going anywhere."

"Last night—" Mr. Atlas starts.

"Was a mistake. I wanted to protect my bandmates, but after speaking to them, I realized it would only hurt them. We started Sanctuary together, and if it were to end, then it would end with all of us. I'm sorry to have bothered you."

"We understand your stance on this, but we request to remain together. We will await your decision on the suspension." Dash stands and nods his head. "Let's go home."

Blinking at his sudden stubborn streak, I stand as Fox takes my hand, and we head out. Downstairs, however, Po catches us.

"I knew you'd make the right decision." He grins at Fox and then us. "I managed to convince them to let you carry out your prior engagements, so the ads and your charity concert." He moves closer, lowering his voice. "It's your chance."

"Our chance?" I frown, unsure what he means.

He sighs as he looks between us. "The public got you where you are now—obviously you're talented—but they are the reason you were noticed. Let them do that again. Let your story be heard and bring it into the light rather than hiding in the shadows. Don't give the label a choice."

"Why would you tell us that?" Strike asks.

"I'm on your side. I don't agree with their decision at all, but they went above me, so let's work together on this plan and not give them a choice." He glances around before stepping back. "I'll come by tomorrow to help you with the preparations. For now, do what you're doing and trust me, okay?"

With no other option, we leave the building, and when we're back in the car, Fox smiles.

"What is it?" I ask curiously.

"Po has a plan. I think he's right, but even if he isn't, how about we give our fans one last epic show?"

THIRTY-THREE

FOX

Po asked us to trust him, and we have no other choice. I won't give up Ryker, and my band won't give me up, so for now, we are relegated to ads and our show. That night, we have a party to celebrate staying together—or maybe to drown our misery, I'm not quite sure. Either way, the alcohol is flowing and the music is blasting throughout the house the label bought for us. We know this could be one of our last nights here, so we plan to make the most of it.

We used the company credit card and bought a shit ton of food, and it covers the dining table.

"Fuck them all!" Strike yells as he thrusts his glass into the air, spilling liquor over the edge and onto his arm. His grin is lopsided, and he's already buzzed, but I can't help laughing.

I don't usually drink much, but tonight is the exception.

"Our last hurrah!" Dash nods, clinking his glass with Ryker's where they play some sort of drinking game on the coffee table. "Let's spend all their money and fuck up their house."

They look at me as I sip my beer. Rolling my eyes, I slide from my chair and head over, hitting mine against their outstretched glasses. "If you can't beat them, fuck them!"

Their cheer is so loud, it can be heard over the music. Strike shakes his ass in time with the beat, and Dash quickly joins in, spanking him as they grind and twerk, singing loudly off-key along with the song.

Ryker leans into me as he downs his drink, our eyes on them as they bump into the sofa and knock bottles everywhere. It's getting messy, but honestly, I don't even care. I came so close to losing this.

They are loud, stupid, and rude, but they are mine, and I'm so glad they stuck with me.

"To think you were going to miss all this," Ry teases as he climbs to his feet. "You aren't nearly drunk enough. Let go tonight, baby. One night won't hurt." Gulping down the rest of his liquor, he grabs my chin, tilts my head back, and arches his eyebrow. I open my mouth, and he presses his lips to mine then spits the drink inside. After swallowing it, I grab his neck as he goes to pull away, and I kiss him hard and fast. His gasp fills my mouth as I break away, licking my lips.

"Delicious," I murmur as I climb to my feet. "Let's dance, baby."

I tug him to me and grind along to the music, gripping his hips until he sways with me, and then I grip his ass, dragging him closer, his thigh pressed against my cock as we dance.

His smile is wide and wicked as he leans into me. He slides his hands all over me as we move, but I grab them and swing him out and back in. His laughter erupts, filling the air, and then Dash and Strike dance around us. Strike grinds into me while Dash twirls Ryker. I laugh, and another drink is shoved into my mouth as the music keeps changing.

My inhibitions lower with each drink, and I let go like Ryker said. I don't worry about prying eyes or what tomorrow will bring, I just let the buzz flow through me and give into it as I climb onto the table with Strike. Ryker pulls out his wallet and starts throwing money at us as we dance. Grinning, I shake my ass for them as Strike slides his hand down my chest and slut drops, and when the song ends, we pose. Dash and Ry toss more money at us, and Strike throws himself off the table. Dash and Ry try to catch him, but they tumble back to the floor, giggling as the next song starts. I lower to my ass on the table, grabbing another drink and tossing it back.

The rest of the night is a blur of laughter, games, and more drinks. At some point, more bottles appear, and by the time I'm too exhausted to continue, it must be early morning. The music is still pounding, but I can't take it anymore.

Grabbing Ry, I leave Dash and Strike confessing how much they love each other and head into the hallway.

"No, I want to party!" Ry cries as he hangs onto my neck. He moves so much, I struggle to walk, or maybe it's the walls that are moving. I'm not sure since we fall into them. Blinking, I try to get us back to our feet, but I fall again, and this time we sprawl across the stairs and descend into laughter.

"Let's fuck here." He wiggles his eyebrows, and I barely raise my head.

"Baby, you couldn't even get it up," I scoff, and that makes him laugh again as he flops and lies across me.

"Fine, sleep." Within seconds, he's snoring.

I stare at the spinning ceiling before wrapping my arms around him and giving in.

"Seriously?" The loud voice makes me open my eyes, and I groan at the bright light. My head is pounding, my skin feels way too hot and sticky, and my stomach is churning something fierce. Po stands above me, looking unimpressed.

"Why are you in my room?" I grumble.

"I'm not. This is the hallway," he scoffs, and I glance around to see I'm lying across the stairs. No wonder my back and ass hurt. Ryker is still snoring, clinging to me like a teddy.

"Up now," Po demands as he rolls his eyes and stalks into the living room. "You've got to be kidding me!"

I slide Ry off me, watching as he turns and hugs the stair post as I stumble to my feet and lean into the wall to see him gaping at Dash and Strike.

Strike is completely naked and sprawled out on the table, surrounded by food and empty drinks. Dash is half on, half off the sofa, his head on the floor and his legs tossed over the back.

"Where are his clothes? Never mind." Po points up, and I see his boxers hanging from the light. "Kitchen, now. Wake them up. I told you I was coming to plan today."

"Can I shower first . . . or maybe vomit?" I mutter.

"No. Kitchen. Now," Po snaps and turns on his heel as I scrub my face, wondering how the hell I'm going to wake them all up.

SANCTUARY

THIRTY-FOUR

RYKER

"It's too early," I whine as I lean my aching head on Fox's shoulder. He looks far too put together to be hungover like us, but he's slightly green, which makes me feel a little better. I didn't even hear Po come in, but he looks annoyed as he makes his way through the messy kitchen, throwing us dirty looks every few seconds as he tries to make himself coffee.

"Why the hell is someone's shirt in the fridge?" Po grumbles as he grabs milk.

"Oh, I remember. I was warm and thought it would cool me down," Strike tells him, his eyes still half closed as he hugs his glass of water like it's his lifeline.

Sighing, Po turns to us and cups his mug. "Well, you certainly have partying like rock stars down. What happened?" Po says as he leans against the kitchen island.

"We figured we'd make the most of last night in case it was our last. It seemed like a good idea at the time," I admit as I rub my aching head. Fox passes me some water and pills, and I gag as I swallow them.

"Fox, really, you're usually the smart one." Po sighs in disappointment.

Fox shrugs, rubbing my back. "I was with them on it. We might lose all this, so why not enjoy it for once since all we've done is work?"

"I'm glad you're finally all on the same page and working together. I just wish it weren't about partying," Po grumbles. "Fine, I came to help you. I meant what I said. We have the concert to show the label they are wrong and it's what the fans want, so do you want to hear my plan to save your careers, or would you rather go back to sleep?"

We all perk up despite our hangovers and share a look, but it's Strike who speaks.

"How do we save our band?"

"Well, for starters, I'm going to need you to . . ."

We listen as he speaks, the plan coming together. It might not work, but we have nothing else to lose.

Besides, we never played by the rules before, so why start now?

I'm terrified, but I'm also excited.

We have been preparing for this charity concert for two weeks, and I still don't feel ready, but as I look into Fox's eyes as we linger in the wings, I know I have to be. It's our last shot. We are working on Po's plan and hoping that we've made enough of a connection with our fans that they are on our side, which means exposing everything.

It means exposing us.

We haven't been together long, and I worry it will wreck our relationship. Fox must read the concern in my gaze because he heads over, grips my chin, and drags me close for a quick kiss. "We will always have each other, okay? Just focus on me out there, no one else."

"I'm happy to tell the truth. I'm not ashamed of us. I'm just worried the fallout will pull us apart," I admit.

"Never," he murmurs. "That will never happen. Trust in me. Trust in us."

I close my eyes, soaking in his strength as we get the notification in our ear.

"Take the entry lift please."

I nod at Fox and kiss him again, and Strike, Dash, Fox, and I head under the stage and kneel on the rectangle part that rises. Taking a deep breath, I hear the crowd scream and chant, and then everything falls silent as the lights die.

The drumbeat sounds, and the screams erupt again as the lights above us flash red and then purple, and we slowly start to rise, smoke billowing around us. Halfway up, we stand in unison, and the screams are so loud, they rock the arena. I could barely believe we sold out such a huge place, but I guess the hype surrounding the concert is huge. The faceless crowd filling the seats shocks me, towering into the sky, and then the pit writhes with so many bodies, I can't even see a gap anywhere. Shaking my head, I pose just before the light hits us.

We change poses as it hits us again. Our names are shouted, and I try to hide my smile as the drum stops and I grab a mic. I let out a long, high note, and when it tapers off, Fox's guitar shreds for a second, and I hum into the mic as I step from my mark and walk down the extended stage slowly and deliberately. The crowd moves closer as I stop at my mark at the end and drop my head back, letting out the highest note I've sung. When it fades, I pose like that with the mic in the air before I open my eyes and look at the crowd, letting them feel the heartbeat in the silence.

"I'm Ryker, and this is Sanctuary!" Flames erupt from the stage, and the lights turn on behind me, illuminating my bandmates in their spots. Running as the first note of the song hits, I begin to sing as I walk back to them. I catch sight of myself on the big screen for a second before I focus on Fox, letting everything else fade away.

The music and Fox are all that matters, and I don't stop until I lean into him, singing the chorus along with Strike.

Once the first song is over, I head to the front of the stage and blow a kiss to the audience. "Are you ready to have a good night?" I cup my ear and sigh after their screams taper off. "You can do better than that. I said, are you ready to have a good night?"

The screams get louder, and I nod, gesturing upward until it's all I can hear. I wait for the volume to lower a bit before I say, "That was incredible. I suppose you know who we are, but how about we say hello one by one?" I wait for the screams to die, and the light hits me. "I'm Ryker, and I'm your singer for tonight." I grab my crotch and grind as I smirk.

The light hits Dash next, and he smashes the cords, dragging out the notes. "Hello, lovers, I'm Dash."

The light switches to Strike, and he hammers the drums before standing. "I'm Strike!"

The lights illuminate Fox, and he smirks into the cameras as he strums the guitar before sliding his hand up the mic stand. "I'm Fox, and I'm ready to have the night of my life. Are you?"

The volume of the yells shocks me, and he chuckles.

"I take that as a yes. What do you think, Ry?"

"I think they are, but let's test them." I nod as I head to the edge of the stage. "Okay, let's practice for this next song. When I say 'sinners, beware,' you are going to sing back to me 'sinners everywhere.' Are we ready? Let's try." I take a deep breath. "Sinners, beware!"

I hold the mic out, and they scream it back. Shaking my head, I wag my finger. "Not good enough. I said, sinners, beware!"

They scream it back louder, and I grin. "Okay, let's try the left side." I run over and test them. "Now the middle! Finally, all together!"

When their shouts taper off, the drumbeat begins, and we dive straight into the next song, and then into our third.

Once it's done, I lick my lips, and Fox heads to the edge of the stage and grabs a bottle of water. He brings me one, and I take a drink. When I'm done, he downs the rest and smacks my ass as he walks away again, driving the crowd crazy.

"You dirty birds seem to like that, so how about we show you more? Let's rock!" I yell as I dive into the fourth song. Fox moves over to me as he plays, and I lean back into him as I sing. His hand leaves the guitar and slides down me suggestively before gripping my dick, and the crowd goes wild. Turning, I shove his chest teasingly, my eyes on him as I sing, and his hand slides around my hip and grips my ass, squeezing in a familiar way. Desire pulses through me, and he smirks before he lets go and swings his guitar around.

When I sing the ending, the stage goes dark, and I breathe quickly as the next song kicks in. This time, we all move down the extended stage and dance and sing at the end. I reach for the crowd as they hype me up, and when it comes to the chorus, I hold the mic out to them, mouthing the words.

Tears fill my eyes as the crowd screams the chorus to us, their voices beautiful and in sync. I drag the mic back to my mouth, making the most of every moment since it could be our last show.

Wiping a tear off my cheek, I sing the rest of the song and turn away. Fox finds me and hugs me for a moment before he takes the mic, giving me time to compose myself.

"Are you having a good time?" he yells, and the response is immediate. "Good, because we are too! I'm so thankful for all of you coming tonight to support us. Every cent of the proceeds will go to three amazing charities that support male abuse victims through their trials, medical procedures, and recovery, something that is very close to my heart." Turning back around, I see him licking his lips nervously, so I take his hand. Dash wraps his arm around Fox, and then Strike hugs him from behind in a tackle. He chuckles into the microphone as tears fill his eyes.

"I'm so thankful for my band and their support. I never would have been brave enough to speak about what happened without them and without you. The love you showed me after what occurred . . . it blew me away. The people who reached out to me, who shared their stories, filled my heart, and I knew I couldn't sit back and do nothing. I had help and a support system, but most people don't, and some people are scared to speak. I will be their voice and their support, just like my friends and you were for me. Nobody, and I mean nobody should ever have to be touched without their consent. Gender, religion, or race doesn't matter. Here, we are all one, and we stand together. We are the voices for the suppressed, the survivors, and those who are still suffering silently. Tonight is for them. Thank you all for being with me, and for all of the survivors out there, you are not alone. You're strong, and if you need help, please reach out to anyone you can. Now, how about we say a big *fuck you* to everyone who ever hurt us?" he screams into the mic, and the crowd cheers. "Okay then, let's go to church!"

He passes the mic back, and I hold his hand as I pour the lyrics into it. The crowd shouts along until the arena is filled with our anger for those who would do others harm. When it ends, Fox has silent tears streaming down his face, but I realize they are from happiness. He is healing and sharing his journey with millions, since it's streamed live, and when I glance back and see Po leaning out of the wing, I know it's time.

"Tonight is very special for another reason," I begin, and Fox looks at me. I wait for his permission, and he nods, stepping up to my side. Dash and Strike join us, knowing exactly what's going to happen. "Tonight might be our last show."

I hear the confused murmurs and screamed questions, and I wait for the audience to calm down. "We are Sanctuary. We always were. We started this band to become a home for the broken, the lost, and the misfits. We would be lying to you and ourselves if we didn't do this now and admit the truth, and we never want to lie to you." Licking my lips nervously, I look at Fox. "The reason it may be our last show is because I fell in love." I smile at the audience.

I'm not afraid or shy. Instead, I'm so certain of this that it gives me the strength to face it head-on, even with millions of eyes and ears hanging onto my every word.

"I fell in love with the one person I wasn't allowed to, and when it comes down to it, I'm not even sorry." Grabbing Fox, I turn him to me and kiss him.

It isn't for the cameras.

No, it's a declaration, a promise of the future, and love.

THIRTY-FIVE

FOX

As I pull away, the noise of the crowd fades, and all I see is Ryker's love for me as he declares it to the world without a hint of hesitation. It's been a long road, but I know we are in this together, and I won't allow him to face this by himself. Grabbing the mic, I kiss his head before I turn to the crowd.

"Ryker is telling the truth. We are in love. I'm in love with Ryker and have been for a long time, but we refuse to hide anymore. I know you all saw the photos of us and, well, they are true. We weren't trying to hide our relationship, but to keep it for ourselves while we figured out where it fit in our world and careers, but that choice was taken from us. Because of this, we will be taking a break as a band. We were given no other choice. Our label feels our relationship will hinder our performance and upset fans, and that is the last thing we want to do. Our lives have been about making music and sharing it with the world, and when you all fell in love with the music just as much as us, we were so happy. You gave four lost men pouring their souls into their instruments and voices their dream, but our entire life isn't music. I will never apologize for falling in love with my best friend." I look at him and smile.

"Our label, our fans all shipped us, using it to sell myself and products. They didn't care if it was real or fake as long as it got them what they wanted, but now that they are faced with the truth of us being together, they don't want it. As a band, we have decided that if we can't have this future together, then we will walk away. We have been together since the beginning, and we'll be together until the end. I won't say sorry for falling in love. I'm in love with my best friend, and I have never been happier. He makes me a better man than I ever was, and for a short time, we got to live our dreams together, and that's enough for me. My entire future was focused around music, but now it's around my family." I glance at Strike and Dash. "We refuse to back down on this or hide."

Ry leans into the mic. "I also won't apologize for falling in love with my best friend. We've had the happiest few years of our lives when we started this band together, performed, and became Sanctuary. The idea of walking away from this terrifies me more than you'll ever know, but the idea of losing him terrifies me more. I hope you all understand. We aren't going to say goodbye—not now and not ever. We will always be Sanctuary and always be there for you when you need us, and I hope that you still love us the same after tonight and support us no matter where our journey takes us."

Dash takes the mic. "We love you all, and we support our best friends. This choice was easy for us to make. I am so happy to see them together and in love."

"They are right," Strike chimes in. "I watched my best friends struggle to hide what they felt and not cross the line, but seeing them together? How could that ever be wrong? We are with them until the end."

Fuck, I won't cry again.

I take the mic back and breathe deeply. "So, my lost souls, music lovers, and our family, tonight we are going to sing until we lose our voices and play until our fingers bleed. Tonight, we will give the show of our lives and hope there will be more in the future, but if there isn't, know that tonight is what we have always dreamed of, and we will never forget the love you have shown us. We love you all no matter where we go next, so let's make tonight last forever. What do you say?"

We wait anxiously as the cameras pan over the crowd, and we glance up at the screens. I see some crying faces, but I also see so many screaming our names. I recognize worry and love, and suddenly flashlights fill the crowd. My eyes widen as more and more light up until a river of lights stare back at us, illuminating the arena as stomps fill the air and a chant begins.

It's our name.

Sanctuary.

The entire arena stands behind us, and I know Po is right. Our fans will save us, but even if they don't, we have tonight.

I know we are all feeling the same way in this moment, supported and loved, and no matter what happens, we will never forget this. Clearing my throat, I try to compose myself as much as I can as Ryker steals the mic with a grin.

"Since we aren't hiding anymore, how about listening to a song we wrote about falling in love?" The crowd shouts, and he chuckles. "Baby?"

"Let's do it." I nod and peck his cheek.

There are no drums in this song, only a guitar and a singer, so Dash and Strike plop their asses on the edge of the stage facing us, giving us thumbs-up.

The spotlight hits us, and there are no pyrotechnics or fancy lights as Ry croons about falling in love with your best friend. I never take my eyes off him, and he never takes his off me. This is for us. We are done hiding. Whatever tomorrow will bring, we will always have this.

When the last note dies off, he steps into my side, and I press a kiss to his head as we breathe through the intense emotions.

Dash and Strike huddle around us for a moment before we break apart, and Dash takes the mic. "Okay, enough wallowing in our feelings. Let's bring this house down! Let's make this night last forever!"

The crowd screams with him, and they hurry back to their positions while Ry and I follow them.

We perform every single song we have ever written. It isn't perfect, and we make mistakes, but I've never had so much fun. We dance and play, and we do this for us and our fans, not the label, money, or fame. We do this for the love of the music, and I hope that comes through.

We perform two encores, but before long, we are told to come off stage, and I know we can't put it off anymore.

None of us want to leave, knowing it will be our last time on stage, but we have no choice. The curtain is falling, so as we finish up the second encore, we form a line at the end of the extended stage.

"We are Sanctuary, and we will love you forever. Thank you for making our last performance the best night of our lives!" Ryker yells.

"We love you!" Dash and Strike shout, and I lean into the mic.

"Thank you for saving my life. We'll always have this night."

Waving, I memorize the screaming crowd. This could be the last time I experience this, and I never want to forget it, not for as long as I live, but more importantly, I never want to forget who is at my side during it.

Gripping Strike's hand, I smile sadly at him as he looks from me to the screaming crowd. Ry is on my other side, holding Dash who is crying, and I swallow my own tears, tugging them into my embrace as we say our final goodbye.

As the lights turn off and we walk off stage, we still hear them chanting our name.

SANCTUARY

THIRTY-SIX

RYKER

None of us wanted to get up the next day. Our last gig is over, and we know what that means. Technically, we are still on suspension, but that's just a fancy way to say fired, so when we finally drag our asses downstairs, we freeze when we find Po waiting for us in the kitchen, one hand holding a mug, the other his phone.

"It's about time." He smirks as he glances up at us. "What's with the long faces?"

I share a look with Fox. "Isn't that obvious?"

Sipping his drink, he watches us carefully. "I'm guessing you haven't been online yet."

"We are avoiding our phones," Dash admits. "No phones, no way for them to call us and let us go."

Po shakes his head and drops his cell, turning it and pushing it across the table. We crowd closer. Fox wraps me in his arms as Dash and Strike huddle around us to see the tiny screen.

It's a local news station, and despite the muted volume, the headline running across the bottom is clear as it switches between a reporter and a massive crowd chanting and screaming.

"Fans revolt as the up-and-coming rock band, Sanctuary, announced that they are disbanding following their label's lack of support over the lead singer's and guitarist's relationship. Fans are outraged and rebelling downtown, demanding justice."

Po taps the table, and we look up at him. "The news and entertainment industries have blown up overnight. Fans are angry on your behalf. They went straight from your gig to protest outside the label. The news had no choice but to attend. It has spread worldwide that Sanctuary is done because their label won't support a same-sex relationship between their artists. Rage is filling every platform over the fact that they used that same relationship to sell you. You started a fire last night. There is no way to ignore this."

"What does it mean?" Dash asks worriedly, glancing back at the phone. The crowd is huge, and behind them is our label's office.

"They will have no choice but to cancel the suspension and change your contract"—Po shrugs—"or face the wrath of the public. In music, the public is everything."

"How do you know?" Fox asks, his eyes tight as he tries to hide his hope.

"Because I'm going to show them that. Do you think I've just been sitting around? No, I've been collecting evidence and support. I'm not going to leave them with a choice. Do you trust me?"

We share a look, and I speak.

"Yes."

"Good. I'm going to make sure Sanctuary has a long life on stage. Just give me a chance, but until then, don't do anything stupid, okay?" Standing, he fastens his suit jacket then pockets his phone and rounds the table. "That means no statements. In fact, don't leave the house for now, okay? Just put your game faces on because when they call you in, the cameras will be waiting."

"Sir, yes, sir!" Dash yells, excitement in his eyes. We've all been given a new lease on life, a hope that this might not end despite our thoughts last night.

Chuckling, Po looks us over before stopping in front of Fox and me. His hands rest on my and Fox's shoulders as he smiles at us. "I told you, I'm always on your side, even when you weren't discreet."

"What do you . . . You knew?" My eyes widen.

"Darling, I'd have needed to be blind not to know, but you weren't hurting anyone. I want you to be happy. It's my job to make that happen. I might work for your label, but my loyalty lies with you. Now, shower and wait for the call. I have some arms to twist." Stepping back, he straightens his shoulders and strides past us with a cocky smirk.

Po wasn't kidding. He went to war. We only sat around for two hours before the call came. Dressed to kill, we get in the car they sent for us and head down to the label. Nervous energy fills us. Fox's hand presses against my bouncing knee, trying to stop it, before he blows out a slow breath. "Breathe with me," he murmurs.

Nodding, I copy his breathing, trying to slow my racing heart, which can't seem to tell the difference between heading to our label and the end of the world. I'm so close to having everything I want that I'm worried it will be snatched away.

It doesn't stop me from falling into the beauty of my boyfriend though. His hair is down and slightly wavy, his eyes are darkened with liner, and his lips are tinted the same color as mine since he kissed me to apply it. His chest is bare in his unbuttoned white shirt, the sleeves rolled back to expose his thick, veiny forearms—which I know he did on purpose since I have an obsession with them—and his incredible thighs are encased in gray pinstripe slacks. He looks good enough to fucking eat.

"Have I told you how stunning you look today?" I whisper.

"No, but it can't be as beautiful as you, baby," he murmurs as he twines our fingers and kisses the back of my hand.

"Oh, Dash, look how pretty I am," Strike teases.

"Not as pretty as me," Dash responds, and I raise a brow at them.

"Don't make me come over there," I hiss.

"Try me, pretty boy." Strike blows me a kiss, and I jerk forward in my seat, slapping him. Our laughter breaks the silence and nervous energy, until the car stops and we drop into silence again, staring out of the tinted window.

Our label's building towers above us, but the crowd surrounds it. Security forms a path, and then Po knocks on our door, his smile in place. That has to be a good sign, right?

Fox slides to the edge of his seat and looks at us. "Ready?"

"Ready." I nod, and Dash and Strike confirm they are prepared as well before he opens the door. The screams are insane and shocking when Fox slides out, then he turns and offers me his hand. I place my shaky one in his and let him pull me from the car. He keeps hold of me, interlacing his fingers with mine as Dash and Strike follow us out. Security instantly surrounds us, their arms out to form a path through the yelling crowd.

Po nods at us. "Follow me." He navigates the path, and we have no choice but to keep up.

Our names are chanted, and words are screamed.

"We love you!"

"No restrictions!"

There are signs shoved over security, and I read them as I pass.

Love is love!

Artistic Freedom.

No Sanctuary, no fans!

There are so many words of support that by the time we reach the door, there are tears in my eyes. We are hurried inside and escorted to the elevator. Po stands before us until the door shuts, then he whirls.

"I've made the path, now you need to walk it. It's your choice. Whatever you choose now, I am with you," he promises as we ascend.

We barely speak after that, and we are shown to a familiar meeting room where the board and Mr. Atlas wait across from us.

Déjà vu hits me as I sink into my seat. They don't look happy, but I suppose being backed into a corner will do that.

"I am sure you've seen the crowd outside," Mr. Atlas begins, his hands steepled. "After speaking to some advisors and Po, we believe it is in our best interest for us to speak again. Last time, we put you on suspension, but we would like to lift that now and return you to your normal activities."

"Just like that?" Fox asks, suspecting a trap.

"Yes," Mr. Atlas mutters.

"And our relationship?" I press.

"We will allow you to continue dating—"

"How kind," I deadpan.

"But you will keep it private," he says.

"No deal." Standing, I head to the window and look out at the fans, knowing this is about more than us now. This is about change and love. "We will date publicly and decide what we want to show to fans and when. We will allow you to sell our music like you did before, but on our terms. It's that or we'll walk. We won't have you dictating our relationship. Not now, not ever again."

"He's right. If you want us to stay with you and would prefer to avoid a media outcry, then our contract will need to change. We will continue to be your band, and we will work twice as hard as every other artist out there to make it, but in return, we get freedom with our relationship," Fox demands, "or we'll walk out right now."

"I agree," Strike adds.

"It's that or nothing at all," Dash says, serious for once.

"Po said you would say as much," Mr. Atlas grumbles as he pulls out four contracts and slides them across the table. I sink back into my seat, scanning them, just like we did the first time we came here, only now Fox looks at me to make sure I'm happy.

The clause about us dating is gone, and in its place is simple wording that band members can date and dictate their private lives as long as it doesn't negatively affect their work.

"Happy?" Mr. Atlas asks.

"Ry?" Fox murmurs.

Grabbing a pen, I squiggle my name on the line. Smirking, he follows suit, and then Dash and Strike as well before we push the contracts back. "Happy." I nod. "Thank you."

"We had no choice." Mr. Atlas huffs. "Your plan, I'm betting."

"No, we just wanted to keep making music together. There was no plan. We didn't want to cause any trouble. We just wanted to live our lives," I admit. "Thank you for giving us that."

He seems to soften, sighing as he grabs the contracts and stands. "Cameras will be waiting downstairs. We'll announce your reinstatement now before this gets out of hand." Hesitating, he looks us over. "We really didn't do this before to hurt you or because we had an issue with you two being in love. We were trying to protect you from a world that isn't always kind to those with love like yours."

"I know, but the world is changing, and so should we. I won't apologize or hold back in fear of what some may say. This is my life, and I will live it however I want. The fact that you are supporting us means a lot, and you have paved a path for new artists like us."

I know they are doing it to save their own asses and earn good PR, but they are also making their side clear. They are with us, and we will prove why that was a good choice.

"Let's hope you're right. Come on." We head back downstairs together. Cameras and a microphone stand are waiting outside in front of the crowd. Mr. Atlas steps up first, and the crowd and reporters fall silent.

"My name is Jeremy Atlas. I am the CEO of Atlas Records. There has been some public upset at a mistake made with our latest band, Sanctuary. Yes, they were on suspension. It wasn't because we are a homophobic company, as we have been accused of, it was simply a breach of contract we had no choice but to uphold, and the situation would have been handled the same with any artists found dating after signing what they did. However, we hear you, we see you, and moreover, we support our artists. Just now, Sanctuary has signed a new contract and agreed to come back to work with our full support, both publicly and privately. We hope you will show them the same love and undying loyalty for many years to come both in their music and their love. Atlas Records is happy to announce our support and trust in Sanctuary." Turning to us, he smiles. "Would you like to say some words to your fans?"

"I want to thank you." My statement is awkward, and I can see them waiting for more. There are so many people all here for us, fighting for us in a battle we couldn't have won without them.

We owe them everything.

"It is thanks to all of you," I continue, my voice growing in confidence, "that we get to keep our dream, but more than that, we get to keep our family. I vow that we will continue making music until the day we die. We have and always will be Sanctuary."

"Ryker is correct," Fox offers. "We would not be here without our fans. You were the reason we were noticed, and now you are the reason we get to stay together. We owe you everything, and we'll make sure to give back all the love and support you have shown us."

"Fox, Ryker!" We blink as people scream for us, and I nod, picking someone at random.

"Are you two staying together?"

"Yes." I smile without hesitation. "Fox is my boyfriend, and that won't change." Looking up at him, I can't help but soften. "He's the love of my life."

Dash and Strike fake gag, making the crowd laugh, and Fox leans in and kisses my cheek. "My beautiful boy," he whispers. "You did so well."

"Yeah?" I lower my voice so the crowd doesn't hear. "Then you can show me when we're home."

Chuckling, he takes my hand behind the mic stand as we answer more questions, and for the first time since those pictures were taken, I feel the sun rising with hope.

I see our future, and it's fucking bright.

THIRTY-SEVEN

FOX

We are celebrating.

A feast is spread across the table, and drinks flow in our private room in the restaurant Po took us to. He's chatting away with Dash and Strike, who grow increasingly more drunk. When I lay my hand on Ry's thigh under the table, I feel him jump. His eyes swing to me as he spills beer over his arm. I lick it clean, watching his Adam's apple bob as he swallows. Chuckling into his skin, I slide my hand higher on his thigh until I cover his cock and squeeze.

"I need the bathroom." I stand and head out, hoping he gets the idea.

After all, I have a promise to keep.

Leaning into the stall door in the empty bathroom, I check my watch when the door bangs open, a wide-eyed Ry standing on the threshold. His gaze clashes with mine. "Fox." It's all he gets out before I'm on him, shoving him back into the door as I lock it before turning him and pressing him to the wall. Our kiss is sloppy as he gasps into my mouth.

"We don't have long." I undo his pants and tug them down before lifting him. His legs wrap around my hips as I press him back into the wall. "Be good and scream for me."

I'm inside him in one thrust. He gasps, and I kiss him until he relaxes and rolls his hips, urging me to move. Our kiss turns messy as I grunt, pull out of his tight ass, then slam back in. The force presses him back as I move fast and hard, knowing they'll eventually come looking. His leaking cock is trapped between us, and I shift so I can hold his length in my fist. He thrusts into it as I take his ass, my name on his lips.

His head falls back into the wall as he holds onto my shoulders, his groans filling the air as he arches his back, taking me deeper.

"God, look at you, baby, so goddamn perfect," I praise as I bite his neck. He jerks in my fist, and I hammer into his ass, wanting to come when he does. "My baby, aren't you? Mine forever, and now the world knows."

"Yours," he promises, swelling in my fist. "Fox, I'm going to come."

"I know. Come for me, baby. Let me feel it." I squeeze my fist around his cock. He cries out, squirting on my hand as he comes, and I keep up my rough pace, fucking his ass. I'm unable to look away from him, and when his eyes open, it sends me over the edge.

Groaning his name, I fill his tight ass with my release and slump into him. He drapes his arms over my shoulders, still breathing heavily.

"I wonder if they heard," he teases.

"If they didn't, I didn't fuck you well enough," I retort, then I kiss him. "I love you."

"I love you too," he murmurs, kissing me deeper before I pull away. Dropping him to his feet, I lift my fist and lick his release from my fingers.

"Fox," he murmurs, sounding scandalized as I laugh.

"Baby, I've tasted every inch of you, and every single drop is perfect," I purr.

"Idiot," he mutters, but he's smiling. I help him back into his pants, and we clean up before looking at each other in the mirror. For a moment, I remember every time we would sneak away and hide in the bathrooms at clubs and bars we were playing in just for five minutes of peace with each other. He must remember, too, because his smile is wide.

"Even back then, they were my favorite five minutes of the day," he says.

"Mine too," I agree as I circle my arms around him and rest my chin on his shoulder. "You were and always will be my favorite part of any day, Ry."

"Even when I'm being a pain in the ass?" he teases.

"Even then," I reply as I kiss his cheek. "I have been in love with you for so long, I don't think I could ever stop loving you."

"You better not," he grumbles as he turns and kisses me. "Because I'm not letting you go ever again."

"Promise?"

"Promise." He nods. "We wasted so much time, but we won't waste any more. We got everything we wanted, Fox, so now let's just enjoy it." He kisses me softly, and I can't resist kissing him back.

When we rejoin the table, Dash, Strike, and Po look at us knowingly, and I simply smile as I sink into my seat, tugging Ry until he's sprawled over my lap. "I couldn't find the bathroom," I tease.

"Sure," Strike scoffs. "The walls aren't soundproof."

"Which reminds me, Po, we need soundproofing. Ry is loud," Dash says seriously.

Groaning, Ry hides his face in my neck as I chuckle, rubbing his back as I grin at my friends.

I've never been happier.

I have everything I ever wanted and couldn't even dare to imagine.

A family.

A dream.

A love that will never break.

Even if the world tries to tear me down, I have everything I need to fight it because no one can do it alone, and I won't have to ever again.

SANCTUARY

THIRTY-EIGHT

RYKER

Months later...

Life is good. Our label supported us and got us back on tour with Dead Ringers—once Beck Danvers was ready, of course—and due to them and our increasing popularity, more dates were added, which sold out instantly. I know it isn't just for us, but for Dead Ringers as well, yet the love we see every night when performing on stage is like no other.

We are living our dream.

I won't say it's domestic bliss, since Fox and I still argue, but now it ends in us fucking and making up. Dash and Strike are still idiots, but we love them. We've never been closer, and we have so many plans for when this tour is over, the world won't know what hit them.

Grunting, I press harder, my back aching from the position, my arms quivering as Fox groans next to me.

"Oh hell no, not again!" Strike yells as he heads up the bus steps. I lift my head, tilting it curiously as Strike and Dash stare at us. "Shit, I thought you were fucking because of the noises. Remember when we talked about putting a sock on the door? I thought you forgot."

"We're cleaning." I frown as I look at Fox. "Wait, it sounded like we were fucking?"

"Yes!" they yell as my cheeks heat, and I wonder who else passed by and thought we were having sex.

Oh well, it wouldn't be the first time we've been caught and definitely not the last. Despite being together nearly six months now, Fox and I can't keep our hands off each other, on and off stage.

Dropping his cloth, Fox wiggles his eyebrows at me. "You know, if they all think we're fucking, then we shouldn't let them down."

Smirking, I dive at him as Dash and Strike toss something at our backs, their denials fading as I fall into Fox's eyes. "I love you."

"I love you too," he whispers as he hauls me closer. "Let me show you how much."

This time, our moans are from fucking.

I can't even believe it's the last show of the tour. It has gone so quickly, but we will remember it forever. We found ourselves out on stage, and we are never turning back. We might be here only to support Dead Ringers, but along the way, we found love, friendship, and loyal fans who will never leave us.

After Dead Ringers performs, they bring us back on stage, something we didn't plan. Luckily, we are all still dressed, and we hurry down the extended stage. Trav slings his arm around Dash, while Strike clings to Chase. Beck holds Kolt's hand and takes mine, while I keep Fox's, and we bow to the crowd. They scream loudly, and we wave and bow again as Beck takes the microphone.

"I know this tour has been . . . a ride." She chuckles. "But I want to thank all of you for coming to our shows and giving us such amazing support—not just for us, but for Sanctuary as well. I think we can all agree how incredible they are, can't we?" She holds the mic out, and the crowd screams. "I know I'll be looking forward to their very own tour, but for now, I want to thank them for becoming such good friends and for being in our corner the entire time. I couldn't have asked for a better bunch of people to do this world tour with."

We bonded, and I'm going to miss our nights in the green rooms and buses. They've quickly become some of our closest friends in this industry, and their support has been invaluable. When we came back on tour, they included rainbow lights in every one of their shows for us and also encouraged everyone to love who they want.

Beck hands me the mic, smiling widely. "Any last words?"

Taking it, I glance at my band, and they nod. "I want to thank everyone again," I tell the crowd. "We wouldn't be here without you. I also want to thank Dead Ringers, who took a chance on a nobody band. We love you. We've had the best time on this tour, and we are going to look back on these memories for the rest of our lives. We've learned trust, friendship, patience, and forgiveness, but most of all, love and community. We have no plans to make that stop now, so next Tuesday at noon, our brand-new album will be dropping!"

The crowd goes wild, and I laugh as I lean into Fox, waiting for them to calm down. "We can't wait for you to listen. It's raw and brutal, and it's unlike anything we've ever done before. It's our story. It's our home, our sanctuary, and now it will be yours! Until then, goodnight, and remember to rock on!"

We spend a few more minutes waving and blowing kisses to the crowd before we take one final picture, our backs to the audience, and Fox's hand finds mine as we smile at each other. I know it's going to be my new favorite photo.

My family is together, and our future is wide open before us.

What could be better?

EPILOGUE

FOX

One year later...

"Are you ready?" Po asks in the wings.

"Born ready, Daddy!" Dash chimes in.

"Ready to melt their faces," Strike yells.

Shaking my head, I look at Ry as he grins. "Ready, bitches."

"I'm ready." I lay my hand out. "Hands in, fuckers."

One by one, they place their hands in, including Po. "Sanctuary!" we chant as we throw our hands back before turning and heading out to take the stage.

It's the first show of our world tour, and we are brimming with excitement. Our last two albums have done better than the label thought possible, sweeping awards and propelling us higher. Our fanbase has grown worldwide, and our tour sold out in every city in under five minutes. It was terrifying, even though it was exciting, and now I get to travel the world with my best friends and the love of my life, playing music for the masses.

As the lights dip and we wait for our cue, Ryker's hand finds mine, a stolen touch. We don't hide that we are together, but sometimes we like these moments just for us.

Our rings smack, and my smile grows. We were married two months ago in a secret ceremony, and no one else but our immediate friends know. Our love went from private to public, but this is still between us. Our fans get everything else, but not this.

I'm so glad I stopped resisting and took that step because I have everything I could have ever wanted. I've never been happier, and as I lean into my husband, I can't help stealing a kiss.

"I love you, baby," I whisper as the heartbeat backing track sounds. "Let's make rock history."

RYKER

As the last note of our brand-new love song fades away, a song we didn't expect people to love as much as they did, I stare out at the crowd. Their phone lights fill the arena, and I can scarcely believe it. We aren't a supporting act. We are here, and they are here for us. They scream our songs back to us and they wear our merch and know our names. We have seen our fair share of the dark side of fans, but the majority are incredible, and we wouldn't be on stage without them. They gave us our dream, and now I'm going to fight for it for the rest of my life.

I was lost not too long ago, everything slipping through my fingers, but now I have everything I could need. I have best friends who support me in everything and anything. I have an incredible manager who pushes us to be better and a label willing to give into our demands and ideas. I also have Fox.

My Fox.

My husband.

It still feels strange calling him that, but every time I do, he gets this look in his eyes, and I usually end up coming so hard, I can't walk. Our lives together haven't been easy, but we are each other's safe places. With him, I'm just me—not Ryker, a rock god, or a symbol. I'm just me, a man who wanted to be loved and finally accepted that. He took me in, even with all of my flaws and mistakes, and he let me live within his heart and gave me a second chance.

Looking at him now as he slings his arm around Strike, I can't help but fall even more in love with him. "That has to be my favorite song," I say into the mic, and he looks at me as I smile. "For anyone who has ever found their other half, that's for you. Before Fox, I never knew what it meant to be loved. It's in the little things he does for me, like remembering the way I drink my coffee or waking up to warm the house so I'm not cold in the morning. It's the daily, little, mundane things where he shows me he loves me every single day. He is my best friend, a safe pair of arms to catch me when I fall, and now we get to sing our story to you." I look back at the crowd. "This is where we will stay, together and with you. That is what Sanctuary means to me. It's a place of people I love. It's a safe haven, and now we get to share that with you."

"You big softie," Dash teases into his mic.

Chuckling, Fox wraps his arms around me and leans into me to speak into the mic. "I think our lead singer is feeling a bit emotional tonight at seeing you amazing fans, so how about we show him some love?"

The crowd shouts.

"You can do better than that! Scream for me!"

They cheer even louder, and I smile up at Fox as he kisses my cheek and swings his guitar around, shredding the intro to the next song as I watch him. I almost miss my cue, but his eyes find mine, reminding me, and I start to sing, losing myself in those dark depths just like I have since the moment I met him.

I don't know how long this fame will last, but there is one thing I know for sure.

I will always have him, and we will always be legendary.

THE END

ABOUT K.A. KNIGHT

K.A Knight is an USA Today bestselling indie author trying to get all of the stories and characters out of her head, writing the monsters that you love to hate. She loves reading and devours every book she can get her hands on, and she also has a worrying caffeine addiction.

She leads her double life in a sleepy English town, where she spends her days writing like a crazy person.

Read more at K.A Knight's website or join her Facebook Reader Group.
Sign up for exclusive content and my newsletter here
http://eepurl.com/drLLoj

OTHER BOOKS BY K.A. KNIGHT

CONTEMPORARY

LEGENDS AND LOVE *CONTEMPORARY RH*
Revolt

Rebel

Riot

Resist

PRETTY LIARS *CONTEMPORARY RH*
Unstoppable

Unbreakable

PINE VALLEY COLLEGE *CONTEMPORARY*
Racing Hearts

Crashing Hearts

DEN OF VIPERS UNIVERSE STANDALONES
Scarlett Limerence *CONTEMPORARY*

Nadia's Salvation *CONTEMPORARY*

Alena's Revenge *CONTEMPORARY*

Den of Vipers *CONTEMPORARY RH*

Gangsters and Guns (Co-Write with Loxley Savage) *CONTEMPORARY RH*

FORBIDDEN READS *(STANDALONES)*
Daddy's Angel *CONTEMPORARY*

Stepbrothers' Darling *CONTEMPORARY RH*

STANDALONES

The Standby *CONTEMPORARY*

Diver's Heart *CONTEMPORARY RH*

DYSTOPIAN

THEIR CHAMPION SERIES *Dystopian RH*

The Wasteland

The Summit

The Cities

The Nations

Their Champion Coloring Book

Their Champion - the omnibus

The Forgotten

The Lost

The Damned

Their Champion Companion - the omnibus

PARANORMAL

THE LOST COVEN SERIES *PNR RH*

Aurora's Coven

Aurora's Betrayal

Book 3 - *coming soon..*

HER MONSTERS SERIES *PNR RH*

Rage

Hate

Book 3 - *coming soon..*

COURTS AND KINGS ^{PNR RH}

Court of Nightmares

Court of Death

Court of Beasts

Court of Heathens

Court of Evil

THE FALLEN GODS SERIES ^{PNR}

Pretty Painful

Pretty Bloody

Pretty Stormy

Pretty Wild

Pretty Hot

Pretty Faces

Pretty Spelled

Fallen Gods - the omnibus 1

Fallen Gods - the omnibus 2

FORGOTTEN CITY ^{PNR}

Monstrous Lies

Monstrous Truths

Monstrous Ends

SCIENCE FICTION

DAWNBREAKER SERIES *SCI FI RH*

Voyage to Ayama

Dreaming of Ayama

STANDALONES

Crown of Stars *SCI FI RH*

SHARED WORLD PROJECTS

Blade of Iris - Mafia Wars *CONTEMPORARY RH*

CO-WRITES

CO-AUTHOR PROJECTS - *Erin O'Kane*

HER FREAKS SERIES *PNR Dystopian RH*

Circus Save Me

Taming The Ringmaster

Walking the Tightrope

Her Freaks Series - the omnibus

THE WILD BOYS SERIES *CONTEMPORARY RH*

The Wild Interview

The Wild Tour

The Wild Finale

The Wild Boys - the omnibus

STANDALONES

Kingdom of Crowns and Daggers *Dark Fantasy RH*

The Hero Complex *PNR RH*

Dark Temptations *Collection of Short Stories, ft. One Night Only & Circus Saves Christmas*

CO-AUTHOR PROJECTS - *Ivy Fox*

Deadly Love Series *CONTEMPORARY*

Deadly Affair

Deadly Match

Deadly Encounter

CO-AUTHOR PROJECTS - *Kendra Moreno*

STANDALONES

Stolen Trophy *CONTEMPORARY RH*

Fractured Shadows *PNR RH*

Shadowed Heart

Burn Me *PNR*

Cirque Obscurum *PNR RH*

CO-AUTHOR PROJECTS - *Loxley Savage*

THE FORSAKEN SERIES *SCI FI RH*

Capturing Carmen

Stealing Shiloh

Harboring Harlow

STANDALONES

Gangsters and Guns *CONTEMPORARY*, IN DEN OF VIPERS' UNIVERSE

OTHER CO-WRITES

Shipwreck Souls (*with Kendra Moreno & Poppy Woods*)

The Horror Emporium (*with Kendra Moreno & Poppy Woods*)

AUDIOBOOKS

The Wasteland

The Summit

The Cities

The Nations

Rage

Hate

Den of Vipers (*From Podium Audio*)

Gangsters and Guns (*From Podium Audio*)

Daddy's Angel (*From Podium Audio*)

Stepbrothers' Darling (*From Podium Audio*)

Blade of Iris (*From Podium Audio*)

Deadly Affair (*From Podium Audio*)

Deadly Match (*From Podium Audio*)

Deadly Encounter (*From Podium Audio*)

Stolen Trophy (*From Podium Audio*)

Crown of Stars (*From Podium Audio*)

Monstrous Lies (*From Podium Audio*)

Monstrous Truth (*From Podium Audio*)

Monstrous Ends (*From Podium Audio*)

Court of Nightmares (*From Podium Audio*)

Court of Death (*From Podium Audio*)

Court of Beasts (*From Podium Audio*)

Unstoppable (*From Podium Audio*)

Unbreakable (*From Podium Audio*)
Fractured Shadows (*From Podium Audio*)
Shadowed Heart (*From Podium Audio*)
Revolt (*From Podium Audio*)
Rebel (*From Podium Audio*)
Riot (*From Podium Audio*) Coming soon...
Cirque Obscurum (*From Podium Audio*) Coming soon...
Kingdom of Crowns and Daggers (*From Podium Audio*)
Diver's Heart (*From Podium Audio*)
Racing Hearts (*From Podium Audio*)

FIND AN ERROR?

Please email this information to thenuttyformatter1@gmail.com:

- *the author name*
- *title of the book*
- *screenshot of the error*
- *suggested correction*

Printed in Dunstable, United Kingdom